The Empty House

THE EMPTY HOUSE

Stories
Nathan Oates

LOST HORSE PRESS
Sandpoint, Idaho

Acknowledgments

Grateful acknowledgment is made to the following publications in which these stories originally appeared:

Alaska Quarterly Review: "In the World Below"

The Antioch Review: "The Empty House," "Running Rapids," "Hidden in the Trees," "Famous for Crabs," "Looking for Service," "Nearby, the Edge of Europe" & "In the Ravine."

Best American Mystery Stories 2008: "The Empty House"

Best American Mystery Stories 2012: "Looking for Service"

Forty Stories (Harper Perennial): "The Highline Highway"

Hot Metal Bridge: "The Yellow House"

Witness: "Developing"

Cover Art: *High Rise Living* by Mel McCuddin, adapted from the original 48" x 44" oil on canvas. Permission graciously provided by the artist and Art Spirit Gallery.

Author Photo: Vera Nieuwenhuis

Book & Cover Design: LeAnn Bjerken, Tim Grassley, Preston Ham, Marie Hoffman, Dorian Karahalios & Tim Pringle

FIRST EDITION

The Spokane Prize is made possible through the partnership of Lost Horse Press and Willow Springs Editions. This and other fine Lost Horse Press titles may be viewed online at www.losthorsepress.org. Previous winners of the Spokane Prize as well as WSE's annual chapbook can be viewed at http://sites.ewu.edu/wseditions.

Willow Springs Editions staff who contributed to this book: Jaime Baird, LeAnn Bjerken, Polly Buckingham, Casey Fowler, Tim Grassley, Preston Ham, Marie Hoffman, Christopher Howell, Merideth Jeffries, Dorian Karahalios, Tim Pringle, Cat Sarytchoff, Kati Stunkard & Holly Weiler.

LIBRARY OF CONGRESS CATALOGING-IN-PUBLICATION DATA

Oates, Nathan.
[Short stories. Selections]
The Empty House / Nathan Oates.—First Edition.
    pages cm.—(Spokane Prize in Short Fiction)
"Willow Springs Editions."
ISBN 978-0-9883166-7-6 (alk. paper)
I. Title.
PS3615.A355A6 2013
813'.6—dc23
                              2013026955

for Amy

TABLE OF CONTENTS

Nearby, the Edge of Europe

ONE OF THE YOUNG MEN who worked on the ferry said they might want to go below; it was a windy day and the ride wouldn't be the smoothest. But Jenny said she wanted to stay up on deck, and Ethan, who was only four, wanted to do whatever his sister did. Caitlin frowned at Martin, as though he was indulging the kids again. Then she touched Jenny's head, said, "Be good," and with Boen the baby around her chest in a sling, joined the trickle of passengers going down to the seats.

The ferry left Rossaveal on time. Though the day was overcast, Martin could make out Inishmore.

"That's where we're going," he said, squatting between Ethan and Jenny, pointing out to the island that rose like a whale's hump. The mist and haze were so thick, he thought, the island very well might slip back under the waves.

"Where?" Ethan said, resting his forehead on a low white rung.

The ferry rocked as it sped up and Martin put a hand down on the deck. "The gray shape," he said. "Out there."

The boy squinted, biting his lip. "I don't see it."

"Your cousins live out there. That's where we're going." The pride he felt, filling up his throat, so intense it was almost as though he could cry, was a little silly, sure, but also heartening. He was bringing his children to a part of their past, his past. With the oblivious ease of the average American, they could have lived with no thought of their relatives living here on the far edge of Europe. Though he tried not to hope for too much, he found himself imagining Jenny writing letters to his cousin Sharon and her husband Thomas's daughters about life in America, replies arriving in battered white envelopes, cursive writing on yellow paper telling of the fierce soccer games between the island's three schools, how Patricia had scored a goal. And beneath what he hoped for the children, Martin maintained a small hope that his wife would see something through his family on this remote island off the Irish coast that would make her love him again: he would offer up his past, his family. Doubtful, but worth a shot. He was willing to do anything.

"I see it," Jenny said, grabbing the bar just above her head. "I see it, Daddy."

"Me too!" Ethan said, stomping his foot.

"No you don't." Jenny glared at Ethan. Then, as though it had just occurred to her—an inspiration—she added, "You dumb-dumb."

"Jenny," Martin said. "I'm sure he sees it."

"I do," Ethan said, starting to cry.

The ferry hit the first large wave and they all rocked back, Ethan just barely keeping his grip on the bars, though he could easily slip between them. Martin put his arm beneath his son's sagging backpack and lifted him up.

"Come on, Jenny," he said, touching his daughter's blonde hair, wet with spray from the waves.

"I'm fine," she said, fixing with little pats the hair he'd ruffled.

Thirteen years ago, Martin's father had visited these same cousins out on the Aran Islands. While he was visiting, Thomas was out fishing (he'd been raised on the island, his family having always been fishermen) and his boat was late coming back after a strong storm that had rattled the windows and doors while Martin's father sat with the family, trying to talk jovially, all of them watching the clock. At one in the morning they were called down to the harbor. Thomas was standing against the wall in the harbormaster's office, dripping. He didn't look up when Sharon and Martin's father (who was carrying the one-year-old Patricia) came in. Thomas's brother had been washed off the boat in the storm. Martin's father said that, back at the Collins's house, Thomas hadn't changed out of his wet clothes and had sat in the kitchen, drinking tea until morning, a puddle spreading around him over the yellow linoleum.

In the morning they started walking the coast, looking for the body. They searched for days, traveling over to the Galway shore to walk through the piles of brown seaweed, the sand cold and gray, the sea-side quickly becoming impassable so they were forced to climb up through wet grass to then peer down over the eroded shore into the water. It sounded like something from one of Caitlin's novels: a dirty flock of seagulls squalling away from a pair of searchers, crabs picking at swollen white fish bodies. He hadn't told Caitlin about Thomas's brother for exactly this reason. He was possessive, childishly so—he knew—of his connections to his Irish relatives. He didn't want Caitlin using their stories in her next novel. What he wanted was to mediate between his family and his relatives out on the island, to become somehow a crucial link. In a way, this was why he'd begun writing a nonfiction piece (he didn't want to call it a book yet) about his family and Ireland. Maybe it was partly driven by jealousy, but he wanted to produce something that had the effect of Caitlin's novels on her readers, on him. By the end of the trip, he might have one hundred pages. At any rate, he was trying something new. He was a scholar, a historian, not a memoirist, but he was willing to try, to branch out. This was, he thought, one of his more admirable qualities.

On the deck of the ferry, Ethan wrapped his arms tight around his father's neck and Jenny clutched the rails, her mouth open. She smiled (she was beautiful, so much like her mother) and shouted, "Daddy! It's salty!" Then she turned and opened her mouth again as they hit another wave. The ferry rose up the crest of a swell and fell rapidly into the trough. On the Aran Islands he felt sure, as his stomach lurched, he'd find the Ireland he'd always hoped for.

❖　　　❖　　　❖

"I hope they don't get sick," Caitlin said twenty minutes later when he took the kids down the slick steps to the airplane style seating. "They're soaked." She rubbed a napkin over Jenny's head furiously while the girl ducked away, digging in her backpack.

"They're fine," Martin said and leaned down to retrieve a pair of balled socks that had fallen from Jenny's bag. While bent over, he looked at the legs of an old woman several rows forward. Her boxy brown shoes, which didn't quite touch the ground, had rubbed through her thick pantyhose, abrading a red patch of her heel. They were the same shoes his grandmother had always worn, the same dense pantyhose with the bulky seam up the back.

"Did you tell them any good Irish fairy tales up there?" Caitlin said when he straightened up. She'd let Jenny loose and was smirking at him. Her hair was pulled back beneath a bandana, making her look older and more tired.

"I don't know any fairy tales," he said. He kept his voice down. Everyone knew Americans were loudmouths, but Caitlin apparently had no problem living up to stereotypes.

"None? I thought that's what being Irish was all about. *Fairies and leprechauns,*" she said in her terrible fake accent, far too loud. She crumpled the napkin and looked as though she might chuck it at him.

"No," he said, not allowing himself to get angry. "No leprechauns." He'd have suggested she quiet down, please, but he knew exactly where that'd get him.

"Ah, well," she said. "'Tis a shame, then."

"Okay," he said, and turned to check on Ethan.

She knew he hated her intentionally bad accent. Her talk of leprechauns. Caitlin's inspiration was the tour bus driver who'd taken them out to the Cliffs of Moher two days ago. All day the idiot driver had talked about fairies and leprechauns, as though they were at some Disney version of Ireland, instead of in the place itself. Any Irish person would have found everything the driver had said idiotic. Caitlin had been teasing him with talk of leprechauns ever since, and though it was ridiculous, petty, childish, it drove Martin crazy.

They'd rented a house in Connemara, outside Galway, for three weeks (extending spring break on either end with canceled classes). Though their trip was almost over, this excursion to the Aran Islands would be their first overnight stay out of the rented house. All other outings had been to places they could do in a day, because Caitlin's exhaustion, which had begun the first day as jet lag and a hangover from four airplane sized bottles of wine (the stewardess had begun to look a little distressed), had worsened no matter how little they did. It was the drinking, of course. Each night she drank herself to sleep and then said she couldn't possibly do anything for more than a few hours. She was ruining the trip. Driving the rental car down the street to the small shop where they bought rich milk, tea, and biscuits sent her back into the bedroom where she lay with an arm flung over her face. It was the accents. It was all this left-side-of-the-road driving. It was the wet chill always in the air—it was March—that the small European heaters do nothing against. Instead of doing all the things Martin had planned, she played with Ethan and Jenny in the small backyard. Late one morning Martin had gone out back—he'd been writing for three hours (the day before he'd walked down along the harbor where boats had taken away thousands of emigrants, including his grandmother)—and found Jenny, Ethan, and Caitlin on their knees beside a newly poured patio, pressing hands into the wet concrete.

Caitlin smiled at him and showed her palms, smudged gray. Ethan and Jenny squealed, delighted, on either side of her.

He'd done everything to convince her they should take this trip. He'd said it would be a chance to get away so she could get some writing done. She'd asked what difference it made to him if she got writing done. Why was it any of his business?

"It's not my business," he'd said, thinking that since her advances and royalties helped feed their kids, of course it was his business.

"Right you are. None. Of. Your. Business," she said, poking his arm with each word. But he was undeterred and eventually, unhappily, she'd given in. Perhaps because it was the first thing in years he'd insisted on. Perhaps because she wanted to ruin the trip once they were there, to show him what a fool he'd been to suggest this outing all along. To think they could be happy . . .

They'd met seven years ago at a faculty party. She'd come up to him and said, "I read your book." It seemed like the kind of thing *she* must hear all the time. The reading she gave as part of her job interview had been jammed, and when her first novel came out during her first year, people called her a "great writer." She was fast-tracked to tenure. Her novel was on the cover of Sunday's *The New York Times* Book Review.

Along with everyone else, he'd read it and been impressed. Each piece of the novel was perfectly clear: the tightness with which the mother wound the narrator's hair each morning into a pile atop her head, the embarrassment of new white laces in battered shoes. But despite the clarity of each scene the novel had carried him farther and farther into uncertainty. When he finished reading his hands had been shaking. How had he gotten here, to this awful final place? Though he'd known it was silly, he hadn't been able to resist some of the speculations everyone else indulged in. How autobiographical was it? The violence, the poverty, the sex. Had any of it actually happened to Caitlin?

Students paused in their conversations to watch her hurry from the parking lot to the Humanities building, head down, a manila folder in one hand like a weapon. Her classes were the first to fill up, and the artsy female students began imitating her style of dress—long black skirts, high heels, tight blouses—and her manner of walking, a headlong charge, and her fast, under-the-breath manner of speaking. "A little slower and a little louder, please," he'd been forced to ask with increasing frequency in his classes. So it had seemed strange that she should approach him (he'd harbored, like most academics, fantasies of being the hotshot on campus when he was hired right out of his PhD program at

Johns Hopkins, only to have such illusions quickly dashed) and ask about his book. He'd published a history book through the University of California Press on the Irish manipulations and adaptations of the cultural orthodoxies of the Catholic Church to undermine the political repressions of the English in the nineteenth century, and the political implications for resistance movements in Central America.

The party was at the house of the college's other creative writer, a loud-mouthed poet who was holding forth to an unwilling crowd across the room about Ashbery's grammar. Martin felt the other faculty glancing enviously at Caitlin and him. Absurd, how good it felt to be talking to her, to have been chosen. Pathetic, but also wonderful.

"Have you been to Ireland?" she asked. There was a mole on the right side of her upper lip, like Madonna's.

He told her he'd been to Dublin twice for research. Most of the time, those trips had actually been spent in London, with only two quick days in Dublin to collect information: not nearly enough time to visit family or even see much of the city. But he'd love to just go and stay.

"I've never been," she said, sipping her wine. He was surprised, considering the fearsome reputation she'd gathered on campus, how it felt being this close to her. The word *sweet*, which he hoped wasn't in any way condescending, came to mind. She was short, which didn't match how he'd seen her from afar—only five-two or -three—and she was thin, with muscular arms and calves. Her brown hair was cut short and held back with small pink butterfly clips.

"I think you should take me along, next time you go to Ireland. How about it?" she said. Despite the directness of her words, she'd blushed and held her wine glass up near her mouth as though to hide.

They began seeing each other. First for coffee, then drinks, then dinners out. After two weeks he invited her over and cooked salmon with capers. Afterward they watched a movie—a romantic comedy that she'd brought over—and she'd taken his hand, squeezed the tips of his fingers, then pulled him across the couch to her. Her breath had shuddered against his neck while he unbuttoned her blouse. She leaned forward so he could reach around and unclasp her bra. He kissed her nipples, which, he soon learned, she liked to have pinched, softly at first, then harder as she came to orgasm.

After six months they married at the courthouse. He was in love with her, he knew, but other than that, did he know her at all? She never talked about her past and he'd taken to rereading her novel compulsively, thinking within it must be hidden some crucial part of her. Perhaps there was, but he'd never found it. Thinking back, he felt foolish, but then at the time it wasn't idiotic. It was driven by love and romance and excitement and mystery. He found himself aroused by the scene in the woods with her boyfriend: he told her to lie down, then tied her arms around a tree. Bark scraped the back of her head while they had sex. He could see Caitlin doing this, but it seemed almost like another Caitlin, as though she'd lived many lives and this time with him was just part of who she was. Her mysteriousness was, he knew, part of the reason he loved her.

After the courthouse, faculty friends threw a reception and his parents flew in, as did her sister, Alice, the only sign he'd seen in all their time together of any family. Her sister did little to clarify the truth of Caitlin's childhood. She was a lawyer and was pretty, like Caitlin, though taller with long hair. Alice had worn a blue business suit and insisted on talking about law. He'd listened to a long monologue about giving up the hope of becoming a litigation attorney and her new interest in tax law when what he wanted to ask her was: *Is any of what she wrote true?*

Those first few months after they were married he'd thought, despite all the mystery that shrouded her campus persona and how little home life dispelled it, they had a happy marriage. But he was never able to get beyond that deep sense of isolation and otherness she exuded. At dinner she might be silent, eating her chicken (she liked it overcooked, dry and fibrous), or at other times she'd be garrulous, energetic, full of plans for trips, articles, stories. Not once did he feel he could predict her mood. Then she was pregnant and it had been hard—three months of bed rest—and the gap between them widened. A year and a half later Caitlin's second novel, set in North Carolina during World War II, came out to less acclaim than the first (though he'd been deeply moved and shaken by it) and she went on tour. Not long after the readings and signings were over, she was pregnant with Ethan. Since then she'd been at work on a third book. She obsessed over her work, filling a computer with her files, a new file for each day, perhaps a hundred files for a few dozen pages of progress. He imagined her other readers waiting for her next novel, but it had been five years and still no draft had been sent to her agent. Since Boen's birth, even though the breast-feeding had only lasted six months, half the time she'd fed the first two children, she'd been drinking more. Two glasses of wine after dinner at first, then a bottle, then double bottles. She woke late and wrote for four or five hours. Or at least sat in front of the computer for that long. There were times he'd walked, slowly, past her office and not heard a single key clack.

He'd honestly thought Ireland would help her. A friend of his with depression had been told by his doctor to travel and, while he wasn't certain Caitlin was depressed (she refused therapy), travel always helped. He'd bought her the conversion plugs and he'd carried her laptop (along with his own) onto the plane. But in Ireland she stopped writing altogether. Days went by when she didn't open the laptop, though he plugged it in for her each morning while she was still in bed. When he heard her waking, he put a cup of tea beside the computer. One morning, while she'd sat in front of the laptop, sipping, he'd asked if she was going to write today.

"Writing!" she shouted, sitting up, tea slopping onto the carpet. "That's right. I forgot." She opened the laptop and tapped wildly at the keys, whistling, bobbing her head with a ridiculous smile. "This is great," she said, looking up at him. "Just great."

Far from helping, Ireland had only brought more fully to the forefront that Caitlin no longer loved him, didn't even like him as far as he could tell, and now he was unsure if she ever had. Maybe this was why she'd wanted to always have kids. She loved the kids.

"So," he said, wanting to get away from these thoughts, "do you know what you want to see on the island?"

"I'm not sure," she said, leaning back to look at him as though he were a strange photograph. "You've probably got an endless list already drawn up."

"No. I mean, what do *you* want to see?"

"Well, if you put it *that* way," she said, putting a finger to her lips and tapping, "I guess maybe the bottom of a pint of Guinness."

"Well—" he started, but she cut him off.

"And then another pint, and another," she tapped her lip in rhythm. "Another, and another."

"I get it," he said.

Jenny hopped out of her seat and whined for money for snacks. "We're almost there," Caitlin said, shaking her head.

"Please, Mom," Jenny said, looking at her father.

"We're almost there," Caitlin repeated.

"Please, Mommy," Jenny said, hands balling into fists.

"Here," he said, reaching for his wallet, but Caitlin slammed her hand on the armrest. "Fine." She dug into her bag. "But only two Euros."

Jenny ran down the aisle, tottering with the pitching of the boat.

"Do you want me to take him?" he said, pointing at the sling around her neck in which Boen slept.

"I'm fine," she said, rubbing her eyes. "I just can't wait to get the fuck off this boat."

She wouldn't meet his smile, so he looked across the rows of seats to the window, though there was nothing to see but the churning gray sea.

◆　　　◆　　　◆

His cousin Sharon was waving at them, smiling, as he led his family down the wobbly gangplank, his arms full of two backpacks and the baby cradle. Sharon was a tiny woman, five feet tall, with a crop of short red hair and a kind, worried face. She wore a red raincoat against the mist.

"I knew it was you," she said. "This is why I told you to take the islander ferry. You'll be the only Yanks aboard." She kissed Caitlin's cheek, kissed the kids, and shook Martin's hand. "So many babies," she said. "You'd think you were Irish."

"My father says hello. He wishes he could have come," Martin said. Why did he feel so nervous? His voice was shaking.

"Oh," Sharon said, nodding. "How is he, your father?"

"Oh, he's great."

Sharon squinted at the ground and said, "How many years ago was it he was here?"

"I don't know," he said. A lie: it was thirteen years, when Thomas's brother had been swept away. He wouldn't bring this up, of course.

They piled into Sharon's small red car, Caitlin up front and Martin jammed in the back with the kids. The car smelled of mildew and exhaust. Sharon tugged and forced the stick shift through the gears. "I forgot," she shouted over the clanking engine, "to pick up petrol. I hope we can make it." She smiled at Caitlin who stared straight ahead, clinging nervously to the door handle as they wove up through the town that sat on a slope above the harbor. The town buildings were low and square with black tile roofs. *The American Bar* was written in large black letters on a red stucco wall. Out of town high stonewalls closed in the road.

Sharon told them, shouting over the engine, that the walls had been built, in part, to hold the soil in place. "There wasn't any soil when the first settlers came. They made the soil out of seaweed."

"Dad," Ethan screamed, clutching his father's knee, "what's seaweed?"

"Don't worry about it, sweetheart," he said, not wanting to interrupt Sharon, but she didn't add anything else.

They drove in silence for longer than he'd have expected (wasn't the island only nine miles long?) and, as the narrow road continued to climb the island's hump, he got a better view through the rain flecked window: bright fields within the dense patchwork of walls. Every once in a while there would be a cluster of houses, white walls, small windows, and occasionally older gray stone buildings with roofs fallen in. It was too bad they no longer used thatch. He'd have liked to have seen that. Sheep spotted a few of the fields and he pointed these out to Ethan and Jenny who said, "Where, where?" leaning across him. The windshield wipers creaked over the glass.

Sharon turned onto a narrow side road, then drove off onto the grass in front of a house like the others: white stucco, a green door, two square windows far apart.

"Let us help you with the bags," she said, jerking up the emergency brake, the engine wheezing a final breath.

The front door of the house opened and a thick, bald man came out. He wore dirty blue jeans, into which he'd tucked a green sweater. The collar of a shirt escaped the sweater on one side, the other half-trapped down beneath the wool. This must be Thomas. He looked so much like what one would expect from a man born and raised on the Aran Islands. His face was wrinkled and tufts of gray hair stuck out around his big ears.

Sharon had the trunk open by the time Martin got Jenny and Ethan out of the car. "And then this is Thomas," Sharon said. Thomas nodded shyly, then took the cradle his wife held out to him and disappeared into the house.

The Collins family was gathered in the kitchen around a small vinyl-topped table with cups of milky tea. Sharon and Thomas had three girls: Patricia, Sibhoan, and Mary, all with long, straight, black hair. Martin was surprised at the shabbiness of the house. The curtains, surely once white, had gone yellow with age, and the yellow-topped table was streaked with years of use. The kitchen was dominated by a large black stove—a cooker, he remembered his grandmother had always called it—that seemed to be the room's only source of heat. Atop the stove a tea kettle hissed softly, its silver handle fixed on with a loosening wad of black electrical tape.

All three of the Collins girls wore tired looking clothes. Patricia, the oldest at fourteen, wore a loose white and black striped shirt stretched out at the neck, and the other two had on thin sweatshirts. They all wore jeans patched at the knees and rolled up, as though they'd been bought at a charity and didn't quite fit. Sharon shooed her daughters out of the chairs around the table and told Martin and Caitlin to sit and warm up with a cup of tea.

They sat with the tea and stumbled through awkward conversation. Thomas sat in a straight-backed wooden chair by the door, not saying a word. His daughters huddled about him. Thomas's hands, on his knees, were thick and wrinkled. Fisherman's hands. Did it make the grief worse for Thomas to give up fishing after the loss of his brother? Or did a loss so deep dissolve all other minor attachments? Martin was an only child. It was one of the reasons he'd wanted several children, but then Thomas was a reminder of what it could bring. He felt himself becoming, once more, stupidly romantic. Thomas noticed Martin staring and glared, then snorted, as though insulted.

After ten minutes of fumbling for conversation, Patricia said, "And do you like *Seinfeld*."

He was about to ask, *What?* but Caitlin said, "Oh, I love it. I watch an hour of it every night."

"It's brilliant, isn't it?" Patricia said, nodding happily. Her fingers fussed at the dirty sleeves of her striped shirt.

"We have a tape," Mary—the youngest, perhaps Jenny's age—said, poking her head out from behind her father's shoulder. She was missing her two top front teeth, and smiled to show off the gaps.

"The girls," Sharon said, "love *Seinfeld*. Would you like to watch it?"

This was about the last thing Martin wanted to do, but the conversation had been so strained, so uncomfortable—Thomas and Sharon acted as though he was the local English landlord, here to evict them, rather than family—that when Sharon walked off to the living room, he followed.

"Well," he said, while the Collins girls went on giggling in front of the television. What should he say? One wall was taken up by a large set of mostly empty plywood bookshelves, tattered paperbacks fallen over on one another. Between the books were picture frames. He'd have liked to get up and look at those pictures, to sit (maybe there was an album somewhere) and talk with Sharon and Thomas about their family, about Thomas growing up here, about Sharon moving out here in her late twenties to marry an islander, and about what life was like here now.

"I was thinking—" he started to say, but Thomas coughed and nodded at his daughters who finally managed the tape into the VCR's mouth. There was no way not to feel that Thomas disliked him. While they'd sat in the kitchen, the man had thrown him unhappy looks and had seemed affronted each time Martin spoke.

While they all watched the crumbling black screen, Patricia, standing beside Caitlin said, "You watch an hour a day?"

"Repeats," Caitlin said. "You could watch two hours, if you wanted." She patted the couch as though there was room for everyone.

"Really?" Patricia said, perching herself on the couch arm.

The other two girls down on the orange shag carpet watched the exchange raptly.

"Daddy," Ethan whined.

"What's wrong?" Martin said, but just then the show started abruptly in mid-scene.

"I'm hungry," Ethan groaned, bumping his forehead against his father's arm.

On screen George and Jerry sat in the coffee shop.

Everyone in the room watched the TV except Ethan who knocked his forehead harder against Martin's arm.

"Honey," Martin whispered. "Quiet."

"I'm hungry!" the boy screamed.

Elaine had joined the two other characters on the television and they were gesturing wildly. Ethan groaned and pounded his feet against the couch.

"Does he want something to eat?" Sharon said, putting her hands on her knees, about to stand. "Because I can get something from the kitchen."

"No, no," Martin said. "He's fine. He's just tired." Ethan groaned and Martin leaned his head down and said, "Quiet, sweetheart." Ethan rammed his forehead into his father's jaw. As his eyes watered the boy began to scream.

"The boy's hungry, for Christ's sake," Thomas said, loudly. His arms were folded over his chest, staring at the television.

"Sorry," Martin said, staggering up from the sagging couch. "Sorry." He reached down and grabbed Ethan. "He's just tired," he said, then realized he was blocking Thomas's view of the TV and stepped back, toward the door.

"No!" Ethan screamed, flailing, smacking his father in the head, kicking.

Caitlin watched with a bemused smile from the couch, her arm around Jenny. "Come and sit up here," Caitlin said to the other Collins girls as he went out into the hall.

From the kitchen where he stood near the door pinning the writhing Ethan to his chest, he could hear laughter, the show's soundtrack, Caitlin's familiar twitter, and the voices of his cousins.

✦   ✦   ✦

"I'm too tired," Caitlin said, sitting on the bed in the room they'd been given where he'd sat with a fussing Ethan while the rest of them had watched the show. All three of the Collins girls were to sleep in the same bed in a room down the hall. Sharon had brushed aside his protests that they could stay in a hotel. Now she wanted to take them up to Dun Aengus, the Neolithic fort atop the island cliffs. She'd worked as an archaeologist at the site during the recent excavations and wanted to show them the three iron rings she'd found: the centerpiece of the artifact collection.

Boen squirmed on the bed, staring at the ceiling, his mouth pursed, as though he were considering whether or not to scream. *Why not*, Martin thought. *Go for it, kid.*

"I'm too tired," Caitlin repeated. "Boen needs a nap." She touched the baby's foot.

"Sweetheart, we're only here one day. We might not get another chance."

He'd already been forced out of the room with Ethan, and he wanted to do *something* with his cousins. While in here with Ethan, he'd noticed, on a little white bookcase, paperback British editions of Caitlin's novels, the spines heavily creased. He wondered what Sharon had thought of them. He imagined the Irish thought of America as a place of exuberant wealth, pop stars, and bankers, so what would they make of Caitlin's filthy homes, indolent fathers, violent mothers, sex in the backseats of rebuilt cars, no consolations in the narrative, a spiraling down into confusion, darkness, and often death? Caitlin wrote about the kind of life one knew existed; at least he knew *of* it, but he had always regarded it abstractly through the heavy filter of history. Her novels made it palpable. He couldn't help but see his wife as the narrator early on in the first novel, slipping on the floor in the dark kitchen on a February morning after the pipes had burst, the kitchen floor a sheet of ice, her elbows bruised purple. Her mother had hit her over and over with the belt, senselessly sure the ice was the girl's fault.

"How many days," Caitlin whispered, slumping forward, "how many days till we can go home?"

He wanted to tell her to grow up, stop complaining, but he was overcome by the thought that perhaps when they returned to America she was going to leave him. This trip, then, was the last straw. He loved her, but what good was it, his love, if it went nowhere? Like the priests hidden in the countryside along the Dingle Peninsula when Cromwell came through burning the towns, killing, banning Catholicism; in barns, or fields, parishioners had knelt on straw, or rain-wet grass, heads bowed to receive the Latin blessing. Dedication against sense was, at times, the only freedom—the only happiness—one had left.

"Just take a nap, okay?" he said.

Without answering she shoved her shoes off her feet and carefully lay down beside Boen who began fussing. She whispered to him and laid her face against his small head. Martin had seen Boen so rarely on this trip: Caitlin kept him cradled in the sling about her neck.

Ethan and Jenny crashed into the room waving their toothbrushes like swords.

"Careful," he said, but they weren't listening. Leaving the wet toothbrushes on a nightstand they fished through their packs to gather supplies for the hike. Jenny took the small magnifying glass Martin's father had given her and binoculars, a present from Martin's mother, an avid birder. Ethan found his plastic army knife with its flimsy black plastic belt and set about, biting his lip, fixing it around his waist. Then they were ready.

"Oh, are you staying?" Sharon said sadly, looking past Martin at Caitlin.

"I'm going to take a nap," Caitlin said.

"Well," Sharon said. "Are you sure? It's not far. You should . . . come."

"No. No, I'm going to stay."

"Please, then, won't you come?" Sharon said. Martin cringed at the pleading tone.

Caitlin shook her head and smiled in a way meant to convey her utter exhaustion.

"Oh," Sharon said, picking at the zipper on her coat, "well, then." She sounded as though she were about to cry.

Why was she so upset? What was the big deal? *He* was still going. "We should get going," he said.

"Have fun," Caitlin called as he pulled the door shut.

◆   ◆   ◆

Through the visitors center, up the long hike to the fort, and then while they were within the curving black stone walls, near the two-hundred foot cliffs, Sharon relayed bits of history he knew, but he didn't interrupt her, not wanting to be rude and because he didn't feel that Sharon disliked him yet. Not that he imagined she liked him. She seemed nervous and unsettled around him, as though he were famous for rude outbursts. She pointed out how spongy the ground was, that the walls kept the grass from blowing away. He tried to act interested, but felt worn out. Why was she so hesitant with him but seemed to take so much to Caitlin? Caitlin was the one people should be afraid of. She was the one who couldn't be counted on to act in a rational, reasonable way. Well, maybe that was overstating it. A little. But she was the one, unlike him, who often acted out of a kind of animal selfishness, rather than out of concern for those around her.

There were only four other people up at the fort that day, young Americans or perhaps Germans in expensive Gore-Tex coats and hiking boots. The four walked carefully toward the edge of the cliff and then, ten feet from the lip of rock, they dropped down to their knees and crawled, then finally shimmied along on their stomachs to hang their heads over the edge.

"Dad," Jenny said, squinting at the four who scurried back from the ledge, laughing and happy, "can we do it?"

"No, honey."

"Dad, please?" Ethan said, tugging again to free himself from his father's grip.

He scooped Ethan up with one arm and said, "Sweethearts. It's too dangerous."

"Mom would let us," Jenny said, glaring.

"That doesn't mean it's right," he said. "Just because Mommy would do it doesn't mean it's right."

He was too tired to make chitchat on the descent. Ethan whined: Why couldn't Daddy carry him? "Because Daddy is tired," he said.

          ✦   ✦   ✦

Caitlin wasn't napping. She was in the kitchen with Thomas and an open bottle of whiskey. Martin had bought the whiskey in Galway to bring as a present. Thomas's glass was watered down to pale yellow, two melting flecks of ice bobbing, and it sat almost a foot from his hand, as though it were his only reluctantly. Caitlin clutched her glass. Boen's baby cradle was on the floor beside her. She gestured hello with her glass. "Did you have fun?" The kids ran to her; Ethan pulled out his knife and stabbed the air to show how he'd killed the barbarians; Jenny tried to quell him and tell Caitlin what she'd seen with the binoculars: a boat out on the ocean. Far, far out.

"How's Boen?" Martin said, squatting beside the baby. He wanted to reach in and pick the boy up, carry him out of there, but he was sleeping peacefully.

"Sleeping," Caitlin said, not looking at him.

Sharon stood behind Thomas and whispered in his ear.

"What's that?" Thomas shouted, quieting everyone. Martin watched Boen squirm toward consciousness, the shudder of his arms, the twisting of his mouth, as though inside it was a small, slick minnow.

Sharon flinched and whispered again.

"They went down to the wormhole," Thomas said, waving his hand in the air. He looked angry and tired.

Martin wondered if Caitlin had said something insulting.

"Maybe," Sharon said, "if you're not too tired, we should go down to the wormhole?" Her mouth was pursed and she kept reaching up nervously to pat her hair, trying not to look at the bottle of whiskey. What was Caitlin doing getting drunk in the kitchen in the middle of the afternoon?

"Good idea," Martin said, not sure what was meant by "wormhole." He stepped between Thomas and Caitlin, grabbed the cap and screwed it back onto the bottle.

"Thomas," Sharon said. "Will you come along?"

"Jesus," he said, leaning back in his chair, flopping his mouth open and gasping loudly. Heaving himself forward and to his feet, nearly knocking the baby cradle, he said, "I suppose I will. We have to entertain the Yanks, now don't we?"

He stomped out of the room. Martin picked the whiskey bottle off the table—there were only a few inches gone—and followed Caitlin back to the bedroom.

"What were you two talking about?" Through the door, he heard Sharon, down in the kitchen, talking to Ethan and Jenny.

"Excuse me?" she said, arranging the sling about her neck.

"What were you talking about?" He set the bottle carefully on a dresser.

"It's mostly a secret," she said, settling Boen into the sling, "but, you know, childhood, siblings, stuff like that."

"Childhood? Must have been an interesting talk."

"Oh, yes," she said, stepping past him and out into the hallway. "He lived in New York, you know."

"Is that right?" he said. His stomach sank.

"Yeah," she said. "He worked as a gravedigger in Queens." She told him about Thomas leaning on the shaft of his shovel, while, a few dozen yards away, a family stood sobbing near the pile of earth he'd soon be dumping into the hole.

Maybe later he'd ask him about this. He didn't have the time now to ask the questions he'd need in order to write it (where had he lived, how had he gotten there, what did the bodies smell like?), but he could feel that tingle in his chest, the seed of an assuredly good story, beginning to crack. But then Caitlin already had it. Already she was probably molding it into some piece of a story. She'd stolen it out from under him.

"His brother," she said, "went with him. But that was before the accident."

"And I'm sure you had lots of good stuff to tell." His voice was shaking. An image from her first novel came to him: The narrator was fourteen and her younger brother, a waifish, delicate, often-beaten-up little boy had been bitten by a brown recluse spider while they were visiting relatives in Missouri. The mother wouldn't take him to the doctor, saying it was too expensive, even as the red welt turned black. There was a terrifying scene in which they heated a spoon and scooped a rotted chunk from the boy's arm. The brother never recovered. What if she'd had a brother who'd died? A part of him had always wanted to protect and care for Caitlin. What if any of those things *had* happened to her? But now the tangle of truth and fiction seemed all part of an elaborate obstruction she threw up, not only against him, but against the world, closing it out. Exactly, he thought with a sudden surge of self-righteousness, the opposite of the book he was writing, which sought to commemorate, to describe, to remember, to tell the truth.

He watched her go down the hall, calling when she reached the kitchen, "The lazy Yanks are all set! Aren't we my little lovemuffins?"

❖   ❖   ❖

Gusting wind pushed rain into their faces. Caitlin had pulled on a green poncho to cover Boen and she walked up ahead with Sharon and Thomas chatting away while he was forced to stay back and help Ethan and Jenny through the muck. His shoes—and the kids' pants—were soaked. Ethan's lips, when Martin bent to pull his son's foot free from a mud-hole, matched his blue raincoat.

The path degenerated to a set of wheel ruts before fading altogether and they were walking through fields avoiding cow patties. Jenny took his hand. "Are you tired, honey?" he said.

She shook her head and squeezed his fingers. He smoothed his hand over her wet hair, then arranged her hood more tightly over her head. "I'm sure we're almost there."

He was carrying Ethan by the time he could finally see the three dark shapes of the Collins girls running toward them through the rain. Then, behind the girls, through the earth, rose a spray of white.

Sharon's girls gathered around her, talking together quietly, so that it sounded, with the rain pelting Martin's hood, like a tree full of birds. Caitlin walked on ahead, toward where the mist had spouted. Squinting, he made out the shape of the wormhole.

"Mommy!" Jenny shouted, as though Caitlin was about to hurl herself into the hole. Pulling her hand from Martin's she ran over to Caitlin.

They shouldn't have come to Ireland. What might have been beautiful under different circumstances was all strain and danger (the driving, the cliffs, the wormhole). Certainly they should not have come to stay with Sharon and Thomas. Perhaps they could make the evening ferry back to Galway. Caitlin could get drunk in their rented house while he sat in the living room watching Sky Television, or pretending to read while staring over the rim of a book at her beer, as though he could, if he just focused, will it away and along with it all the unhappiness and anger and hatred. Which is, he was surprised to find, what he felt, watching Jenny and Caitlin walk slowly toward the wormhole.

He hated his wife. Well, there was love, but there is so often love. So often there's hatred, as well, but he'd never felt it before. And along with his wife, he felt he could easily expand his hatred to include Thomas. Martin had wanted to believe the man's gruffness was some endearing trait of the shy Irish, but it wasn't. It was mean-spiritedness, part of the man's sense of superiority. He'd been a grave-digger in Queens, a fisherman in the Atlantic Ocean, and his brother, in front of his own eyes, had been washed out to sea and who knows what else. And what did Martin have? What had he ever done?

He followed the Collins family over the shale rock to the hole. "Here we go!" Caitlin shouted and up shot a cloud of mist. Jenny screamed with delight.

In the hole he could see the sea frothing, slamming into the rock walls. He set Ethan down on the ground and the boy ran to Caitlin. She squatted down and wiped rain out of her son's face.

"In the summer," Thomas said, "when the tide is out, the girls like to climb down there."

"You should come," Sharon said, putting a hand on Martin's arm, "in the summer. It's beautiful then."

"Ah, but it's too crowded," Thomas said. "The Germans and the Italians. And the Yanks, of course." The smile he gave Martin wasn't friendly. "Always the

Ship To:

Valeria A Garcia Tufro
6917 Charade Drive —
DALLAS, TX 75214

Order ID: 114-2276427-5479413

Thank you for buying from EastTexasBooks on Amazon Marketplace.

Shipping Address:
Valeria A Garcia Tufro
6917 Charade Drive
DALLAS, TX 75214

Order Date:	Mon, Oct 3, 2022
Shipping Service:	Standard
Buyer Name:	Valeria
Seller Name:	EastTexasBooks

Quantity	Product Details	Unit price	Order Totals
1	The Empty House (Willow Springs Editions) [Paperback] [2013] Oates, Nathan **SKU:** 03112022-0470 **ASIN:** 0988316676 **Condition:** New **Order Item ID:** 47018395344178	$23.84	Item subtotal $23.84 Shipping total $3.99 Tax $2.30 **Item total** **$30.13**

Returning your item:

Grand total: $30.13

information about the return and refund policies that apply.

Visit https://www.amazon.com/returns to print a return shipping label. Please have your order ID ready.

Thanks for buying on Amazon Marketplace. To provide feedback for the seller please visit www.amazon.com/feedback. To contact the seller, go to Your Orders in Your Account. Click the seller's name under the appropriate product. Then, in the "Further Information" section, click "Contact the Seller."

14,702

Yanks. Coming back to find their *roots*. But I tell them, there aren't going to be any roots here on the island. The soil is only a foot or two deep at the best." The smile split his wrinkled face in half.

"Well," Martin said, stepping toward the wormhole, leaning forward to look down into the gray-blue water, "you know how the Yanks are. *Fuckin' idgits.* Right?"

"Oh, no," Sharon said. She looked startled, her thin lips pursed, red hair wet and flattened. Mary and the other girls stared at Martin, shocked.

He hurried over to his family, nearly slipping on the wet rocks. A spray of mist shot up through the wormhole and fell over them like a thick, fluffy rain. He stood close to Caitlin and said, "They climb down in there. In the summer time."

"Really?" Jenny said, frowning through the water running down her face.

"Do you want to scoot up to the edge?" he said. "Like up on the fort?"

"Daddy," Ethan said, clutching Caitlin's leg.

"Honey, don't worry. It'll be fine. We'll crawl."

Jenny stared at the wormhole and Ethan pushed his face into his mother's leg.

"Fine," he said. "I'll do it."

The echo of the water on the rocks swelled as he neared the hole, blotting out everything else. When he could see the entire circle of water rushing in and sucking back out, he dropped to his knees. The rocks were slick and pocked with puddles. His entire body was soaked. A spray shot up before him, a wall of white, hanging, then falling over him. He lay in the water breathing hard, and then crawled out until his head hung over the edge.

The wormhole wasn't a pure drop into the loud, churning water: there were levels of rock, every five feet or so. He looked back at his family. Sharon and Thomas were standing beside Caitlin. Ethan had his face pressed into his mother's leg and Jenny was sitting down on a rock. Through the rain he could see her face was twisted up, crying. Boen, of course, was hidden away inside the sling. He waved to his family and then pulled his legs around and slipped them over the edge so he was sitting. Bracing himself with his hands on the rock he lowered his feet down to the next level. The ledge below was maybe four feet wide, plenty to stand on, but small enough that, if he wasn't careful, he might fall. Stretching his foot down to touch the wet rock, he clung to the wall and slipped beneath the rim of earth. He huddled against the wall, the roar of the tide pulling in and out, smashing against the rocks, as though the water was trapped, and maddened. At the far end of the wormhole he could see the cavern through which the water came, a dark path of rushing water. As he watched another large wave poured, swelling and pushing against the small path of the cave, into the wormhole, the water writhing then slamming into the walls below him, deafening, the spout of water rising, drenching him.

He smiled and clung to the wall. He waited there for someone to come and get him, to creep up to the ledge and look for him. The water churned and a few moments later another large wave rushed in and washed over him with greater force this time, so he dug his fingers into the black rock and clenched his eyes shut. He imagined himself letting go, falling into the water, and being sucked by the undertow into the narrow cavern and out to sea. His body would never be found. There was nothing between here and North America but thousands of miles of cold water.

But he didn't fall. And no one came to the edge above to look for him. He pressed his body to the wall and straightened up and was just able to see over the edge. Sharon and Thomas were still there, but Caitlin was gone. Then he saw her. She was walking back the way they'd come with the children, theirs as well as the Collins girls, all gathered around her.

"Caitlin," he screamed, but with the roar of the water he could hardly hear his own voice. He knew now what she was doing, what she'd always been doing. She was stealing his family. She was stealing everything. He felt as though he'd been tricked. Throughout their marriage he'd worried that Caitlin was on an edge and that he needed to hold her back or else she'd tip over into the darkness, all that darkness she wrote about, but this wasn't true, he saw, watching her walk away. It was a lie. She'd done it to put him off balance, to unsteady him, to push him out onto the edge while she drew back away, with their family all gathered about her, a family that was nothing like the world of her fiction, a family of happy, smart, gentle children.

He put a foot on the wall, figuring a way to pull himself out. Caitlin and the children continued to walk away, without looking back. If there had been any hope of them hearing him, over the roar of the water, he'd have screamed again. Instead he grabbed at the loose rocks for a grip and then, eyes clenched shut, gasping for breath, pushed himself up and his hand slipped. When his elbow struck a sharp rock, pain flared across his eyes. Clutching his elbow he huddled down on the ledge. His arm was throbbing, as though it had suddenly grown its own heart, small and furious.

He didn't notice the hand, thrust down near his face, because he was crying. Then there was the voice, "Take my hand."

Above him, squatting on the edge, was Thomas. Rain ran down his wrinkled face and he held a hand down to Martin. "Put your foot on the wall and take my fuckin' hand."

With no time to wipe away his rainy tears, Martin stood and held up his injured arm. Thomas grabbed it and, with a grunt and a snarl, hauled Martin's body up.

LOOKING FOR SERVICE

As soon as they called the First Class passengers, I stepped to the head of the line, hurried down to my seat and braced myself for the crowd that came slumping past minutes later with their loose, swollen bags. Any of them could stop, pretend to cough or adjust a strap, and a runty hand could pull out a cobbled together shank which he'd stick into my chest, my neck, my cheek where it would clatter against my teeth, again and again, sinking through the soft meat of my eye. I left my seatbelt unbuckled, ready to fly up and fight my way back to American soil. When the stewardesses began their pantomime of safety, I was able to relax a little—probably only because by that time I'd finished two vodka tonics. I was hoping to drink myself to sleep, but as we reached cruising altitude and the ice in my drink tumbled under the collar of my shirt, I knew I wouldn't be so lucky this time.

When I was first told they were sending me to this country to do an accounting of the Canadian mining firm's books, I told them I couldn't. I said, "My wife is sick."

There was silence on the other end of the line and I was suddenly unsure if I'd ever met the man to whom I was speaking. I'd assumed he was the same Steve we'd had over for dinner a few years earlier. My wife had made enchiladas with mole sauce. Steve had picked around the plate, eaten half his salad and a few scoops of refried beans, leaving two perfectly formed enchiladas like a big old fuck-you to his hostess who'd spent hours in the kitchen lifting the skin off broiled peppers.

The man on the phone eventually said, "I'm sorry to hear about that." Another pause, as though this made what came next acceptable, "Your flight's tomorrow, at seven."

"Seven?"

"A.M." he explained.

As turbulence wobbled the plane I leaned my head into the oily leather seat and breathed deeply, but this made the pressure in my chest expand into a lead weight.

Half-way through the flight the woman beside me turned and grinned until I stopped pretending to be asleep. She was an American, a Mississippian, she clarified, and was going down to visit her daughter who was about to marry a young man from the country's elite. She wore a beige suit like an ill-fitting exoskeleton. Every inch of exposed skin—face, neck, hands—was layered with foundation and powder so a smell of petroleum oozed out from beneath gusts of perfume. Her eyes were small and a beautiful blue, startling to find rooted in that puffy, twitching face.

"They're very nice people," she said, then admitted that in fact she'd never met them. "But they own three coffee plantations. The wedding is going to be at one of them."

Despite her grin, she was clearly horrified that her daughter was about to be swallowed up by a family of brown people, no matter how rich they might be, no matter how comforting the word *plantation*.

"You know, they're not actually Hispanic, they're Spanish. I mean, they have no Indian blood at all."

Eventually, she left me alone and began searching through her cavernous plaid handbag, setting off an incessant clinking of lipstick cases against her cell phone, wallet, and makeup case, accompanied by the tinny rattle of loose change. At one point she pulled out a photograph in a gaudy metal frame. In it a beautiful young woman in a tight fitting white dress leaned against a stone wall. The woman stared for a few minutes; then, with an elaborate sigh, she dropped the frame back into the purse.

I'm sure I looked like a compatriot, an overweight, middle-aged man with thinning hair gone white except a few strands of black that looked permanently wet. The starched collar of my button-down shirt, the faint pinstripe on my suit pants, and the shine of my black shoes all suggested not only that we were both Americans, but also that back home we might even have been friends, would've invited each other over for dinner parties where we'd drink too much, flirt clumsily at the fridge, then turn our energies to moaning about our ingrate children, the awfulness of youth in general, and the folly of anyone who disagreed with us about anything. And, I knew, we *were* compatriots of a sort, but I was too tired, too angry at being on that plane when I should've been home with Joyce.

I'd promised no more trips after she got sick. I told her I'd work from home, or at least from the American headquarters of the firms I audited. But it turned out this wasn't possible, and so every few months I was off again—Zimbabwe, Peru, Bolivia, South Africa—in each place working to make sense of the tangle of fraud that constituted the local office's financial records. I had a particular talent for this, an ability to see through bureaucratic madness and to articulate a legally defensible financial record. Typically, I went down to the capitals of these godforsaken places and took a limo to my hotel—the nicest in the country, holdovers from colonial days—and the next morning another limo would ferry me to the offices that were always staffed half with gringos who looked like they'd had too much local rum, and half by locals who hadn't quite learned how to smother their bitter scent. I was given my own office, usually that of some recently fired executive, and I would make sense of the confusion they'd all bred in their frenzy to pull minerals from the earth.

We descended through a scrim of clouds. The city clung to a tangle of ravines at the foot of sheer, black mountains, the lower slopes of which were smothered with shanty-towns. The downtown was marked by dull gray buildings and a few half-finished concrete towers. Our plane touched down with a jolt, the seatbelt cut into my gut, then we seemed to be rising again before slamming down a second time, the engines whirring, the smell of burning rubber filling the cabin. Then we were there, trembling on the runway.

◆　　　◆　　　◆

None of the three men holding name-signs were waiting for me when I came through customs. The glass doors weren't tinted and the near-equatorial sun set off a pulsing headache behind my eyes. When I checked my cell phone, set up with world-wide access, it said, *Looking for Service.*

Maybe it was my exhaustion, my hangover, or the soldier who stepped away from the wall, eying my bag, but I felt suddenly weightless and lost, as though waking from one dream into another when I should've been back in the real world, not caught in this greasy airport with the high, rising scream of a woman at the customs point as soldiers tossed her underwear, her socks, her shirts to the floor, then held up a pair of blue jeans and scythed them in half with a knife. Whatever the reason, I panicked and joined a clump of passengers heading for the glass doors.

"Excuse me?" an American voice said. There beside me were two young hippy travelers, a boy and a girl, both grinning like idiots. They wore loose, dirty clothes that might've been hemp and stank of patchouli and sweat. Loose leather sandals showed off filthy feet, toenails blackened with grime, feet they surely planned to tan before going back home with dysentery and a few snap-shots of indigenous kids atop a trash heap.

"Do you know which way the train is?" the girl asked.

"There's no train," I said, hurrying after the crowd.

As we rushed along, the tall, thin boy held up a travel guide and said, "No, it says there's one that goes into the city center." He said this with a kind of desperation, which was understandable. Stretching out around the airport was a dead zone of warehouses with metal shutters pulled over the doors. Power lines sagged from leaning poles. All this made it look like if there had once been a city here, it had long ago been abandoned.

"No," I said, "the book's wrong. There's no train." I quickened my pace, hoping in their confusion they'd fall away.

"So, how do we get to the city?" the girl asked, scurrying to keep up.

"Take the bus," I said, pointing at the crowd ahead of us, which bulged around the doors before squeezing out, like a clot of blood from a narrow wound. "Or a taxi."

"Dude, isn't that expensive?" the boy said.

"Depends on what you think of as expensive," I said.

The girl was still smiling, bobbing her head as though we were listening to a good, thick reggae beat. Then we were outside in the too-bright light. Sitting at the otherwise empty curb was a black SUV and in it were two men wearing sunglasses. They leaned forward and though it was possible they were just trying to get a better glimpse of the American girl's thin white shirt, I felt sure they were waiting for me and so I started walking faster, pushing through the crowd. Behind me the American kids were shouting. I hunched down and jogged to the orange bus. In that SUV a rifle could be sliding up between the men, scope swirling out of focus before sharpening in on the white hairs at the back of my head.

The bus driver was leaning in the open door and for a moment my Spanish abandoned me. I gestured at the door and nodded. I glanced back at the SUV. One of the men was standing in the street, pointing. Finally, I found the word, "*Abierto.*"

"*Lo siento,*" the driver said, stepping aside. I sank into a narrow green seat, my legs pinched up against my gut, suitcase and briefcase piled to my chin.

At that moment, I finally paused to wonder what in the hell I was doing. My limo driver was probably inside right now, he'd probably just gone to the bathroom, but here I was, in the open, jammed into this bus which was already filling up with peasants hauling bags of all shapes and sizes they'd managed to smuggle past the driver who screamed at everyone to toss their luggage onto the roof.

"Is this taken?" The American girl was smiling at me, pointing at the empty six inches of seat.

Once settled, her leg pressing against mine, she held out a hand. "I'm Allie."

"Robert," I said. Her hand was slim and cool and in the midst of my confusion, I held on too long, until she was forced to pull back with a pitying smile.

Soon, every seat was full and the aisle was packed. The American boy, who I later learned was named Billy, was pinned between two fat ladies, his spiky blonde hair brushing the ceiling as the bus lurched away.

"Is this your first time here?" Allie said, leaning across me to look out the window so her breast rested on my arm. I tried to see the road behind us, to see if the SUV was there, but the angle was wrong.

"No," I lied, because it was easier.

"It's mine. But I was in Mexico last year for a couple months. In the Yucatan."

I tried to smile, though my mouth was so dry my lips stuck against my teeth.

We passed a few dozen warehouses and pulled up onto a truck clogged highway. Men bent beneath enormous piles of sticks or stones walked along the road, their faces gray with the diesel and dust kicked up. We passed a line of auto-body shops where cars sat stripped and piles of tires leaned toward the street. Mangy dogs and naked children scampered in and out of the open garages while shirtless men hefted greasy tools and wiped their sweating faces with handkerchiefs.

"Dude," Billy shouted, leaning toward our seat. "Have you ever been to Tonterrico? I hear the waves are awesome."

I didn't answer. All my energy was focused on ignoring the puddle of what was possibly piss sticking my shoes to the floor.

◆　　　◆　　　◆

At the bus station, I paid for my ticket and those of the kids, who patted their pockets as though they'd lost their wallets. I'd hoped this generosity would be enough to get rid of them, but they followed me to the hotel shuttle. There was no sign of the SUV, and as I was ushered to a plush red seat by a man in a tuxedo shirt and bow-tie, I felt a measure of calm returning. While the driver stood in the door to see if there were other passengers—there weren't—I noticed that neither of the kids had backpacks, or, for that matter, bags of any kind. They looked tired and unwashed, though that, I knew, might be an affectation.

"Are you staying at the Palacio?" I said. These kids were pretending to be vagabonds, and so I knew they'd never put up the cost of the room, which was, considering the general destitution of this entire region, extravagant. But now that my confusion had receded, I felt sorry for them. They were scared and lost and I could help them out, a little.

Allie said, "We don't have a reservation, but maybe. Is it nice?"

I said it was unquestionably the best.

"Well, so maybe we will," Billy said, plastering his face against the window.

As the shuttle pulled away, Allie started telling a story about the time she'd traveled to Saint Petersburg and ended up getting in a cab whose driver promised to take her to a club.

"He said it was the hip new place. Then we got off the road and were driving through these warehouses and I got pretty nervous. I mean, I thought he was going to rape me or something, but then we turned a corner and there was this one warehouse, with lights and techno music. I guess I was just relieved, so I didn't think it was so weird when the driver got out of the car. The music was so loud it was like shaking your head apart, and he opened the door for me. I didn't step inside. I could see that the place was empty, I mean, almost empty, except this huge speaker stack and these towers of strobe lights and then I noticed like four or five guys, all holding baseball bats and on the ground in front of them was this guy, all beaten up. The guy on the floor looked up and shouted, 'Help!' He was American. I started running. If I'd been wearing sandals I'd be dead. I ran and ran and that fat fuck of a cabbie couldn't keep up and eventually I hid in this empty warehouse. I could hear the men go by, looking for me, and they came by again later. I was hiding behind this stack of metal barrels, but if they came into the warehouse they totally would've seen me. It was the middle of the night, you know, but I ran out and went to another warehouse, in case they decided to search that first one and I heard them, shouting, a ways off. When it was light I snuck out and walked back to the city along the train tracks. It was pretty goddamn scary, though."

In all likelihood this was a myth she'd heard while traveling, or one she'd read on the internet. That it wasn't true didn't matter, what mattered was telling the story and the practice this gave her. In a few months she'd come down from the remote mountains to get drunk in gringo bars on the coast and talk about all the crazy stuff she'd seen. It wouldn't matter if anything she said was true, because facts weren't important, what was important was the idea of herself that traveling confirmed: she was brave and adventurous and open-minded and now she could go home thirty pounds lighter and filthy, which would frighten her parents enough to allow her to live off their money for a few more years.

"That's totally fucked up, man," Billy said, his face up against the window as we pulled past the gray government buildings. "Hey, isn't that the Department of Interior?"

"So, are you traveling, or what?" Allie said, picking at the dirt ground under her nails.

"No, I'm here for work."

"Where do you work?"

"I'm a consultant."

"For what, the government?" From the hardening of her consonants it was clear she had me figured out: I was a bad guy and she was more than eager to judge, not all that different from my daughters, both of whom fancied themselves world savers. They had the security to use their educations and opportunities however they saw fit—one was an assistant D.A. in New Jersey and the other was a school teacher in Brooklyn—all because I'd worked my entire life to make enough money so they could attend Columbia and Brown.

"Not the government," I said. "Independent companies."

"What kind of companies?"

"A mining company. I'm auditing their operations here." I said this in a rush as though I was flustered, which I guess I was. That's how I got any time my daughters started in on universal health care, or how awful American foreign policy was. Susan, our oldest, the teacher, was home helping Joyce while I was away and for her I'd pounded a sign into the front lawn: *Thank You, George Bush.*

Allie just stared, as though waiting for horns to sprout from my forehead. Billy was still muttering about this building and that building and the civil war.

"*Aqui, El Palacio,*" the driver said, easing to a stop.

I left the American kids frowning at the glimmering facade of the hotel and hurried into the revolving door. The lobby, with its slick stone floors and dribbling fountain, was empty except for a cluster of boys in bright red jackets and black pants who looked desperate to snatch my bag away.

In my reserved room I went to the drawer of the bedside table and found the promised handgun and shoulder hostler. I splashed cold water on my face, dried it on a plush towel, lay down on the slightly lumpy mattress, and watched the jerking ceiling fan.

◆   ◆   ◆

I woke to the knocking at the door and groped for the gun, nearly falling out of bed, shouting, "Hold on. Just hold on."

Through the peephole I saw a bellboy. He was barely five feet tall and so thin his arms and hands looked withered, his fingers long and spindly. He rattled away in Spanish, spraying spit.

"What?" I said. "English. Speak English."

"Guests, down." He pointed at the floor. "Wait. You. Guests."

"Who? Who is it?"

He shook his misshapen head and pulled his lips up into what he must've imagined was a smile.

"Why didn't you call?"

"No phone work," he said, pointing into my room. "Guests. Down. Bar." Then, probably sensing I wasn't going to tip, he shuffled away.

I checked the phone. There was no dial tone, just a blank space. I checked my cell, hoping to call Joyce and make sure Susan had arrived. The phone said, *Looking for Service.* Before leaving the room I grabbed my briefcase. You could never be sure with these companies. They were often frantic and might want to see something to comfort them right away.

The bar was off the lobby, through a frosted glass door. I let my eyes adjust to the darkness, taking in the sour smell of bleach, half-full ashtrays, and rum. An oily sunset was smeared across the one window.

From a booth near the window a woman waved. It was Allie, and beside her was Billy. They were drinking tall, fruit-adorned cocktails.

"We were waiting," she said, pointing at their drinks in which quivered flecks of poisonous ice. "Someone's got to pay for these drinks, after all."

Still in something of a daze, I joined them, settling the briefcase on my lap. The waiter appeared and soon we were sipping a round of beers.

"Are you staying here?" I asked, not quite able to pull myself fully into the waking world.

"Dude, are you crazy?" Billy said. "This place costs a fortune."

"We found a hostel," Allie said. "Not too far away."

"Well, that's great," I said, tipping my bottle at them, then taking a sip and trying not to gag.

"But we thought we'd come and meet you for dinner." She reached across the table to pat my hand, as though they felt sorry for me. At that moment her smile reminded me of Susan, with that smug twist to her mouth. I'd assumed these kids were in their early twenties, but now I thought they might be the same age as my daughters, late-twenties, on the cusp of realizing that life wasn't a game, that it was hard and ruthless and that the main thing was to keep from getting completely and totally screwed over by others.

"Sure," I said. "We can get some dinner. I bet the food's okay here."

"Don't be silly," Allie said, leaning forward to slap my shoulder. "Not here. We know a great place nearby."

"Is that a good idea? The food can be pretty dodgy down here." I touched the gun under my arm.

"Come on," Billy said, biffing me on the shoulder. "We'll be fine, man. It'll be an adventure." He stared at the briefcase on my lap, seemed about to say something, then just grinned like a dope.

I should've gone to my room and back to sleep. Maybe it was exhaustion, or maybe, like that idiot Billy said, I just wanted to do something different, something that might help me slip for a moment out of my life.

"Just don't order salad. You'll be fine," Allie said. "And you better get the check, big guy," she said, then threw back her head and chugged the rest of her beer, clinking the bottle down on the table. Gasping for breath, she said, "Ready?"

❖   ❖   ❖

They refused my offer of a taxi and so we walked, gathering attention on every street—three gringos ripe for a mugging, or, if the locals were feeling more industrious, a kidnapping. The chances of this increased the farther we walked, out of the governmental area, through what counted here as a "middle class" neighborhood, and past a hostel with a few gringos hanging around out front. I asked if that's where they were staying and they smiled dimly.

We walked on, into a slum. The narrow passageways between crumbling concrete walls were littered with garbage and an open sewer trickled down the middle. All the children were barefoot and ravenous, dark eyes glittering as they displayed their stumpy teeth. A clutch of them gathered around us, tugging at our pockets and sleeves and smearing swarms of bacteria over my fingers and the brass lock on my briefcase, so eventually I cradled it against my chest. I kept thinking, *What the hell am I doing here*, but I didn't turn back. I began to wonder if I'd picked up some tropical bug and was in the early stages of delirium. Sweat soaked my back. I touched the handle of the gun again and again for comfort.

This was probably just the sort of thing Susan had done during her recent trip across India. She'd come back with a new wardrobe of saris, a streak of red dye in her light brown hair, and stories about the noble poor and our responsibility to them. Like Allie and Billy, Susan had played at destitution, renting rooms from families in remote villages where she could've easily been raped or killed. During her recent visit she'd worn me out with her stories and self-righteousness. One night, after listening to awful, jangling music for an hour, I'd helped Joyce to bed, hooked up the tubes, and said, "Well, that was quite a performance."

"Performance?" she said, in the raspy near-whisper that was all she'd been able to manage for the past year. The brittle strands of her hair clung to the crisp pillowcase.

"Susan," I said, kissing her papery cheek. "That music."

Joyce closed her eyes and said, softly, "I thought it was beautiful."

"Beautiful?" I said. She opened her eyes and at that moment she looked frightened of me. I tried to calm myself. "Don't be silly, Joyce. It was awful."

"No," she said, closing her eyes again. "No, Robert." And then she was asleep. Music leaked up from below for hours and I ground my teeth until my jaw throbbed.

I told myself that Allie and Billy weren't much different from my daughters, which is obviously part of the reason I went with them: I wanted to protect them and, in so doing, I thought maybe I could teach them something useful. The longer I was around them, the more ragged they looked. Both were severely underweight, especially Allie, whose jaw was drawn so tight it looked painful, and she had the wild look of hunger, the kind of fear that could get her into real trouble. There was something black and feral in her eyes, as though they didn't quite see you, only what she could get from you. She'd carried her Central American adventure too far, and soon, if she wasn't careful, she would end up truly lost.

At the door of the restaurant, the urchins fell away. At first, my relief they were gone was so great I didn't notice that the restaurant doubled as a brothel, but by the time we were seated at a rickety plastic table, I'd noticed the sickly girls, none older than sixteen, lined up against the far wall, shifting their legs apart so their tiny dresses rode higher. The bar stools were full of heavy men wearing cowboy hats which they tipped back on their heads to peer at us through the smoke-haze.

"Apparently," Allie said, scooting up to the table, "the tacos here are killer."

A tiny Indian woman with wildly unkempt hair took our order. I lied and said I'd eaten but that dinner was on me, of course. A few urchins approached the door warily, eager for us to emerge as drunk, easy targets.

When the food came the American kids bent over the paper plates and crammed everything into their mouths, even the lettuce, sauce dripping over their dirty hands, which they licked clean like dogs. I signaled to the waitress for another round of tacos, and they tore into them, letting out little groans of pleasure. Wiping their mouths on their sleeves, without a word of thanks, they pushed their plates away and grinned at me.

"Hey," Allie said, sitting up straighter. She pointed at me. "Do you have any money?"

"What?" I said. "Of course."

"So, like, do you think we could borrow some?" She cocked her head and grinned and when she did I noticed she was missing several teeth, as though they'd been pried from her raw, red gums.

"For what?"

"To buy stuff," she said, so brightly, so stupidly that I pulled out my wallet.

"How much?" I said, peering at the lump of nearly useless local money and the crisp American bills behind.

"I mean, whatever you can spare." She was still smiling, but it had a harder edge now. This wasn't the first time she'd asked someone for money.

I pulled out two American twenties and handed them across the table. She squinted at them as though not quite believing I was so cheap, then slipped them beneath the table.

"That's great. Thanks," she said.

"Hold on." I pulled out another two twenties.

"Thank you," she said softly, folding the bills carefully and tucking them away. "I'll pay you back."

"Don't worry about it."

Done with me now, the American kids started yakking about something. Music, I thought, though the arcane names of bands, or brands, or TV shows proved impenetrable. I fell into the role of observer, watching men slip in from the street, skirt the far wall until they reached the line of girls, one of who would peel off and lead the man through a curtained doorway. One of the girls had noticed me watching and kept catching my eye, smiling, maybe thinking I'd be good for a big tip.

"So, are you like actually going up to the mine?" Allie said, cutting Billy off in the middle of one of his stories.

"Excuse me?"

"The mine, are you going there?" She was squinting, as though I was far away.

"No. There's plenty of work to do at the headquarters."

"Yeah, I bet," she said, propping her knobby elbows on the table.

Like my daughters, this girl clearly had some fantasy about a world made up of good guys and bad guys. This was a liberal delusion, one that sensible people eventually realized was a limited and immature way of seeing the world.

"I've heard about that mine," Allie said.

I knew she meant in *Harper's*. Susan had mailed me a copy of the issue. The article focused on the displacement of the local population, and the tensions this generated within the community and the possibility that it might reignite the civil war. In truth, I'd only skimmed the pages, bloated as they were with nonsense.

"I guess that makes you an expert, doesn't it?" I said.

"I think it's pretty fucked up," she said. "I mean, how can you work for that company? They're stealing those people's land."

"Those people don't own the land. That's the point."

"That's such bullshit!" she shouted, slapping the table. The men at the bar turned on their stools.

"Don't be ridiculous," I said, just above a whisper. "The opportunities that mining presents for this country outweigh the concerns of a few subsistence farmers." I hated myself for getting sucked in, but I'd never been able to stop myself. Thanksgiving dinners always ended in acrimony at our house.

"Of course it does!" Allie was shouting now. Everyone was watching us. "Opportunities for the rich who've raped this country for hundreds of years, and for North American corporations. Which I guess is what your job is, right? Grease the fucking gears."

There was something in her tone that made me think she wasn't just someone who'd stumbled across an article that had mentioned, now that I thought about it, the presence of international human rights organizations serving as observers and even human shields for the local communities when the mining company sent in men to burn the villages. Seeing her indignation, I began to wonder if maybe she was one of those. Even brainless Billy could've been an activist.

"I think you're simplifying things. The world isn't that easy," I said.

"It's not?" she shouted. "What's so complicated? Thieves come down and steal land, property, goods, and call themselves a company. That's how it's always been." Her face was red and the cords of her neck stood out. A little vein pulsed along her forehead. Billy watched all this with a bemused smile, as though we were speaking a foreign language.

"That's how a child thinks," I said. "Just because you read something in a magazine doesn't mean you understand anything."

"What the fuck are you talking about? What fucking magazine? I guess you," she lunged forward, trying to poke me in the chest, but the table caught her in the stomach, "are just naturally full of fucking wisdom, aren't you?"

Before I could say anything she stood and stomped to the bar, squeezing in between two men. Billy fussed with the label on his bottle, then followed. They whispered together furiously while I finished my beer and gestured for another. Little peaks of their bitching rose into audibility every now and then. When I'd nearly finished my new beer, they went and sat at another table, back near the prostitutes.

Maybe at that point I should've left. But I'd seen the way the men in the bar were looking at the American kids, and though they were strangers, I felt responsible for them. I ordered another beer, told the waitress I was paying for everything the Americans had, and snuck a look at my cell phone, which was still getting no service. Though the lopsided clock on the wall said it was only six o'clock, dark had fallen. Back home, Joyce would be exhausted, barely able to shuffle to the bathroom where she'd strain to urinate and then brush her teeth. Susan would have to help lift her mother into bed, hook up the tubes and set the level of the oxygen. These are things I'd done every day for the past year when I was home and I'd come to think of them as rites no one knew how to enact but me. I hated when reality imposed on this feeling, as it continually did when we had to hire nurses to help while I was abroad. This time, Joyce said she didn't want a stranger. She couldn't stand another bored, tired nurse changing her bed pan, lifting her frail shoulders from the sheets to slip her nightgown off before sponging her down, massaging her legs and slipping a clean gown over her head. I'd written out how to do all this in explicit detail for Susan, but I was worried something would go wrong. Joyce might die and even though I knew this was inevitable, knew that soon enough she'd be gone, I wasn't ready for it and couldn't accept it. And now I was here, thousands of miles away and out of touch. I wanted to be there, to take care of her, to sit up in bed when I heard her sighing in pain or just shifting her hips. I was alert in a way I hadn't been since Susan was born and for the first few weeks had only been able to sleep nestled between us. All that time I slept thinly, always aware of her delicate body on the mattress. Instead of thrashing around in the sheets as I usually did I was suddenly calm and careful, and it was how I felt taking care of Joyce, the slight weight of her body in my arms as I cradled her and lifted her up and set her down in the soft seat of her wheelchair. But what was I supposed to do when the man who might've been Steve called? If I'd refused to come down here, they'd have fired me, had nearly already done so because of my "personal conflicts" that were "hindering my accountability," and if that happened we'd be left without health insurance.

Distracted by these thoughts, I didn't notice the two men join Billy and Allie. The men looked about the same age as the Americans, but were of a whole other world. Both men had cowboy hats tipped down over their narrow faces. I'd seen men like this all over the world, charming enough on the surface, but an inch down they were criminals. I could tell from the way they sat in their chairs that beneath their shirts were knives, or guns. The two men laughed, stood up, and gestured to the Americans. Allie and Billy complied. They knocked at a door on the back wall, which opened a crack, then let them in.

By the time I fumbled up out of my seat and across the room, the door was closed. The nearest prostitute grinned at me, tugging down the neck of her blouse.

I knocked and waited. While I did, I reached into my jacket and lifted the gun half an inch out of the holster, then let it fall back. In my other hand I gripped my briefcase, full of financial papers and spreadsheets and my laptop computer. When no one answered my knocks, I turned to the bartender, who avoided looking at me. "*Abierto la puerta,*" I said. The bartender smiled at me, then nodded and stepped around the bar and unlocked the door.

"Dancing," he said, speaking Spanish slowly, as if I was a child. "Good dancing."

A steep flight of stairs led down into a room that pulsed with blue light and a dense, throbbing music. The stairwell was smothered with water sodden posters—political ads, deodorant advertisements, and what looked like rock bands, men and women studded with piercings, sticking their tongues out and flicking off the camera as they danced atop blood red letters that had blistered and burst apart. The door above slammed, a lock thrown.

The music was too loud to hear voices in the room, the walls of which seemed to be shaking with the violent strobe light, and it took me a moment to recognize Allie and Billy at a table near a low wooden platform out of which rose a greasy metal pole. The Americans were laughing, bent doubled over as if in pain, and the two men they'd been talking with were smiling and smoking, holding what must have been joints out as the kids straightened up. There were half a dozen other tables, only one of which was occupied by a single man in a long trench-coat, a baseball cap pulled low over his face. I sat at the table nearest the stairs, turning my chair so I could see if someone came down. A tiny, shriveled woman stepped from the shadows, her old body grotesquely squeezed into a leather bra and panties, her loose, cellulite thighs quivering as she stepped beside me and glared until I ordered a beer. Watching her slink back to the bar in the corner I noticed a wall, covered with leather straps, whips, and a long, thin machete.

I jumped when the music cut off, just long enough to hear Allie say, "Exactly. That's exactly what I'm—" and then the music erupted again, a crashing heavy-metal that felt as if it were scraping the inside of my eyes. A silvery cloud drifted along the low ceiling filling the room with the overripe stink of marijuana.

At the far end of the wooden stage a heavy black curtain was pushed aside and a young woman walked out unsteadily on high, silver stilettos and nothing else, her small, high breasts not moving even when she tottered into the bright puddle of a spotlight. She stopped in the middle of the stage and stood smiling shyly, her skin shining blue with sweat or oil. She stared straight ahead, blinking heavily in the spotlight, smiling. One of the men at Allie and Billy's table stood up, stretching his arms over his head, leaning down to whisper something to Allie, who laughed and nodded. Slowly, as if everyone weren't watching, the man walked to the wall beside the bar and took down a short-handled black leather whip with three strands that sagged at the ends. Hefting it to test the weight, he walked back to his table, made another joke, then, as the music rose to an even more frantic pitch, stepped onto the stage beside the woman.

I stared at my beer, but I could hear the wet, heavy snap of the whip and once I heard, through the din of the music, a single cry of pain. Only when the music shifted between songs and I heard a woman's voice, "No, I'm serious," did I look up.

Allie was being pushed toward the stage by one of the other men, his mouth open, teeth flashing. Allie tried to turn, but the man grabbed her arms and spun her around to face the stage on which the naked girl was bent over, her face hidden by a fall of hair. Allie shook her head, but the man on the stage leaned down, grabbed her wrist, and jerked her up. Billy, I noticed, was staring at his hands in his lap, as if about to go to sleep. The man on the stage held the whip out toward Allie. She turned to step down, but the man grabbed her arm, pulled her back, and thrust the whip into her hand. I couldn't tell, with the flashing light, with the blue haze, with the pounding music, but I thought she might be crying as she looked down at the whip in her hand, but I know that as she stepped up beside the kneeling girl she looked up, back at me, as if she'd known all along I was there. I put my hand on my gun, out of fear I guess, but also because I felt sure at that moment that I was in danger, that after she was done with the girl, she'd come for me. Then the fear left her face and Allie twirled the whip around her head and gyrated her hips. Beneath the music I could hear the men cheering as I scrambled out of my seat, knocking over the untouched beer on my table. I ran up the stairs, slipping and hitting my knee so hard that I limped through the door after knocking wildly until it was opened.

Outside the bar I got lost immediately, but kept hobbling until I found a larger street, lined with auto-body shops, against the fences of which snarling black dogs hurled themselves. I walked along the side of the road, tucking the gun back into the holster, my briefcase in the other hand, glancing back until I spotted a cab and flagged it down.

✦   ✦   ✦

Now it's nearly morning. Allie and Billy are surely dead, raped and tortured and robbed, all because they thought life was a game. In a few hours, the men from the mining company will come for me. We're having breakfast here before heading to the office. It's all there on my itinerary. The phone in my room is still dead. My cell phone still has no service and of course there's no internet, so I can't check on Joyce, can't make sure Susan arrived, that they're all still safe.

There's nothing more to write. But I can't stop thinking about what must've happened to Allie. I can't stop thinking there must have been something I could have done to save her, to keep her safe.

In a few weeks her mother will start to worry. In a month she'll call the embassy and her daughter's degenerate friends to see if they've heard anything. She'll sit up for hours, staring into the brittle, suburban dark, unable to even begin to imagine what might have happened, or what the world that swallowed her daughter was like. With no answers, there'll be nothing she can do but wait and hope for some final word, for anything other than the silence.

.

THE HIGHLINE HIGHWAY

DRIVING ACROSS THE COUNTRY had been Jacob's idea, but Sheila was the one who insisted they return along the Highline Highway. Throughout the trip she'd navigated and he'd done most of the driving, a compromise he'd insisted on to keep her from behind the wheel where she turned into someone else altogether: obscene, misanthropic, possibly homicidal. The route she plotted was circuitous—revenge, he suspected—always avoiding interstates, opting instead for old two-lane highways. The Highline fit right into that.

Jacob had suggested they just go south a bit, get on I-90, which would take them through Bozeman. He'd show them where he'd lived and the stadium where he'd played cornerback for the football team. But Sheila said no, they'd stay up where they were. They hadn't come on this trip for a nostalgia tour.

Other than the miles that passed through Glacier National Park, there was nothing to look at except endless fields of low-cut barley, broken only by the syncopated thuds of telephone poles, and pathetically small towns named after lonely men. Sheila said, "I can see why you left this place."

"I didn't live here. Bozeman's in the mountains."

"I know, I know, so pretty, all that skiing, blah, blah. But this," she rapped the window with a knuckle, "is what I always sort of imagined. This is what I thought you were running away from." Her window was cracked open and dark hair blew around her face. She kept pushing it behind her ears, but in seconds it was free again.

"It sure is bleak," he said, to get her to be quiet, though he wanted to say he hadn't been running away from anything.

In the back seat, Janey had her headphones plugged into the iPhone they'd bought her as consolation for coming away all summer with her parents. For the past few thousand miles she'd poured her attention into the little screen as if it were her last link to a dying civilization. He'd known Janey wouldn't want to come on the trip, but he hadn't expected the almost imperturbable sheen of indifference she'd put on since the second day. She pretended not to hear them when they asked her questions, and remained bored and annoyed even as they'd visited the Grand Canyon, the La Brea tar pits, and through the hike in the Redwood Forest. She wanted to be home with her friends from fourth grade, lying around the public pool, watching the older kids flirt in their too-revealing suits. And though he'd been relentlessly upbeat all trip, even Jacob was ready to get home. The Accord, which he always kept immaculate, was littered with food wrappers, tourist flyers, ripped up maps, and the seats were sticky from spilled soda and mashed crumbs.

"Did you ever come up here?" Sheila asked.

"No," he said, too quickly.

"Never?" He didn't look over, but could tell she was smiling at him.

"Maybe, I don't know."

She picked up the map and ran a finger along the page. "But isn't Bozeman just down here? It's not far at all. For you Westerners."

"I said maybe." He knew he sounded defensive, but he couldn't help it. Twenty years had passed. Half his life. This place had nothing to do with him anymore.

"When? When did you come up here?" She always knew when he was hiding something, and could never let it alone.

"I don't know. One time, I think."

"For what?"

The lie surged up in a welcome rush. "With the football team. We played an exhibition in Saskatchewan. I think it was a recruitment thing. Up in Regina."

She turned the map over to the yellow mass of Canada.

The memories came steadily: Jacob had answered the door in his boxers, mouth sweet from a night of beers, and blinked. Standing there was a man with a white beard who said they'd been watching him at practice. For a second he'd thought the man was a scout, but that didn't fit with the coarse black suit, the beard with no mustache. In the old man's hands was a large black hat with a wide brim. Behind him was a younger man with the same hat, only on his head. They had a proposition for him. Why didn't he get dressed and they'd take him to lunch?

"It's kind of mesmerizing." Sheila said. "Just goes on and on and on. I think you'd go a little nuts, living here."

"Sure would."

"And there we go, one of the local crazies." She pointed to a horse and buggy, standing in the breakdown lane. "What're they, Amish?"

"I don't know." He sped up, but the cart lingered in the rear-view.

"They live up here all winter? Without electricity? With wood stoves?"

"I guess."

"That must be so cold. The poor kids."

"Must be."

Sheila turned and looked out the back window and when she straightened out said, "Hey, why don't you stop."

He looked in the rearview, thinking she meant to help the cart. An old man with a thick white beard had been kneeling beside the wheel. "Why?"

"Just stop," she said.

"I can't, we're on the highway."

"What? Just do it, Jacob. There's no traffic."

"Jesus, Sheila, it's dangerous. And Janey's watching her thing."

"So what? Janey can pry herself away for five seconds."

"What do you want to stop for?" He could no longer see the cart. It was probably miles back by now.

"I want a picture. Just stop."

Easing into the breakdown lane he said this wasn't a good idea, but she turned back to Janey and snapped her fingers in front of the girl's glassy eyes. Wind slammed into the door when he opened it. As he made his way around the car a semi roared past, shaking the air.

"Here," Sheila shouted over the wind, holding out the camera. "Get one of us."

Janey held her mother's hand, dazed and compliant. They climbed down the gravel slope so that when he looked at the camera they were framed entirely by the yellow fields. They were beautiful, his ladies: both with thick dark hair, pale skin, and translucent blue eyes. The backs of their legs, he'd seen as they walked down the slope, were red and impressed with the criss-cross seat-pattern, but through the camera lens they were perfect, the finished version and the smaller replica, both prettier than he felt he had any claim to hope for.

"Smile," he shouted into the wind.

Sheila insisted on checking the image, wanted another, but he refused, imagined the buggy catching up to them, imagined Sheila striking up a conversation with the man. He walked around the car and got behind the wheel, started the engine, and because he was rushing he didn't check the mirror and so didn't see the truck, passing so close it seemed to hit him in the eyes, the horn blaring, the wheels within inches of the hood, then the second set of wheels, and he turned them back into the breakdown lane, wheels spinning in the loose gravel. Only at the last second did he manage to correct the turn and head back out onto the road, but too fast, so that they hit the ridge of asphalt with a crack.

The truck disappeared into the distance. They drove in silence.

"Oh my God," Sheila said

"We almost died," Janey shouted. "We almost had an accident!" She leaned forward, clutching Sheila's headrest.

"Yes," he said, pushing on the accelerator. Then, "Put your seat belt on, right now."

"What happened?" Sheila said.

"That truck just came out of nowhere."

"You almost killed us."

"On purpose, Sheila. I did it on purpose."

When he looked over she was crying. "I'm sorry," he said. "That just scared the shit out of me."

In the lull that followed he noticed a rattle coming from the back of the car. The noise got louder. Soon he could barely hear Sheila shout they should probably stop next time they found a place.

◆　　　◆　　　◆

The mechanic wiped his hands on a rag and said there was a crack in the manifold. Could they drive? That was all they needed, just to get home. They could, the man said, but if they hit a bump the whole exhaust system might just fall out on the road.

"So how long to fix it?" Jacob said.

"Well," the man said, looking back into the shop. "I'm pretty full."

Jacob said he'd pay whatever it took. The man frowned, squeezing the oily rag. "For another five hundred, I could probably do that."

"Good. Great, fine," Jacob said. With the cost of the labor and parts that brought the total over two thousand, but what were they going to do, sit it out in this road-bump town for a week until the mechanic got around to them? Sheila would be pissed and blame him. But she was the one who'd insisted on the Highline Highway. If they'd gone his way they'd be in Bozeman, strolling through campus, or driving slowly around his old neighborhoods. Now they were in this nothing town, which he'd realized, as soon as they drove past the welcome sign, he had been through before.

Twenty years ago, he'd taken the bus up from Bozeman with the ticket the old man with the white beard, Elisha, had handed him across the diner table. The bus would be more comfortable, the old man assured him, than riding all the way up with him and his son, Adam, in the buggy. They'd pick him up in this town, where I-15 hit Route 2, and take him the rest of the way out to their community.

He'd heard of these people before, some sort of Amish, or Mennonite, or Anabaptists, he wasn't sure exactly. He'd seen them a few times while riding to football games in the bus.

How familiar was he with their community? the old man had asked over lunch, which it turned out only Jacob was eating. Not very, Jacob admitted, chewing a strip of bacon. They wouldn't bore him with the details, but one thing about their life was that they were isolated, out in the plains above the Highline. The old man seemed to be winking at him—a tick, but it drew attention to the old man's eyes, sunk into a thicket of wrinkles, the whites distinctly yellow and thatched with red veins.

"Must be tough," Jacob had said, stupidly, as the man seemed to want a response.

"We manage. By working together. We are a very close community."

And that was also the problem. Elisha had hired a researcher at the university to study their bloodlines and had been told that if they didn't get an infusion of new genes, the community would begin to degrade. The truth was they'd already started to see this: stillbirths, defects. "Mental retardation," the old man had said in his weird accent, as if he'd come over on a boat from Germany.

Jacob was about to say he didn't have any interest in joining their community, but the old man held up a hand. "You would only need to come and live with us for one week, and we will pay you very well for this."

"Pay me for what?"

"Three thousand dollars," Elisha said, leaning forward, clearly awed by the number.

"For what? Three thousand dollars for what?" At the time, Jacob had twenty-seven dollars and nineteen cents in his checking account.

"I explained," the old man said. "We need new blood. You will be the new blood."

"For one week," Jacob said. They wanted him to come up to their community and give some of his blood. No, his genes. Fuck that, his sperm. He almost laughed, but looked over at the old man's son, Adam, who was glaring with just-contained hate. Jacob wondered if he'd be screwing this guy's wife.

"That is all the money we have," Elisha said, holding his calloused palms up, as if to prove it. "We cannot offer more."

"Okay," Jacob said, sipping his coffee. "That sounds like a deal to me." Even that afternoon he'd wondered why he said yes. The money? The plain weirdness of the offer? But he didn't think it was even as rational as that. He'd been hung over, which made him both euphoric and depressed, and it was this swirl of feeling that had made him say yes, a surge of hysteria. Then, as soon as he said yes, it seemed there was no way to back out, though of course he could've at any point.

There was no one he could tell about the proposition. His friends wouldn't have believed him, and what if they had? That might be worse. So he was on his own to wonder, increasingly, why he'd said yes, and why they'd chosen him. How long had they been watching him? Just this weekend, or had they been watching him walk to class, watching him head in sweatpants and sweatshirt to the gym each morning for weight training, head out to the fields in the afternoon for practice? Had they followed him back to his apartment and watched him through the kitchen window, shoveling mac 'n' cheese into his mouth? And what had they seen that had made them settle on him? Why not any of the other guys on the team? He knew he was good looking, had always had an easy time with girls, could just wait for them to drape themselves across the hard slabs of his shoulders and soon they'd be moaning beneath him on whatever creaky bed or sofa was on hand. He was six foot three, two hundred twenty five pounds, with a thick head of light-brown hair (which, in his mid-thirties, had started thinning, leaving him bald on top, a trait Elisha and Adam probably weren't yet aware of), and he had a strong jaw. His mother had called it a movie-star jaw. "My little leading man," she'd called him. They must have chosen him for his looks, since they propositioned him before meeting him. His personality, such as it was, didn't matter in the slightest. He could've been anyone, a murderer, a sadist. The old man's plan was stupid and even dangerous. For them, and for him. Out in their community he'd be surrounded. They could kill him and bury his body in some barren field. But still he'd packed a small duffle bag and, as soon as the semester ended and the cold had gripped all of Montana, he walked through the creaking snow to the bus station.

After the mechanic settled up with Jacob's credit card—"I'm afraid in this case I'm going to have to get it all now," he'd said—Jacob asked if there was a car he could use.

The man led him out to a back lot, through a chain link fence to a battered old Datsun with South Dakota plates. The car barely ran, the engine dry and raspy, and the seats smelled like body odor and mold. Jacob honked for his wife from the lot of the diner and had to step out of the car to wave when she didn't recognize him.

As they drove to the motel, a low-slung building like a super-sized trailer, bound on all sides by a field of weeds and small, wind-shaken trees, he explained the situation.

"We have to stay here?" Janey said, glaring out the window at two boys standing up on the pedals of their bikes.

"Just for tonight. It'll be fine."

"How much is it going to be?" Sheila said, face already hardened with blame.

"Enough, honey, okay? It's going to be enough." Thankfully, she let it go.

In their room, which cost eighty dollars a night, he asked what they wanted to do.

"What exactly is there *to* do?" Sheila said. "Did I miss something? All I saw was a Dollar Store and that disgusting diner."

"There was that movie theater. Or we could just drive around."

"To look at cornfields?" Sheila said, sitting on the creaking bed and turning on the television. "I think we've done that."

"Barley," Jacob said.

"Whatever. The answer is no. I'm staying right here in our lovely room."

"Well, I'm going to go drive," Jacob said. "If that's okay."

"Whatever," Sheila said, waving him away.

"Janey?" he said. She shook her head vigorously, as if otherwise he might scoop her up and subject her to some arcane torture.

"I'll be back," he said, hurrying out.

As he backed out of his spot the Datsun coughed and clattered, exactly like a car he'd driven back in college, a clunker he'd bought from a graduating senior for four hundred dollars, a car you could drive drunk and not worry about, because what was the worst that could happen? You'd crash the thing, but that was no big deal. They were nineteen, twenty, invulnerable. He felt for a moment that sense of his old self, his old confidence returning, as if the fabric between the man as he was now and the man he'd been was lifted by a strong wind. But then he caught a glimpse of himself in the rearview as he backed out: his wrinkled face, the tanned top of his head, dusted with the remains of his hair, grown too long on the trip, and the curtain fell heavily back in place and he was once more a thirty-nine-year-old high school teacher and football coach in rural Pennsylvania.

He passed the garage where he saw his car parked in the lot, the windows all rolled down, two other cars up on the jacks. The town dwindled away to nothing after that.

When he'd come up on the bus twenty years ago, Elisha had been waiting for him at the station. Elisha explained he wasn't allowed to park the buggy in the lot, but it wasn't far. Jacob noticed people eying them as they walked out onto the main street. Maybe Elisha had come here first, made the offer to a few of the locals, before heading farther down to Bozeman and the gullible college students who had nothing at stake. All he'd had to do was call his parents back in Pennsylvania and tell them he had to stay after the end of the semester, but only a few days, for a football thing. Anything having to do with football had always been good enough for them. Throughout high school, when he'd been a varsity starter from sophomore year on, they'd prepared him for his time as a star, but by mid-junior year it was clear he wasn't good enough for Penn State, or any Big Ten school, so he started looking through the letters sent him from schools he'd never heard of, including Montana State University. On the cover of the brochure there'd been a red brick building and high, snow-capped mountains in the background, students walking through pristine air. He'd known no one in Montana and though he'd always made friends easily and did on campus, he'd felt completely alone the entire four years he was out west. Maybe Elisha had seen something of this. Maybe the old man's spartan, religious life had allowed him some insight into the person Jacob was. Maybe he'd be able to let Jacob in on what he'd seen.

Had they talked on that buggy ride out to the community? It'd taken hours, but he didn't remember saying a word. What he remembered was feeling, as they rumbled along, that he was doing the right thing. Elisha's people needed one of the most basic things in life, and he could provide it. But what the hell was going to happen, exactly? Since that breakfast in the diner Jacob had masturbated many times to fantasies of sleeping with young women, virgins, but also older women, widows, or maybe even married women. But as they pulled out of town and started along the breakdown lane of the highway, he started worrying about the details. Would there be specific rules? Was someone going to be watching, to make sure he didn't do anything forbidden? As they turned onto a narrow road marked by two white mailboxes—which were still there when Jacob drove in the Datsun; he braked hard, just making the turn—he started to get afraid. What if this was actually some sort of death cult, some sort of ritual sacrifice? He'd thought about getting a gun before leaving Bozeman, of hiding it in his duffel, just in case. In the buggy, as they were enveloped by the endless fields, he wished he had.

There was another turn off the state road to get to the community, but he couldn't remember where. He'd have missed it if not for the family walking along with their cows, the mother leading the way, two young girls beside her, all three women with black bonnets on their heads, long black skirts brushing around their ankles. Behind the cows were a father and son, the boy no older than five or six, the father probably not much older than Jacob had been when he'd been brought out here, which was how old his child, the child he'd been brought to make, would be now. He'd been twenty and that was nineteen years ago. His kid would be eighteen. Father and son wore straw cowboy hats and stiff black pants that rode up above boxy black shoes. They held long switches they brought down gently on the swaying rumps of the cows. Jacob backed up and turned onto the narrow dirt road. As he passed, the father looked up and touched the brim of his hat.

When they'd arrived in the buggy, Elisha had taken him directly to the house where he'd be staying. The building was behind Elisha's house, in the center of the community, a tidy cluster of white houses. To Jacob it looked more like a glorified shed, a single room with a bed, a wooden dresser, a single wooden chair. There was one window without shutters or a curtain. On the wall beside the bed was a pot-bellied stove, a funnel running up to the ceiling, and beside it, a pile of chopped kindling. An outhouse was just down the path, and a bedpan was under the bed, Elisha said.

"Does this look acceptable? We thought you might like this better than staying in the house. We thought you might want privacy."

"Of course, it's fine," Jacob said, tossing his duffle bag onto the bed, which creaked under the weight. When he looked back at Elisha the old man was frowning, as if he'd expected something more from Jacob. Thanks? Excitement?

"Everyone is at a meeting. They are waiting for me. Do you need anything?"

Without giving Jacob a chance to respond, Elisha walked out. Jacob thought he heard a lock turning, but when he tried the knob a few minutes later it opened and he looked out. He found what he thought was the church—there was no cross, but it was the biggest building in town—and studied the windows, trying to see in, but from that distance all he could see was the hint, now and then, of a dark shape, and though he strained to hear complaints, shouts, protests, rage in the voices of the men who'd come and find him in this shed and bludgeon him with the sharp edge of a shovel, he heard nothing but wind.

There was a single gas lamp beside his bed, but he wasn't sure how to light it, so he used the flashlight he'd brought when dark came early. He was looking at the white spot on the ceiling when Elisha came in, stepping aside to make room for a woman, his wife. She set a plate, covered with a towel, on the dresser. They'd brought him some dinner. They hoped he was comfortable. Again, without waiting for an answer they left and this time he distinctly heard the turning of a key, and when he tried the door he found it locked. Maybe for his safety. After eating the entire plate of potatoes, green beans, and chicken, he turned off the flashlight and was plunged into solid, depthless black.

Jacob recognized the church, and farther on he saw Elisha's house. Behind it the gray shed looked even smaller than he'd remembered. After that first night he'd thought maybe he was going to be locked up in the shed all week, but the next morning Elisha took him around the community and introduced him to the men. They greeted him kindly, though once or twice the men seemed to squeeze his hand harder than necessary. He wasn't introduced to the women, but they were there, walking past on the roads between the homes, nodding to him, or maybe it was to Elisha. The same was true of the children, especially the little boys, tiny, creepy versions of their fathers with the same hats in smaller sizes.

As he drove past, the doors of the meeting hall opened and children poured out, little boys leading the way, leaping off the four white steps and landing clumsily in the yard, then racing toward the playground equipment, an elaborate dark wooden structure with swings and a bouncy bridge. Back when he'd been here before, there'd been no playground, and from what he'd been able to tell the kids hadn't spent much time playing, but now even the girls were climbing onto the swings, which the boys had left empty, and soon they were rising high, their hair trailing out beneath their bonnets, the thick pleats of their skirts lifting up and falling down. The oldest looked like they were not quite teenagers. Twelve, maybe.

His second night in the community he'd been led back to his shed after dinner with Elisha, his wife, and their unmarried son, Matthew, who was mildly retarded. Dinner began with a long, elaborate prayer, and then followed in near total silence. Matthew kept looking up quickly, as if continually surprised to find Jacob there, opening his mouth, then snapping his thick lips shut again and staring down at his plate. Back at the shed Elisha held open the door for him and looked at his shoes.

"She will be here soon. I will leave you to prepare."

"I'll be waiting," Jacob said, but knew that sounded strange, maybe too eager, so he smiled and tried hard to think of something else to say. Then he saw the lamp and said, "Can you help me with that thing?"

The knock that came a few minutes after Elisha left was barely audible. "Come in," he said, not sure if he should go to the door.

Her hand appeared first, gripping the edge of the door, then her arm, covered in black, then her face. She couldn't have been more than eighteen, and perhaps not even that, he thought, as she came all the way into the room and closed the door. She was at most seventeen. Maybe sixteen. Jesus fucking Christ, she might be fifteen.

"Hi," he said, standing up. The room was too hot: he'd stoked the fire until it was raging, pushing in most of his wood, so he'd probably be freezing later.

She folded her hands over her stomach and looked like she wanted to run, but instead she stepped quickly over to him and put her hand on his chest. She was more than a foot shorter than Jacob, her hair in a thick brown braid down her back. In all his fantasies he'd imagined some demurely beautiful woman, but this girl was plain, almost dowdy, with a wide nose and a gap between her front teeth. Standing in front of him, she was breathing hard, panting, almost, and her cheeks were flushed.

"I'm Jacob," he said.

Rising up on tiptoes, she tried to kiss his mouth, but he pulled away.

"I don't think," he started, but saw her face harden.

"Here," she said, stepping out of her shoes and climbing onto the bed. She hoisted her skirt, lifting her butt to get it all the way up. She had on nothing underneath. Her pubic hair was a light brown, tinged with red.

"Look, I think," he started.

That's when he heard something just outside the door. A man, coughing.

The girl on the bed just stared at him and lifted her hips. He unbuckled his belt, pushed down his pants, and climbed on top of her. He was as gentle as possible, fumbling for a while trying to get himself positioned, almost losing his erection, but then he'd looked at her face and she'd turned to him, and he slid in, watched her gasp, then roll her face away as he began to move.

As soon as he'd finished she slipped out from under him, pulled on her shoes, and left the shed. He thought he heard her talking, but Jacob just rolled his face into his pillow. Tomorrow he'd go home.

But he stayed. The next day he walked toward the more distant farms whose land pushed up against the sand hills. Beyond town he could see men working, leading horse-drawn wagons, repairing the roof of a shed, doing something to a silo. Back at the shed he had nothing to do, so he chopped the logs of wood stacked beside his barn, then moved on to those beside the house. Elisha's wife brought him a bucket of warm water and a greasy bar of soap and shivering behind the shed he washed as best he could.

That night, his third, the knock came at the door after dinner. It took him a minute to realize that the woman standing before him was the same as the night before.

"Wait, I thought," he started, but stopped himself. But what had he thought? Of course it had to be the same girl.

She lay down and pulled up her dress, just like the night before.

"I was wondering," he said, as he unbuckled his pants and pushed them down over his erection. "Maybe you could tell me your name."

She blinked as if the idea had never occurred to her. Then she said, "Rebecca."

"Hi, Rebecca. I'm Jacob."

She rolled her face away from him, toward the wall.

"Well, it was nice talking with you," he said, kneeling between her ankles, but he paused. "How old are you?"

"Shhh," she whispered, reaching down and grabbing his dick.

The next morning, after breakfast, which Elisha's wife left outside the door, Jacob followed a narrow dirt track to the rising slope of the hills where the fences ended. At some point he expected the ground to turn to sand, like at the beach, but instead the crumbly dirt got grittier, looser, the low, yellow grass sparser. Why hadn't he brought water? When he looked up, panting, he saw nothing in every direction but the billowing swells of the hills, the shuddering yellow grass. The sun was straight up overhead, so he couldn't tell which way was east and after wandering a little, he sat down and waited for the sun to drop. By the time he was able to start back his shadow stretched, long and thin in front of him and the wind had turned sharp out of the north. He ended up too far south and had to trudge along the edge of the hills until he found the cow-trail. By the time he reached his shed his lips were cracked, his face red and burned, his ears throbbed from the cold wind, and his hands were numb. He drank the ceramic pitcher of water and lay down in the dark.

The knocking didn't wake him that night, and he only drifted out of sleep when Rebecca poked his shoulder. "Wake up," she said. She lit the lamp beside the bed and he covered his eyes with his forearm.

"What?" Jacob said, forcing himself up on an elbow. "What are you doing?"

"I'm here," Rebecca said, folding her arms across her chest.

"No," Jacob said, collapsing back against his pillow. "Not tonight."

"I," she started, then after a pause, "no, you—"

"Get out," he shouted. He could tell she was standing above him still. "Get the fuck out of here," he shouted, louder, and this time he heard her hurried steps, the door slam. There might have been voices outside and the door might have cracked open, a head peering in at him, then the door closed with a click.

Rebecca was surely still here, in the community, he realized now as he drove out to the edge of the town, and then did a five point turn to start back out toward the road. She'd be in her thirties now, but with the cold and wind and working the fields she'd look older, older by far than Sheila with her faint wrinkles and pale skin. Rebecca probably already looked like an old woman. Presumably she'd been married off and raised the child. His child. Except he didn't really think that. He knew that having a kid wasn't just a matter of shooting your wad.

He slowed until he was barely moving, hoping to see something in the women's faces that would spark a memory of Rebecca, or maybe something of himself in a young man, taller than the rest, with dusty blonde hair, a strong jaw, big shoulders. The young man would be pushing a wheelbarrow in front of one of the white houses and he'd glance up as the battered car rolled past. Through the dusty windshield, they'd see each other.

He'd turned Rebecca away the fifth night as well, and the next morning Elisha had came to talk to him. Was there anything wrong? Was he uncomfortable?

Jacob was lying on his bed, his arms behind his head. Of course not. He was fine.

Elisha considered him carefully, rubbing his white beard. Then he said that it was important to remember that Jacob had been brought here for a job. This was a job they had hired him to do. They had agreed to pay him good money for his services.

"My services? That's what you call it?" He sat up and took pleasure in seeing the old man flinch.

"Please," Elisha said, holding his hands out, "cooperate with us."

"Right, fine," Jacob said. "No problem. I'll cooperate."

That night Rebecca came at the regular time and he was standing naked just inside the door so the wind made his skin prickle.

"Are you ready?" he said. "Because I'm all set to cooperate. How about you?"

She'd stayed by the door. He told her to come closer. Closer. When she was nearly up against him he started to unbutton her shirt. She grabbed at the flaps, trying to fit them back together, but he stopped her hands and told her to behave. He slid the shirt off, then unlatched her skirt and pushed it over her hips. Trembling in her heavy bra that looked more like a bandage and her wide, sagging underpants, she started to cry. He turned her around and eventually figured out how to undo the bra, so that her small, high breasts were free. He ran his thumbs over her pink nipples, watching her face, but she only looked afraid. Then he pushed down her underwear and pulled her to the bed. She lay down on her back, eyes clenched shut. He knelt above her, looking down at her pale, trembling body, then he grabbed her hips. She let out a cry as he turned her over, lifted her ass up, her face in his pillow. Unlike the other nights he didn't finish quickly, held himself back, drawing it out. At first he was angry, but the longer it went on, the more he wanted her to let go of herself for just a second, to moan, to rock her hips back into him, but she didn't make a sound, even when he reached around and rubbed her clitoris. When he finally came she climbed quickly out of bed and dressed. She left the door hanging open behind her so he had to get up to close it against the cold.

Behind a house, framed by a large red barn, a woman was hanging laundry. It wasn't Rebecca. He hoped she never thought of him, but he doubted that was true. Or maybe not. Maybe this kind of life purified your mind, sloughed away all the nostalgia and grasping after youth that was so much a part of his own life.

The last night, his seventh, she came to the shed as usual. All day he'd been trying to think what to say when she arrived, because even after what he'd done the night before, he knew she'd come. What choice did she have? And he had to say something, but all he could come up with was, *I'm sorry. I didn't mean to hurt you, worry you, frighten you.* Those were bullshit, but there was no way he could get at the truth, because he didn't have any idea what it might be. Still, he had to say something. He couldn't leave her with the idea that the father of her child, her baby, was a bastard.

When she came into the room she stared down at her hands.

"Come here," he said, patting the mattress. "Come sit next to me for a minute."

She wouldn't look at him, and he could tell from the tenseness of her posture, and the way she leaned away when she sat down, that she hated him. With good reason.

"I want," he started, but then couldn't think of anything to say. He just stared at her profile, at the slight puffiness of her lips, the perfectly straight line of her nose, her thick eyebrows, which were probably not thicker than other women, but she didn't pluck them.

"I wanted to talk to you," he said.

"All right," she said. "Talk."

"I mean," he said, forcing out a fake laugh. "I mean, I barely know your name, you know? And you don't know anything about me."

She looked at him for the first time, a brief glance.

"I mean, considering all this," he gestured at her stomach, "don't you want to know anything? I mean, anything about me."

She shook her head, then said, "What should I know?"

"I don't know. What do you want to know? Anything. You can ask me anything."

She pursed her lips, frowned and said, "All right. What do you want to do? What kind of work do you want to do?"

Like anyone else, this was almost all he'd thought about during college, but like almost everyone else he knew, he didn't have an answer.

"I guess I'd like to be a teacher," he said.

She looked at him. "A teacher?"

"Yes. High school, I think. Or little kids. Either one."

"What would you teach?"

"History," he said. This was the first time he'd even considered this, but as soon as he said he knew it was true. This was what he would do. He was already majoring in history. So why not?

"What history?"

He laughed and said, "Any kind. American. American history."

She seemed to be considering this, then shrugged. "Okay."

"See, isn't that better?" he said. "Now you know something about me. Come on. Ask me something else. Anything else."

"I don't know."

"Come on. Anything," he said, and he wanted to touch her, to take her hand, to hug her, but instead he just bounced on the bed, making the springs squeal. She shook with the bounce, and he did it again, then again, and her smile widened.

Still bouncing he leaned over and whispered, "Come on, help me out." At first she didn't move, just sat there, shaken by his movements, and then she lifted her butt and brought it down and they went on like that, bouncing the bed, the springs wailing. A few strands of her hair, which had been tied up in a bun, drifted loose around her face, catching in her half-open mouth. She left just as she always did, not looking back at him, and he lay down on the bed that seemed to still be vibrating and he closed his eyes, trying to hold on to that feeling.

He drove back through the community as quickly as he could. Sheila and Janey were probably wondering where he'd gone. They'd drive back to that diner, sit in a booth, play music from the little jukebox on the wall, and tomorrow the car would be ready, and they could finally get out of there and head back home.

A Woman Without a Country

Departure

BY THE TIME THE EPISODE AIRED Colleen was ready to leave. Before her trip to Italy last summer she'd barely seen the reality show about a bunch of twenty-something Americans in Florence, but now it dominated her life. Each Tuesday she turned off her phone, disconnected her Internet, and sat down with a beer to watch. By the time the show ended she was exhausted, and often drunk, especially if the idiot characters had ventured out of their palatial apartment to a club. During those episodes her heart pounded as she scanned the faces in the crowd. Eventually, she'd appear, squeezing through the other American girls until she was close enough to put her hand on his arm. He'd look at her and see that she was willing. And she had been. As far as she remembered. Which wasn't much. Mostly she remembered the lights, the thudding bass, the screech of the obnoxious DJ.

Then, on the first Tuesday in May, there she was: face shiny, eyes loose from too many shots, a Bud Light in one hand. The Colleen on TV was wearing the silver shirt she'd thrown away after that night in Florence, the night replaying itself now. The Colleen on TV slid up against Tony, put a hand on his arm. He looked down, then over at his buddies, and he winked. She hadn't seen him do that. Not that it would've changed anything. She muted the television, then turned it off. She opened her computer, clicked on a new browser—there were probably already emails: *OMG, Colleen, are you watching?*—and bought a one-way ticket to Rome. By the time she was done there were only five minutes left on the show. She wanted to see what the Colleen on TV was doing, but she left it off. There was no reason to pack now. She wasn't leaving tomorrow. But she did anyway.

The Note

On the flight she reread Frankie's email.

> My American Colleen,
> Of course you welcome to visit me. I always space for my American girls.
> You remember where I live? You just push buzzer. Come back, my American
> lady. Come back to Italy where Frankie loves you.

He spoke better English than that, so maybe the semi-literate tone was a joke. What about that "American girls" part? Was that a typo? Didn't it have to be? Because even if it was true—and she wasn't kidding herself, she knew it was the case—he wouldn't write that on purpose. Unless he was teasing her. Unless he'd been sitting at his greasy green kitchen table where he'd made her coffee at five in the morning the night they met, writing the email with some other girl in his bed, or maybe his friends around him, passing a joint of the hash he smoked day and night, laughing at the stupid American girl he'd fucked for a few days and now she wanted to come back for another piece of old Frankie.

The truth was she didn't really remember where he lived. Near the Campo. Around the back of it, as she thought of it, anyway. Maybe it was the front. Down a street, past the Irish pub, and the bar where he'd been working when she stopped there one night by herself after her friends went back to the hotel. She'd ordered a bottle of wine when he came to check on her.

For you? he'd said, in English.

That's right. For me.

You can't drink a bottle by yourself.

Why not?

Okay, okay, he'd said, holding up his hands, as if she was angry.

When he came back he brought a carafe, sat across from her, and poured wine into two glasses.

To my new American friend, he said.

Now, she couldn't remember what he looked like. But she would, she was sure, as she shifted in her tiny seat, the old man next to her spilling his arm almost into her lap. When she saw Frankie, it would all come back to her.

Logistics

On her last trip, her first trip, her only previous trip to Italy—or anywhere, for that matter—she'd traveled with a group of other students from her university and two faculty chaperons. Everything had been pre-arranged for them: buses, hotels, even meals. So now, arriving in Rome alone, everything seemed completely unmanageable. How the fuck was she supposed to get to Siena? It was hours away—she remembered the bus ride with the driver who'd kept turning around to smile at her—and even Rome was a long way and she couldn't waste money on a cab.

Termini, she told the cabbie, slamming the door just as they pulled away from the stand.

As they rushed up onto the highway she fought through the grime of her exhaustion and said, *Quanto questi?*

Eh? the driver shouted.

Quanto? Para Termini?

Quanto costa?

Si.

Settanta.

Settanta?

Si.

Seventy?

Si, seventy. *Settanta.*

Euros?

He didn't bother to answer, turned up his radio. The fucker. She should just jump out when they stopped and run into the crowd. But then he'd find her, beat her, or turn her over to the police. She was no one. Just an American girl on her own. She clutched her wallet in her fist, and stared out at the hideous housing developments along the highway.

Disowned

For half an hour she buzzed the apartment where she was sure—well, pretty sure—Frankie lived. The longer she stood there, the less it looked like the place she remembered. There was just so much she didn't remember. When she'd arrived in Siena on the bus, having figured out that was cheaper than the train, she'd gone the wrong way out of the station and ended up near the wall of the city, then got lost going back, and had to ask directions to the Campo.

How could she get lost when the city was so clear in her memory, the curving streets, the bright sun off the high windows, the open, red-bricked Campo? At least the Campo looked the same, thronged as always with tourists. Around the back of the Palazzo she found Frankie's street. Or maybe it wasn't his street. Maybe that wasn't his buzzer. She stepped back and looked up at the building, at the open windows. All she could see was the corner of a white bookcase with a black stereo on top, the CD drawer open. Frankie hadn't had a bookcase, had he? But she'd been drunk or stoned every time she'd been there, which was only three times. Maybe the buzzer was broken.

Frankie! she shouted. She needed a shower so bad. Standing in that soft sun, just like she remembered it, she felt on the verge of tears. Really, she *should* cry. It was weird that she hadn't. There were so many times she might've burst into tears, like when she'd listened to her mom's voicemail.

Honey, you have to call me. We need to talk. We saw the show. Your father wants to cut you out, honey. He wants to cut you out of the family. You have to call us. You have to tell us what happened.

She hadn't called, instead sent an email saying she was going away and wouldn't be able to check her messages any more. She loved them and was sorry.

Frankie! she screamed, again. Someone was in there, moving around. But no one came down and unlocked the door. She pulled her rolling bag down to an empty playground where she sat in the shade and listened to a radio in the window of an apartment, chattering in hysterical Italian.

Kaput

She was sure this was Frankie's restaurant with its sidewalk tables, if only because the Irish bar was next door. People bustled around inside, laughing, but no one came out to check on her for almost half an hour. The seat was in direct sun and she felt it pricking at the top of her head. Her pale, Irish skin would surely burn. Good, she thought, with a little flare of self-pity. Burn, stupid fucking Irish skin, her father's skin, that fascist asshole with his sexist— but it was hard to stay angry. She should've known what was coming, how her parents would act.

When Colleen was fifteen she'd stayed out on a date past her curfew, and though the boy had tried to talk her into giving him a blow job, it's not like she'd been out all night whoring herself on the streets, which is what you'd think was the case if you'd seen her mother weeping on the couch, clutching a rosary to her snotty lips, kissing the little Jesus over and over. It took her mother almost five minutes to explain that she was just so worried. Didn't Colleen understand? She was so worried her daughter was going to ruin her life, to bring shame into her heart and onto her family. Did Colleen know what that would do to her father? Did she know what it would do to her whole family?

Some time after that her mother had fixed a pin of Saint Agnes of Rome to Colleen's mattress. This seemed to appease her, and though it wasn't long after that Colleen actually did lose her virginity, if not on that bed, her mother didn't have any more weeping fits. They came to a kind of understanding: Colleen would pretend to be the girl her mother wanted so that when her mother went to church on Sundays with her friends she too could have a good, pure daughter, and Colleen could meanwhile do pretty much whatever she wanted, so long as her parents didn't find out. And now, of course, they would. They had. She hated thinking about that. Hating thinking about her mother hearing from someone about the show, then sitting down to watch it, her trembling, blue-veined hand coming up over her mouth in the flickering light of the TV as her daughter writhed around under those silk sheets. She would be shamed. Scorned by her friends, by her priest, her church, her whole world. And Colleen was to blame. She'd done it to her mother. And it must've looked like she'd done it out of spite.

Honestly, it was hard for her to imagine anyone, even parents less crazy than her own, who wouldn't have a problem with their daughter slutting themselves out to some mediocre reality TV star, flirting at the bar, drunk out of her mind, then going home with him, stumbling along the narrow Florentine streets, dropping a beer bottle, the glass shattering right in front of her sandaled foot. Then back in the house, kissing him, his black hair spiked up into a Mohawk she tried to touch, only for him to push her hands away, then lift her arms and peel off that hideous silver shirt so she was standing there in front of the cameras in her skirt and bra, the man sucking on her neck and shoulders. She looked over at the nearest hulking black camera and smiled.

She only remembered bits. Smiling into the camera she remembered, but not getting into bed naked and agreeing to sex. She remembered waking up and the star grinding away atop her. She remembered that he didn't look at her once, and that only after he rolled off did she realize he hadn't worn a condom. But the cameras were there. She couldn't jump up, scream, run out, could only roll away in the red silk sheets and press her face into the pillow.

She'd come to Italy to get away from what had happened, but then it had happened in Italy, so she couldn't get away at all. Probably she should've gone somewhere like Peru, or Thailand, somewhere totally different.

Eventually a waiter emerged, frowning as if she was a derelict. He was young, younger even than she was. Acne still marked his cheeks and his nose shone, as if he'd oiled it with special care. She ordered a glass of wine, then said, *Excuse*, Frankie, *aqui*?

Como?

Frankie, she said, pointing at the waiter. Frankie, *aqui*?

Frankie?

Si, Frankie.

Frankie, no. No Frankie, the waiter said, shaking his head.

No? *Dove*?

Frankie, the waiter said, still shaking his head. Frankie, kaput.

Kaput?

Kaput, the waiter said, drawing a line across his red splotched throat.

Surely he was kidding, she thought as he went inside. Frankie wasn't dead. She'd gotten an email from him, what, a week ago? He'd just been fired, or something like that. Kaput at this little shithole. But not kaput. He couldn't be. He was the only person she knew in Italy. Not that she really knew him. She didn't know him at all. He might as well be a stranger. Fuck, he *was* a stranger. No phone number, no follow up email, nothing. As far as she was concerned, he was kaput. The waiter was right. And with Frankie kaput she couldn't stay in Siena. This was the most expensive city in Italy. Or, anyway, it was expensive.

Before she could leave the waiter returned with a half-carafe, flipped over her glass and poured it half-full.

Good wine, the waiter said, in thickly accented English.

Colleen ignored him, but he just stood there. Without looking up she could tell he was leering.

Drinking alone. Sad.

I'm not sad.

And so pretty.

She sipped her wine and tried to will him away, but instead he pulled out the chair across from her and sat down. After studying the carafe for a minute, he poured some into the glass before him. So it was an old trick. Frankie was just a sleaze. Like this guy.

Cheers, right? the man said, holding up his glass.

Sure, what the fuck, cheers, she said, and banged her glass into his, hoping they'd shatter. No such luck, and so she had to drink the warm wine and sit under the waiter's growing smile.

Itinerary

She left Siena at six the next morning, pulling her bag out of the waiter's apartment, down the stairs, to the street, across the Campo, and over the cobblestones, between which the wheels of her bag kept catching, up to the bus station. The first bus was to Empoli.

Empoli was dumpier than she could imagine anyplace in Italy being, so from there she went on to Milan. She couldn't just shuttle around forever, would soon end up broke. But Milan was a city. She'd be able find work.

Late one night on a balcony of her youth hostel two men joined her, offering a joint. One was an Australian the other an Italian. They were managers of the hostel. The Italian put his arm around her waist. Tattoos of crosses and arrows crawled up from under his shirt, wrapping around his neck, as if to strangle him. She said she was looking for work. The man bent his mouth close to her ear and said he was sure they could figure something out.

Officially, she was a receptionist, but she was always being asked to help overloaded tourists with their bags, and at least once a week she was told to prep a room when the Polish cleaning women she thought might be mother and daughter didn't show. The filth was constant: blood on the sheets, clogged toilets in the hall, shower drains thickened with cum and soap-scum. A year before she'd planned to be a teacher, but after Florence she'd known no one would hire her to teach kindergarten, or first grade, or anything involving children, so she'd moved blankly through her student-teaching assignment, had been scolded several times by the teacher in charge of the classroom, had feigned anxiety and promised to do better, had kept on doing the same thing for another month.

The economy made her lack of interviews explicable, though the real explanation was that she hadn't applied anywhere. When she'd appeared on the show it'd almost been a relief: now she wouldn't need to face graduation, to face all those questions about her future, about what she was possibly going to do. But when she'd left for Italy she hadn't planned on slopping buckets of diluted bleach across sticky bathroom floors, she hadn't expected to be dating the hostel manager who despite his tough-guy tattoos was a complete mama's boy. His name was Julius, but she always thought of him as the Italian. His mother lived two houses down from his apartment and came over every day to clean and cook dinner, which he then ate while his mother hovered around him, scooping extra helpings of pasta onto his plate, even once leaning down to cut up his pork chop. Not surprisingly, the Italian's mother hated Colleen, simply pretended she didn't exist, which in fact seemed like the best approach for everyone involved.

Three months after they met Colleen traveled with the Italian to Lake Como. In all that time she hadn't managed to save any money, had continued cutting into the three and a half thousand she'd left home with, and so, if she was just going to piddle everything away, she thought she might as well do it right. While the Italian slept off a hangover, she took a bus to the nearest station, then another across the border into Switzerland and on into Germany, where, after a few weeks in hostels, she got sick. Her fever was high and she was too weak to eat. Her bed was in the middle of a long row of bunks, and people were always walking past, looking down at her, or clambering around on the upper-bunks, shaking the bed, so she kept waking up terrified the thing was about to collapse. The water from the tap tasted like rust and had a brown tint, but she wasn't strong enough to go out for bottles.

By the time her fever broke she'd lost fifteen pounds and felt as if most of her body had been scraped away. Walking through Berlin, the hot sidewalks squeaking under her shoes, she wondered where everyone had gone. A few cars rolled past, an old woman pushed a wheeled cart over the cracked sidewalk, but it seemed as if the city had been emptied of all but the unwanted and useless. She should call her parents. Beg for forgiveness. Ask for money for a ticket home.

Back at the hostel she paid the outrageous bill, and caught the bus to the train to the airport. In line at a discount airline she studied the destinations. A flight to Dublin left in an hour. She bought a ticket—a last minute deal, not too expensive—and went to the gate. To keep from passing out she bought a muffin at a coffee stand, and put tiny pieces on her tongue, waiting until they dissolved before swallowing. An airy German voice called passengers to prepare for boarding. This was good, she thought. This is where she should've gone to begin with.

Home

Within a week she was in Mount Bellow, thirty kilometers inland from Galway. The outrageous expense of Dublin had driven her immediately to the bus station, and though Galway wasn't as bad, it was still expensive and she kept moving farther out of the city, eventually into a roadside motel in the middle of housing developments left vacant by the burst housing bubble. One of the waiters at the pub in the restaurant where she bussed tables mentioned his hometown, that she should see it, if she wanted to see the real Ireland. She went with him one afternoon to visit, and he showed her the statue of the horse, told her some story she couldn't really understand about some rich British landlord's horse falling in love with the statue, or maybe with the horse that the statue honored. They had lunch in a little restaurant with watery tomato soup and endless pots of tea.

She lived, at first, above a key shop that never seemed to have any customers, but still the owner ran his machines all day, so each morning she woke to the rising whine of metal being cut. She worked at the restaurant where she'd had lunch with her friend, Thomas—the place was owned by his aunt—and on Thursday, Friday, and Saturday she worked at an afterhours club. The nights always ended with a rousing version of The Pogues's song, "Fairytale of New York," played with the lights on, everyone singing along. After the first few nights she joined in, laughing and nodding at her drunken neighbor who was shouting in the incomprehensible, local accent.

Home was what it felt like. That's how she said it to herself. With an Irish accent, which she thought she might be developing a hint of. Everything about her life in Mount Bellow felt familiar: the weak heaters in her rented room that couldn't cut the cold, or the inconvenience of waiting twenty minutes for the water to heat up before a shower, or the fact that the washer-driers at the laundromat didn't get her clothes clean. She felt as if she'd lived this same life, or maybe that this was just the life she'd always been meant to lead. Her father's parents were from up in Roscommon. Maybe there were relatives still there she could visit. Or she could just take a trip up there, get the long-form birth certificates from the parish records office, and become a citizen.

She certainly had no reason to leave. For one thing, she had friends. Thomas, of course, and Margaret, a pear-shaped girl with lank brown hair, and her cousin, Declan, who rarely said anything, and most of all Billy. Eventually, she was sure, she'd fall in love with Billy. His nose was too big, and his teeth were stained and crooked, but he was a kind and generous man. She'd never cared about that back in the States, but then she'd been as mean and stupid as the pretty boys she'd dated. And though Billy was gentle, he wasn't a wimp. She'd seen several men in the afterhours club back down when he'd broken up a fight. He seemed to know exactly when force might be necessary, and that usually it wasn't.

When she'd first come to Mount Bellow Thomas had taken her on a tour of the country and Billy had joined them. They'd showed her the ruins of a Roman tower, half-covered with weeds, the graveyard where both their great-great-grandparents were buried—Billy had stopped and crossed himself and prayed before one of the stones—and the estate of the landlord, whose family still lived in the big manor you couldn't see because of a twenty-foot stone wall. They were a good family, Thomas had explained, so that during the war of independence the house hadn't been burned as so many other manors had.

In March, Billy and Margaret asked if she wanted to move with them into a house a few miles out of town. It was a three-bedroom and they could use help with the rent. Margaret took her out to see the place, which turned out to be dingier than Colleen had expected. Brown stains spread over the ceiling, and apparently the heating was so spotty they'd probably have to keep the cooker going on cold nights. But there was a vegetable garden out back, with a few tomato plants that sagged with rotten fruit, and when Colleen lifted the grasses and leaves with her shoe she saw other things, squashes, or maybe pumpkins.

Moving was no trouble as she still had nothing but her bag. They let her have the room nearest the kitchen—You'll be happy in February, Margaret said, standing in the doorway, looking like she regretted her generosity—and they collected discarded furniture for the living room and kitchen. Plates and cutlery had been left behind, along with a small collection of pots and pans.

Though she worked at the restaurant everyday, she still had plenty of free time. What exactly, she sometimes wondered as she weeded the garden, had she done with her time back in the States? Television, there was that, and of course Facebook. Which she hadn't used since leaving home. In all that time she'd barely been on the Internet at all. Margaret had a laptop, but there was no connection at the house. Once Colleen had gone into town to the library to check her email. There were hundreds of junk emails, and though there were surely notes from friends, maybe even her parents, she logged out. No wonder she'd been such an idiot. No wonder she'd thought it'd be funny, or cool, or ironic to sleep with a reality television star. If in fact it had ever been why she'd done it. She just couldn't remember, but somehow she'd been there in the bar next to him, with his orange-tanned arm around her waist, and she'd leaned in and kissed him. And from there, her life had fallen apart. But maybe it hadn't been a bad thing, in the end, because it'd brought her here, where she was happy.

Some days Margaret worked with her in the garden. One afternoon, after trading off tilling the soil, they sat on the fallen beams of what had been a fence to rest. Margaret offered a cigarette, as she always did, and Colleen said no thanks.

You're not really much of a Yank, are you, then? Margaret asked with the cigarette between her teeth.

How's that?

All the Yanks I've known, and at university in Galway there were loads, were a bunch of drunken sluts. And you're not, you know.

I guess I should say, thanks?

You most certainly should, Margaret said, flicking her lighter and leaning in until the tip was lit. Squinting through the smoke she said, It's a good thing, you know.

Well, thanks.

Sure, you're welcome. Exhaling Margaret added, Though sometimes I think it'd be wonderful. She crossed her legs, uncomfortable. But she went on. Sometimes I think it'd be wonderful to just throw it all off and just fuck whoever. Anybody. All the time.

I don't know about that. I bet it'd get old pretty quick, Colleen said.

Maybe. But at first, it'd be fun. Margaret took a long drag and blew a thin stream of blue smoke over the garden.

I think we're better off like we are, Colleen said, feeling a little thrill, both that she was lying—if Margaret knew the truth she'd consider her a slut of the worst kind, so would Billy, and Thomas, and this whole life amongst people she loved would be ruined—and because she felt it could be true. She could be this other, new person. A person like Margaret.

Easy for you to say, Margaret said, angry, just when Colleen thought they were connected. All the boys are slobbering at your feet, day and night.

I haven't noticed any slobber.

No? Well, that's probably because I've been going around with my towel. Mopping it up. Don't want anyone to slip, you know. Hazard, that.

Colleen could hear the slight waver in her friend's voice, the hurt of not being the one the boys wanted, and so she didn't say anything for a few seconds, then said, I'll have one of those, tapping the pack on Margaret's leg.

Oh, Margaret said, leaning back to smile at her. Maybe you're not so pure after all. Maybe there's a secret Colleen hidden away in there.

Or maybe I just want a cigarette.

Possibly, Margaret said.

She handed Colleen the pack and lighter and watched her get one going. Then Margaret said, Look at you. Like a pro. I'll be watching you, Colleen. I think you might be holding out on us, after all.

Colleen smoked her cigarette, her head spinning.

Surprise

They must've looked at her passport, because when she came back late one night from the club Margaret and Billy were watching a crumbly video of *Ghostbusters* on the tiny black and white television and Margaret sat up and pointed. Hey. You. You're a sneaky little Yank.

Her voice was slurred. Cans of cider covered the coffee table.

Sneaky? Colleen said. She wanted to go to sleep. Margaret had a mean-streak when she drank. In her own mean way, Colleen imagined this was because she was ugly.

Your birthday, you bleeding idgit. Your bleeding fucking birthday, Margaret said, then slumped back against the couch.

What about it?

It's Friday, Billy said, smiling at her to show Margaret was kidding. And we're going to have a party.

Oh, no, shit, don't do that.

We most certainly fucking will do it, Margaret shouted with her eyes closed. Friend of mine, Yank or no, is getting herself a good fucking party. Friday night. Here.

Okay, Colleen said. She smiled at Billy. Her eyes ached. Her feet were sore. Well, good night, she said.

Billy knocked on her door a few minutes later and stuck his head in.

That's okay with you, right? The party, I mean. Because if it—

No, of course it is, she said. Thanks, Billy.

Right, I just wanted. You know.

His smile was crooked and drunk and obvious. He wanted her to invite him in.

I'm tired, Billy. I'm going to sleep.

Right, then, he said, pulling his head back out and closing the door softly.

The Big Smoke

He was someone's cousin, visiting from Dublin. Everyone in Mount Bellow was someone's cousin, she'd already figured out. They were at Barrett's after going to the pub, and she was introduced to him in a large crowd. From Dublin. Trinity College. Was it true she was from New York?

First, they danced, awkwardly, side by side, the way the Irish always danced, and when one of the rare slower numbers came on they went and sat down at any empty table in the back, near where some of the younger boys were debating whether or not to smash the stacks of glasses they'd collected from surrounding tables.

You're not from here, at all? she asked.

Amazing isn't it? We're both outsiders. That's why we're getting shifty looks.

He was joking, but when she glanced up Margaret and Billy *were* watching them, whispering together over pints they clutched to their chests.

Where do you live in Dublin?

Have you been? Then he said, Near Trinity. Temple Bar.

He was handsome, but that wasn't all: he looked like a grown up, in his crisp white shirt with almost invisible black lines, his designer jeans. Instead of scuffed up farm boots, he wore shiny tasseled loafers.

I was only there a couple of days. Too expensive for a girl like me.

Yes. The Big Smoke can be nasty on the wallet. But you should come see it again. I'll show you around. Give you a proper tour.

He leaned closer as he spoke, dipping his handsome face closer, fixing his big hazel eyes on her. Taking her hand he said, almost in a whisper, You don't belong out here. You're a city girl. New York, isn't it?

She almost said, No, New Jersey, then stopped herself, thank God, and nodded. As he slid his fingers along the inside of her palm she glanced up again at Margaret, who was staring now with real hatred. Or maybe it was just concern. Colleen pulled her hand away and said she was going to the bathroom. He sat back in his chair, grinning at her as if they'd just fucked. Which, despite what he thought, they were not going to do. When she came out of the bathroom she found Margaret at the edge of the dance floor and said she was leaving.

But you looked like you were having fun over there, Margaret said.

Not really. And I'm tired, Colleen said.

Your new man over there will be quite disappointed.

Too bad for him, then. Colleen wished Margaret would leave with her, but there was something wrong. At that moment, it seemed like Margaret hated her. Then Colleen realized what must be the problem: Margaret had a crush on the boy from Dublin. Not that she'd had a real chance with that pompous dick, but there it was. And Colleen had betrayed her.

Yes, it really is too bad, isn't it? Margaret said, then chugged the last of her pint and walked away. Colleen went out into the cold and stood at the corner where the shuttle they sent around to Barrett's on the weekends for the young people stopped.

A Taste of Home

She worked the lunch shift on her birthday, and when she got back the house was strewn with streamers, and a massive flat-screen television stood in the middle of the living room. They'd borrowed it, Billy explained. They had a surprise for her, during the party.

Colleen spent most of the party in the kitchen with Declan, barely talking, glancing out at the black screen across which shadows of the party moved. The TV made her nervous, which was justified when Billy called them all—there were thirty or so people there, some of whom she didn't know—into the living room and gave a little speech that ended with:

For so long she's been like a babe in the woods, lost here in the wilds of Ireland, so we thought tonight we'd give our good American friend a taste of her homeland.

The television came on with a loud click, filling the room with gray light, then Margaret got the DVD working. The theme song could be heard while the screen was still black and Colleen had to swallow a mouthful of bile. Then the image came on, the city of Florence, jarring quick-cuts, the faces of the cast, including that man she'd hoped never to see again, and then, amidst the clattering rap music, it zoomed into the group getting dressed to go out for the night in Florence. They were, one of the girls shouted, going to get so messed up. High fives were passed around as they put on muscle shirts and strapped tops. It wasn't the episode in which she appeared. But it was the same season. She put her glass of whiskey down, trying to focus as the group left their enormous apartment and strutted down the cobblestone street.

What do you think?, Billy said, sipping his beer. Feeling homesick?

Sure, she said. Everyone in the States is like those fucking morons. Why'd you think I'm over here?

Billy leaned back, had obviously heard the anger in her voice.

You don't watch this show?

No. It's stupid.

Is it really?

Billy squinted at the screen. The men were gathered around the bar at a club, pounding back bright red shots.

Margaret, he called across the room. Colleen here says this is a stupid show. Not like America at all.

Bollocks! Margaret shouted. I've been there, you know. To New York. This is the stuff. This is just what it's like.

Well, we'll just have to watch, and find out, Billy said, heading over to Margaret.

Watching Margaret whisper something to Billy, Colleen thought maybe somehow Margaret knew, had seen the episodes already. But when Colleen looked over she didn't get that feeling from Margaret's expression. Margaret stuck her tongue out playfully, then gave her a silly thumbs up. It was nothing but bad luck. They were just teasing her. That's what friends did. She should just calm down. Nothing had happened. Everything would be fine.

After the party, as they picked up empty cans, Margaret grabbed Colleen's arm. I hear you don't like the show. What's wrong with it?

It's just stupid, I think.

Bullshit, Margaret said, glaring. You know. We have the whole season. Four discs. And I'm going to watch them. Every one. I'll show you, Colleen. I'll show you they're not stupid.

Good plan, Colleen said.

As she walked away Margaret said, Bitch, under her breath, though perfectly audible.

Departure

The next morning, her head splitting, Colleen found Margaret on the couch, sipping tea, watching the show.

Hope I didn't wake you, Margaret said. But we're going to have to return the TV later this week. I can never sleep after that much drink.

No, of course. Enjoy, Colleen said, going back into the kitchen. Margaret wasn't watching the episode on which she appeared. But her episode was next. She recognized the sequence now.

Her hands shook as she packed her bag, then carried it into the kitchen. Rap music blared from the television. Colleen looked at Billy's closed door. He'd be up soon, with all that noise. Lifting her bag carefully she eased through the back door and went around the side, out to the street. They were on a bus-route and one came every twenty minutes. All she had to do was sit on her bag and wait, then she'd be on her way. She wasn't sure yet where to go. But really, she could go anywhere. Most places in the world were free of people she knew, and in a few hours she'd be somewhere new and once again safely no one at all.

Running Rapids

Brian and Sophia had been canoeing on the Koyokuk River for five days when they came across the raft. Brian was steering in a daze, his stare fixed on Sophia's neck. He'd just noticed a small red pimple at the line of his wife's short blonde hair when they rounded the corner and Sophia said, "Look," pointing with her paddle. On one side of the log raft, the center of which was piled high with green army packs, a skinny guy and a stocky girl with a dark pony tail were dipping plastic paddles into the water. A guy with long dreadlocks sat by a rudder, swiveling it around, the muscles in his back, his shoulders, swelling with each movement. Sophia looked back at Brian, smiling widely. "What?" he said. They were gaining on the log raft.

"Nothing," she said, and turned to face forward.

The people on the raft spotted them, pointed, stood up, waved, shouted. Sophia began paddling hard.

"Slow down," Brian said.

She looked back, still clawing at the water with her paddle. "What? Why?"

"I'm trying to control us," he said. Controlling the canoe—keeping it out of shallow water, clear of the rocks that loomed every once in a while, away from the shore where trees, the shoreline eroded by high water, had fallen, a tight fist of branches into the gray water—had been harder than he'd expected when they'd planned this Alaskan trip. In several situations, when the water ran quick through narrow spaces, only luck had kept them afloat.

"Steer," she said, waving at the rafters. In her excitement she stood up slightly in the front of the canoe and Brian imagined her falling into the fifty-degree water, knocking the canoe over as she went, and in this depth, with this current, they'd both drown. But she controlled herself and was back in her seat, paddling with renewed vigor.

The log raft looked handmade and sloppy, the people looked a little wild: two men and two women. The men were bare-chested and both women wore black sports bras. They were all tanned and filthy and grinning widely. Brian straightened up in his seat, trying to flatten his rounding shoulders.

"Hey there," one of the women shouted, in some kind of European accent.

"Hello," Sophia screamed back, though the distance between them had closed. Brian steered the boat, grinding his teeth at the way it swung into the river's central current where the raft was drifting. He knew part of the reason he'd been having such a difficult time with the canoe was Sophia's inconstant paddling. She'd stroke hard on one side, then switch without telling him, give two big strokes, then lift her paddle up. It meant Brian was continually adjusting, switching sides, turning his paddle this way, that way, no the other way, harder, then even back paddling sometimes, to keep from going in the wrong direction. But now, after five days, they were on the home stretch, only two days from the Bettles Lodge, where they could sleep in a bed, take a shower, eat a hamburger, drink a beer.

"How are you?" one of the women said. She had short red hair and sharply articulated muscles in her stomach.

"I like your raft," Sophia said.

"Oh, no," the guy with the dreadlocks said. Despite his ridiculous hair, the man was, Brian saw, handsome. "This is a terrible piece of shit," he added. The others on the raft laughed and Sophia joined them. The noise rang around the tree line.

"Did you make it yourself?" Brain said. He was having some trouble keeping his canoe even with the raft.

"Yes," the girl who hadn't spoken yet said, with the same European accent. She was short and pudgy, with powerful looking legs and dark hair pulled back in a greasy ponytail. "We chopped down the trees. Then lashed them together. And then we made the raft." When she smiled her teeth were bright white.

"How long have you been on the river?" Sophia asked.

"Oh, fuck," the girl said, waving her hands in the air, at the green line of pines that slipped past on the shore, "forever."

"Two weeks," the guy with the dreadlocks said.

"Wow." Sophia smiled and looked back at Brian. She looked like she was having fun, so he smiled at her.

"We are going to stop," the guy with the dreads said, pointing to a gravel bar they were moving toward. "Would you like to stop? To eat?"

"Great," Sophia said. "We'll stop, right, Brian?" Everyone on the raft looked at him. He nodded and said of course they would, then pushed his canoe past to get to the shore ahead of the raft, thinking if they tried to go in at the same time they'd likely crash and that'd be the end of the green canoe.

❖   ❖   ❖

"So where are you going?" the tall, gaunt guy, Karl, asked. He had a dirty black beard and wore tight blue jeans, cut off at mid-calf.

"Back to Bettles," Brian said. Sophia was talking to Hans, the guy with dreadlocks.

"Oh, yeah?" Karl said, tearing at his beef jerky, or, rather, Brian's beef jerky. It turned out the rafters were nearly out of food. After they'd managed to dock and tie down their raft, they pulled on ratty shirts against the mosquitoes and ran over to join Sophia and Brian, gobbling up all the food Sophia offered, laughing and saying, "We are starving," over and over. "We have plenty," Sophia said, as though in chorus with the rafters, who turned out to be Danish. Though it was true, Brian had felt a tug of resistance to the feasting. What if something happened and they needed that food? It was possible. They shouldn't be reckless, because neither of them, it had been clear after they got on the river, really knew what they were doing. Mosquitoes buzzed around them and Brian hoped the rafters wouldn't ask to borrow any bug spray. Though he'd bought three large bottles, he and Sophia had been using it non-stop and were running low.

As a kid he used to go canoeing with his father and brothers when they lived in Vermont. He remembered running rapids in the rivers around Burlington and, over the summers, long trips in Canada. But apparently he'd forgotten what he'd once known.

Five days earlier he and Sophia had been flown up through the mountains on a loud small plane from Bettles Lodge. Their pilot answered Sophia's many questions with as few words as possible, then guided the plane down onto a small gravel bar. They untied their boat, unloaded their bags, and watched the plane take off. Excited to be on the river, they explored the gravel bar, finding a set of wolf tracks. Late in the afternoon they set off down the river, sure they could find a better stopping point. They paddled too long that evening and by the time they stopped they were tired. Their fingers were cold and they argued about the best way to set up the tent. They didn't have the energy to cook a real meal, so they ate trail mix and went to sleep on a damp patch of sand that soaked through the floor of the tent, through their pads, into their sleeping bags, so they both woke shivering, sore, and exhausted. They spent that first morning on the river eating freeze-dried food, drinking tea, and then spent an hour washing the pans and dishes in the painfully cold river water, breaking camp and packing up the boat, dousing themselves in bug repellent, and finally setting out. But from there the days had gotten easier. They'd fallen into a routine and hadn't argued really until the fourth night when Brian had wanted to have sex.

"But I stink," Sophia said, putting a hand against his chest. They could hear the mosquitoes buzzing at the tent's screen door.

"So what?" he said. "I stink too."

"No, Brian. I don't want to," she said, and turned away, her sleeping bag around her. He looked down at her. They were on vacation. He nudged her shoulder and she said, "Keep your hands off me." Brian got up and left the tent, leaving the flap open so that, sitting out on a rock, he could see Sophia's shape within the yellow tent, crushing the mosquitoes he'd let in. Though he'd never camped with a woman before, he presumed that people, while camping, did indeed fuck. The Danes, sprawling on the gravel bar, tearing through his food, were surely fucking one another.

Getting angry about sex on the camping trip was petty, he knew, but what made him angry was the fact that Sophia's refusal clearly meant that she was angry with him and he hadn't known it. She was probably holding him responsible for her discomfort. She'd wanted to go to the Caribbean. He told her that was something they could do when they were old and lazy. Grudgingly she'd given over. Perhaps, silently, she'd been grumbling about it in her mind and the thought angered him. It was just like her, he thought, to focus on the idiotic, rather than trying to enjoy herself while they were in Alaska. Plus, they'd spent nearly seven thousand dollars on the trip.

Sophia jumped up, talking excitedly to the dreadlocked guy, Hans, and went to one of the packs. *Don't be jealous*, Brian told himself. She dug around in the pack and pulled out a bottle of whiskey, held it over her head like a trophy. The Danes cheered. Sophia looked, for a moment, beautiful, the sun highlighting her dirty blonde hair, the gentle curve of her jaw, her small, pretty lips. She took the first sip and coughed while she handed the bottle around. Brian thought perhaps he didn't deserve her. But so what? They were married and were, like most couples, somewhat unhappy. At least, he told himself, he was still able to appreciate her for what she really was, for the beautiful, kind, and generous person she was. The bottle went round the group. Brian took a big drink and nearly gagged. His eyes tingled and watered and felt bright and he could see, through the watery haze, Sophia smiling at him, holding in one hand a chunk of beef jerky.

"Thank you," the girl with dark hair said, taking the bottle he offered her, pressing her fingers against his with more force than necessary. He smiled and wished he knew a single word of Danish.

❖　　　❖　　　❖

By the time they were done with the bottle, Karl had fallen asleep against a pack, head back, mouth open. Sophia was giggling, sitting at Hans's feet listening to him talk. Hans didn't look the least affected by the alcohol and had been holding the bottle as though it was his, to dispense as he saw fit. Brian got up and walked over the loose gravel to the tree line. While he was pissing someone came and wrapped their arms around his chest and he stumbled, spraying his shoe.

"Sweetheart," Sophia said, pressing her face against his back.

"Jesus Christ," he said, tucking himself in, turning around. "You scared the shit out of me."

She buried her face in his chest. "I'm drunk," she said into his shirt.

"Me too," he said.

"Can we camp here?" She gestured weakly at the gravel bar.

"Are they camping here?"

"I think so," she said, bumping him with her head.

The Danes were sitting on the bags, smoking a rolled cigarette, possibly a joint. They passed it around, laughing, prodding Karl, who was still asleep. Brian couldn't imagine getting back in the boat, paddling, under the sun, trying to steer, control. A headache was building up behind his eyes.

"Okay," he said.

"Good," she mumbled. They went back to the group. Sophia took a few drags on the joint.

After their rough start and despite the lack of sex, Brian had begun to enjoy the busy routine of camping. Days on the river were filled with cooking on the small propane stove, then washing the dishes in the frigid river, pumping water through the hand-held filter, breaking down the tent, stuffing the sleeping bags, packing up the boat, setting off; an hour for lunch somewhere, repacking the boat, making sure everything was strapped down tightly, then, after three or four more hours of paddling, setting up camp and eating and cleaning and pumping more water. The rhythm had made him feel useful. He was more aware of himself, of his body. Unlike the gravel bar where they sat with the Danes, surrounded by a dense line of trees that obscured the mountains, Brian and Sophia had chosen each stopping point for the views they offered. Bald green mountains rising, bright patches of sun shifting across the peaks as the sun dipped toward the horizon, falling, near midnight, behind the ridges, but never setting, so that at four in the morning, when Brian woke to pee, sticking his feet into his unlaced boots, shivering from the crisp cold, the world was lit by silver light. One morning, clouds like pulled cotton lay stretched over the mountains across the river, not moving despite the wind that had kept the mosquitoes off him while he looked.

◆   ◆   ◆

"It's this river," Hans said, leaning over Brian's shoulder to tap the map. After the joint, they'd set up Brian's mosquito tent and everyone was stuffed inside, sprawling, limbs overlapping. Hans tapped the map again so it almost came out of Brian's hand. "Here, there are rapids. Rough water, maybe Class Four, I'm not sure, it depends on the water level." Hans was pointing out a tributary of the Koyokuk.

Across the tent, the woman with short red hair—the prettier of the two Danish women, Krista—stuck her butt up into the air and farted. Everyone laughed and she left her butt up in the air, shaking it from side to side.

"Let's definitely run that tomorrow," Brian said, shaking the map, then folding it up to break his stare from the girl's butt. Hans had been talking about the rapids, how he loved running rapids, but with the raft he couldn't. Wouldn't it be fun to run some tomorrow, he'd asked. Did Brian know how to handle the boat well enough? "It's been a while since I've run rapids," he said.

"That is okay. I know how to steer. I will take the back, you will be up front? Okay?" Hans said and stepped over Karl, who lay humming on the ground, and fell on top of Krista. They wrestled, tugging on the fragile net walls and for a second Brian was sure the whole thing would come down, but they stopped and lay sighing in a pile. Brian felt like an idiot, having been goaded into agreeing to take Hans down the rapids. His pathetic machismo.

"How are you?" he asked, nudging Sophia who lay against him. Someone's legs, he couldn't tell whose, were lying over his own. At first this had bothered him, but then he got used to it, even began to enjoy it, the feeling of strangers.

Sophia groaned and rolled over against his chest. He laid his head back against his pack and closed his eyes. Mosquitoes buzzed outside, wanting in.

❖   ❖   ❖

When he woke up, fingers he couldn't see—Sophia's head was blocking his line of sight—were tugging at the drawstring of his nylon wind pants. Bodies were everywhere. All six people had piled together against one side of the tent. It was impossible to tell where one person stopped and another began. The fingers got his pants loose, then slipped inside, grazed his pubic hair, and grabbed his penis. Brian held his breath. Someone was lying on his legs. His feet were asleep. One of the girls, Krista with the red hair, was down there, near his legs, so it might have been her, but the tall, gaunt guy, Karl, was in the same area, and it might have been, Brian thought, his hand. The hand pulled on his penis, rubbing it, getting it hard. Brian let a breath out slowly and was surprised Sophia didn't wake up, with her head on his chest and his heart pounding so he could hear the blood in his ears. He closed his eyes. The hand around his penis began sliding up and down and Brian focused, trying to tell if the hand was a man's, it was a little rough, but that could have been Krista, the nails were a little long, the fingers slender, but that, again, might have been Karl. There was no knowing. Brian tried to keep his breathing steady as the hand worked him up toward orgasm. He squinted his eyes shut and held his breath, but still convulsed. Colors crashed around on his eye lids and he heard Sophia groan. She sat up a little and the hand pulled quickly out of Brian's pants.

"Lie down," Brian said, almost out of breath.

"What?" Sophia said, blinking at him. Cum stuck his underwear to his stomach.

"Go back to sleep," he said, and she nestled up against his shoulder. Brian let his breathing slow and couldn't stop smiling. A hand, just as he was falling back to sleep, squeezed his leg playfully.

◆   ◆   ◆

If his underwear hadn't been stuck to his skin the following morning, he might have thought it was all a disturbing dream. His back ached. The Danes smiled at him, mumbled good morning, and Hans handed him a cup of tea. Sophia glared down into her aluminum cup and didn't even look at him.

"So," Hans said, standing in the middle of the tent, "here's the deal. Brian and I are taking the canoe down through some rapids. Sophia, you will go on the raft down the main river." She nodded and sipped her tea. Brian stared at her, but she wouldn't look up, as though she knew what had happened last night, but how could she?

"Brian," Hans said, smiling, even winking, or maybe Brian's eyesight was still bleary, "are you ready?" He was wearing, Brian noticed, the same filthy khaki pants, but had put on one of Brian's wool flannel shirts.

"What's the rush?" Even if the rest of them let Hans push them around like a boss, Brian wasn't going for it. Running the rapids, he saw now, was a bad idea. He wasn't sure he could handle the canoe.

"No rush," Hans said, then laughed. The other Danes joined in. Brian couldn't imagine what they thought was funny. Sophia seemed to be getting angrier, shifting around, refusing to look at him, sighing loudly, an almost panicked look in her eyes.

"I have to use the bathroom," Brian said.

"Hurry," Hans said. "It is already getting later."

Brian staggered toward the tree line. He heard footsteps on the gravel behind him and looked over to find Sophia. She looked on the verge of tears.

"Good morning," he said.

"Brian," she said, lifted both hands as though to receive a load of chopped wood, then lowered them to her sides.

"What's wrong?" he said. A mosquito landed on his hands and bit him, another raced straight into his ear.

"I think we should just get going," she said, swatting at the bugs that had found her. They'd been eaten this way, covered in welts, all throughout the trip. The worst was when you had to squat to use the bathroom. Mosquitoes then swarmed over your legs, bit your ass, your genitals, no matter how much you sprayed yourself with repellent. Brian swatted his arm and stepped further from the tree line.

"Just after this thing," he said, smiling, reaching toward her, but she pulled away.

"No," she said, shaking her head. "I think we should go."

"I already told Hans we'd do this thing. It's just a little diversion. Then we'll get back together and we'll be way ahead of these guys before this evening."

"No," she said. A tear was on her cheek running down toward a mosquito, which sucked violently. Brian wanted to reach out, crush the bug on her cheek, but held his hand back. "I don't want to be around these people any more. Last night"—she faltered and looked down at her feet, breathed deep—"it was too crowded."

"We have to just do this," he said, and then turned and started to pee, aiming for the mosquitoes that tried to latch onto him, his hands trembling.

"Brian," Sophia said, "someone was touching me last night."

"What are you talking about?" he said, tucking himself in and turning around.

"Nothing," she said.

"What, Sophia, what?" He tried to remember hearing anything from Sophia, any groans, someone's filthy hand thrusting down her pants, sliding up into her vagina, his wife moving with the hand, twisting her hips. He clenched his jaw so tightly his teeth slid and clacked. He wanted to walk back to the tent, pick up a few rocks on the way, go in through the flap and smash someone across the face. But of course that would never happen. He was stuck, and who was he to get so angry? It seemed the best thing would be to run the rapids. In five years he'd think back on this trip and wonder if maybe he was imagining what had happened in the tent last night, but he'd still have the memory of the rapids, of having gotten something out of the trip. He wanted to believe this, but couldn't look at his wife. Even the sight of her hiking boots filled him with a sense of betrayal, rage.

"Forget it," she said.

"What the hell are you talking about? Forget what?" If she admitted what had happened, what he felt then must inevitably have been the case—that one of those filthy assholes had masturbated her—would he tell what had happened to him? He wouldn't. But she didn't say anything else. "What, Sophia, what?" He wanted to reach out and shake her. He forced his arms to remain at his sides.

"No," she said. "Forget it. Let's go."

Brian felt a sudden, nearly-overwhelming urge to scream, to cry out and throw himself on the ground. Clenching his eyes shut until the feeling passed away he finally opened his eyes and looked at his wife. Without another word they walked back to the tent and stood outside while the Danes wrestled and shouted within.

◆ ◆ ◆

Hans untied the canoe and pushed it into the water, keeping a hand on its prow, to anchor it. "Hop in," he said to Brian, who stood holding his paddle beside Sophia. The Danes stood in a group off to the side, all of them smiling.

"Sophia," Brian said, one foot in the boat, the other on the gravel. He wanted to explain, to say something so she'd be less worried. The Danes, despite whatever might have happened last night, weren't dangerous, he was nearly certain. There was no reason to blow things out of proportion. Things would be fine.

"Hurry up," Hans said, shaking the boat so Brian almost lost his balance.

"Meet you on the other side," Brian shouted back to Sophia, as though he was already cruising down river. "Less than a half hour." She nodded and he added, "You'll be fine. The raft's going the safe way. It'll be fine."

Hans and Brian pushed off with their paddles. The river's current caught them and pulled them away. When Brian looked back, he saw Sophia, her bright blue jacket, walking back up toward the tent.

He paddled hard so as not to have to talk. They were moving faster than he and Sophia ever had.

"There," Hans finally shouted. A dark slip of water cut off the main river and they steered toward it, caught its current, and were swept down between the close rows of trees. "It isn't that much farther," Hans said. Brian paddled harder. If he and Sophia, after this was over, paddled hard for the next day they might be able to reach the pick-up point. The men in the Lodge told them a boat came every day at five to pick up different groups at the dock of Old Bettles, a town now abandoned because of flooding and mosquitoes.

The water was moving faster in the tributary than on the Koyokuk and the sky came through the leaning canopy of trees as just a sliver of gray. It'd rain again that day, but not, Brian thought, for a few hours.

They could hear the rapids before they saw them. Brian back-paddled and looked over his shoulder.

"Okay," Hans shouted. The crash of the water was quickly getting louder. "You watch for rocks ahead. I'll decide which way to go."

"Should we stop to check it out?" Brian asked.

"What?" Hans shouted, looking past Brian down the river.

"Check out the rapids, see which way to go," he shouted. That's what they'd always done when he was a kid, but Hans just shouted, "Look forward," and when he did Brian saw the water rounding a bend quickly and breaking on the rocks into white water. The noise, at that point, made further discussion impossible.

Brian paddled hard, leaning forward in his seat. His arms were tight under the strain of his pulls and for a moment he felt as though this were just the kind of thing he needed to do with himself, to make himself feel something, *accomplishment*. He put his paddle into the water. Hans was screaming something. There were two large rocks on either side of the river and the water funneled between. They were turning sharply to the left, so Brian drew hard on the right side of the boat, and the front, under his pull, swung back straight and there, with the rocks no longer blocking his sight, he could see the full of the rapids. He lifted his paddle out of the water.

The water was an unbelievable mess of white that stood up and crashed down and turned around rocks, which were everywhere, and Hans screamed again, but already the boat had begun to swing around, sideways, heading into the rush completely out of control.

"Steer!" Brian shouted, feeling his paddle twist in his hand. The rapids were unrunable, the water too high, the current too fast. They were rapids you'd portage, if you came across them. The canoe was sideways and tipping and Brian leaned across, to even out the weight, attempt a cross-draw. The bottom of the boat clattered over various rocks, and then it struck one with a hollow thump and pain went all the way through Brian's legs, the paddle came out of his hands, and he tipped head first into the water. He didn't hear Hans screaming. *Neither of us*, Brian thought as the white water came toward him, *have lifejackets*. And then, *At least Sophia isn't here.*

He was sucked under water, slammed against several rocks, got pinned by a washing-machine wave. The glacial water numbed him. He clawed up at the light, up there, and then he turned his body and swam down, away from the air, toward the river bottom, and the current pulled him loose. Already he felt as though he'd lost control of his body. He was pulled along the bottom of the river. His leg caught against a rock, the bone snapped, and though his leg came loose, his body was held down close to the silt and rock on the bottom, and for a moment he was surprised by the appearance of his white hand, floating there in front of his face, bright and clear: the wrinkles of each knuckle distinct. Then the hand was sucked out of sight. He never saw the boulder through the silty water, against which his forehead was crushed. The river pinned his body to the rock, pushing him slowly up until his face was just below the surface, the water humping and piling up behind him, holding him there.

His body, inching along the side of the rock, came loose eventually and bounced downstream. One of his boots, which he'd tied too loosely that morning, came off in the rush of water and was carried away from the body, buoyed up by its lightweight plastic sole. He floated into calmer water. Fish swam past his body, most darting away from the shadows he cast, though one drifted, a large bass, toward the surface and nibbled his finger. A mile downstream, near where the tributary met back up with the main flow of the Koyokuk River, he was pulled toward shore and his body lodged down among the tangled branches of a fallen tree, held there several feet underwater, so if you were to stand on the bank and look down, you wouldn't see any of him, just the gray sky reflected back.

Where the Koyokuk joins the John River, near the town of Bettles, his boot got washed into the shallow joining of the two currents, stuck in the dense black mud against the shore. The water receded with the colder months, and the boot didn't come loose that next winter or spring, when the levels rose and fell, full as it was of rock and mud, a part of the shoreline.

Brian's body was frozen in the branches of the tree that winter, which was particularly cold. His skin, which had swollen in the water, breaking and rotting, froze solid, and when he thawed out with the river that spring, his corpse, cracked and losing flesh, came loose from the tree's weakening hold. In the darkness of April the body floated past Old Bettles. The dark that night was so complete you wouldn't have seen the body, even if you'd been straining your eyes from the edge of the shore. Eventually the body washed into a narrow side stream and bumped up onto a sandy bank, where it was eaten, rotten though it was, by a variety of animals, hungry after that hard winter.

His shoe, however, was found by a group of campers on their last night on the river before getting picked up in Old Bettles, to be taken upstream to the Lodge and those hamburgers, beers. The campers were following a string of bear tracks, the deep imprint of the paw and then, four inches beyond that, the points where the massive claws touched down. They took photos. One of them spotted the shoe and fished it out of the mud with a stick. Everyone, back at camp, agreed it had probably just fallen off someone's boat going down the river. They packed it up in a bag and took it out, threw it in the trash back at the Lodge the next day, before they boarded a plane and flew low over the roadless tundra, back to Fairbanks, where a festival celebrating Native American Heritage was in full swing.

THE YELLOW HOUSE

I DIDN'T PASS THE YELLOW HOUSE EVERY DAY, as I didn't ride that train every day, but, obviously, any time I did ride the train I passed that house and what seems strange to me and the reason I mention it is that what I really mean by *passed* is that I *noticed* it. Every single time we rattled by that yellow house with the six foot security fence that clearly did very little if anything at all or nothing to block out the noise from the tracks, I noticed that yellow, three story house with a wooden fort and a trampoline in the backyard. Amongst all the dozens, hundreds of homes between where I boarded the train in the city—where there are no such houses, at least no houses like the one I'm describing—and where I got off the train, I began to take particular note of *that* yellow house.

In part this is surely because I like yellow houses and once owned one, though that was nowhere near this city where my wife and I live with our daughter and our dog. A great dog, though recently he peed on the floor of our apartment which I attribute to the fact that we live in an apartment, which he's not used to, having spent his entire life up until now in a house (a yellow house). Still, there's really no excuse: my wife stays at home with our daughter and is there to take the dog out five, six, seven times a day beyond the long catch-session I play with him in the park every night.

It wouldn't be accurate to say I coveted that yellow house. It is, after all, in the suburbs and that's what we were hoping to escape by moving to the city. Though our dog might not be happy, longing as he was for his yard (our yellow house had had what I now saw, in my city life, as an enormous yard), but *we* were delighted to be here. And so when I took the train to the university where I taught—the job that'd brought us to this city, that allowed us to live here, though just barely, actually, given the low pay for a professor and the high cost of living, which was made more difficult by the fact that my wife wasn't working in order to stay home with our daughter, at least for the first two years, and which was made even more difficult again by the fact that we lived in the city and not in a suburb, like the one I rode through, which would've been so much closer to my school, but which was the kind of thing we were trying to escape—that was when I noticed the yellow house.

Perhaps I only noticed it because it reminded me of what we'd had and what we'd given up and perhaps it validated my sense that we were right to leave all that behind. Plus, it backed up onto the train tracks. That couldn't be desirable, I thought, though the house was large and looked well kept and probably cost a fortune. What was also likely was that I'd noticed the house once and thought, *That looks like our old place*, and then maybe something like, *Thank God we don't live somewhere like that anymore*, and then after that I might've looked up on another commute and seen the house and thought, *Hey look, that yellow house again*, and then, somewhere along the next few commutes, I'd become obsessed with seeing the house. Maybe that's not the right word. Maybe I wasn't obsessed. But that's what it felt like. A harmless, habitual obsession. It's not as though that was the only yellow house we passed, but it was really the only one I noticed.

I began to be able to prepare myself for the arrival of the house in my line of sight when I became more familiar with the station stops and knew which it lay between. Then I'd look up from my book, or my computer, or magazine and stare out the window at the houses shuttling past and then I'd see the yellow house and think, *There it is.*

For a while, when I was noticing the house, I didn't think anything of it, because it was just a house that I'd picked out and it served, like so many things, as a marker of my progress through the world from here to there to there and back again. There were other such things, like the view of the towers of downtown when the subway crossed over the bridge. The buildings clustered so bright and close and dense, taking my breath away each time though I passed that view several times a week. Every time I did I thought, *Yes, yes, yes, this is why we're here.*

One afternoon, after I'd been making the commute for about three months, I noticed a woman behind the house, bouncing on the trampoline. She looked to be about my age, which I was a bit surprised by, because although I don't delude myself into thinking I'm young, I also don't think of myself as of the age that I'd have kids old enough to play on a trampoline or on a wooden fort as elaborate as the one they had in the backyard. But this woman, bouncing so her short brown hair lifted up above her head and her skirt flared, much like her hair, almost in unison, though it seemed as though the skirt was slightly ahead of the hair in the rhythm, which I thought was maybe because all that fabric was surely heavier than hair, looked possibly even younger than I was. Could she be the daughter of someone who lived in that yellow house? But I dismissed this. She was clearly the owner of the house. You could see it in her face, her vaguely smiling face as she bounced. Of course, racing past on the train, I only saw her bounce once, really, and at that only half a bounce: I saw her falling back toward the trampoline, springing up, and then I was past.

The next time I saw the woman was the very next commute. How could I have taken this train for months and not seen anyone and now, twice in a row . . . but of course it had nothing to do with me and didn't mean anything. Except to me. And even then only in a facile and ridiculous way. This time the woman was with her child, a little girl who looked to be about six or seven. I'm fairly certain that's right and later I would read in the paper and have this confirmed. I have my own little girl and when one has children one notices other children and whereas before I had children I could barely have told you the difference between a two year old and a four year old, now I felt almost able to pinpoint a child's age within a six month span. The woman behind the yellow house was kneeling beside the little girl and they were standing just on the edge of the trampoline and it looked like the little girl was crying. She was rubbing her eyes and hanging her head the way kids do when they cry, as though the tears are so terribly heavy.

That was it. I mean, those were the only two times I ever saw them before the last time I saw them and that time it wasn't behind their yellow house with the fort and trampoline, but floating in the filthy brown pool near the train station. I'd noticed this pool before, but that's not surprising: it comes just before my stop and is a big wide glimmering square with yellow-brown grime on the tile bottom. The water is always untroubled, always empty, so I thought perhaps the pool was closed. Perhaps because it was too filthy to swim in.

I shouldn't even have been on the train that afternoon, but I was going in to do some copying and scanning in anticipation of the coming week and was looking out the window, having just finished the novel I was reading and I thought, *There's the yellow house*, and then, *There's the pool*, and that's when I saw them, floating, face down in the brownish water, their hair fanning around their heads. The mother was wearing a skirt that billowed around her pale legs and the little girl was in a yellow sundress that caught against her skin in the water. The mother's right arm dragged down into the murk, as though she was reaching for something beneath the surface and the daughter, her thin blonde hair in an arc around her delicate head, lay with her fingers straight out, as though trying to fly. They didn't move, except possibly with the dull undulations of the water, still shaken from their entry, or perhaps that was the trembling of the train, the pounding of my heart.

By the time we arrived at the station I was shaking. I felt like vomiting. Later I'd find out the whole story, or, anyway, the official story: the father and husband had murdered them and dragged their bodies to the pool and dumped them to make it look like an accident, though of course no one was fooled. This must have happened just minutes before my train passed, because they weren't in the water long, under an hour, the paper said. The grainy pictures of the dead woman and her daughter were further confirmation that they were the same people I'd seen in the backyard and then in the pool. A month after reading the article, I cut one morning through the tennis courts beside the fetid pool to the streets along the tracks until I found that house and matched its number with that in the article. I read there was another child, an older daughter, twelve, who'd watched her father strangle, with his hands, her mother and sister.

Now, each time the train passes the yellow house, it looks just as it did: well kept, the windows bright, the lawn cut. Maybe a new family lives there. But I don't know for certain, because I do my best, as we pull out of the preceding station, not to look out the window, to keep my eyes fixed on the screen, or the page, following the lines of type, hoping they keep me fixed there so I forget to notice, though they don't and often, despite myself, I look up.

In the World Below

Just as Alain had promised, roadblocks had spread out overnight from Cité Soliel. Each time they approached one of the rubble heaps, Alain took one hand off the wheel and draped his gun out the window for the gangs of men to see. Most seemed not to notice, and those that did lifted their hands to wave, then took the chance to scratch a cheek, or rub an eye. Once they were past, Alain sped up so they jolted and shook over the pitted road.

An hour ago, Donald had had to basically drag his son, Peter, out of bed and now the boy was staring into a book, head shaking so his chin kept disappearing into his swollen, acne-splotched neck. A T-shirt with black and white stripes that looked like a cheap Halloween costume was stretched tight over the boy's jiggling breasts.

"What are you reading?" Donald shouted over the rush of air through the windows. The boy's head wobbled up, his brown eyes stared blankly for a moment, then he held up the book.

"Is that for school?" What Donald really wanted to say was, *Put that goddamn book down and look around. You're in Haiti. This is history.*

But Alain was already slowing for another roadblock, at the base of which was seated a little boy, surely not older than ten, with a long black gun nestled between his legs like a napping dog. The boy smiled when Alain waved: a dark face full of flashing teeth.

As they sped up, Alain reached across the car and slapped Donald's arm. "You see, didn't I tell you? It's the morning shift. They save it for the drunks and kids."

"You're right. Of course you're right," Donald said, flinching in anticipation of another slap that didn't come.

Alain adjusted the gun in his lap, as though it was a favorite kitten. He'd probably been carrying it the entire time Donald had been in Haiti, though he hadn't noticed any bulge in Alain's immaculately fitted Italian suits. But then maybe Donald was simply naive, just another know-nothing administrator who spent his days in his office at Georgetown University surrounded by wealth and privilege.

They were driving up to Alain's château in the mountains where they could wait out "the situation," as everyone had taken to calling it. When, last night, Donald had suggested they might try to get on a diplomatic flight to Miami, Alain had protested. "Things aren't that bad, yet," he'd said, waving a hand as though clearing the slightest puff of smoke. Behind him, the TV showed mobs of men with machine guns down at the docks, jumping and firing off rounds. "This is all just a show. They're too stupid to manage anything real." The television's focus zoomed past the men and out to the long, stiff aircraft carrier with its lines of spidery helicopters.

The carrier had slipped into the bay two nights ago and Donald and Peter had gone up to their hotel roof deck first thing the next morning for the view. A woman in a floral pantsuit had clutched an enormous leather handbag to her chest and said, "Oh, thank God, they're here." As though nothing could possibly go wrong if the U.S. Navy decided to invade Port Au Prince. As though there was any chance they'd actually invade. The ship, the "action," was simply posturing and intimidation and it made Donald's job impossible. He'd come to try to obtain visas for twenty-five Haitian students studying at colleges around the U.S., but the State Department so far refused to grant them. For three days Alain had driven Donald from one office to the next, where bureaucrats—or, more likely, CIA—had watched him beg, then said there was nothing they could do, but he really should consider getting out of Haiti as soon as possible. Was he aware how bad things were about to get? He'd wanted to ask if his stupid American life was worth more than twenty-five young men and women? Twenty-five of the smartest and hardest working students in this country, students who could, with education, with contacts, come back and help rebuild this . . . But, apparently, once the engines of the warships were warm, nothing mattered.

Peter peeked over the top of his book out the window. They appeared to be passing a landfill. Two children picked their way over a mound of trash, bending now and then to fish things from beneath their bare feet. Lines of black smoke knit loose weaves over the neighborhoods. It no longer seemed plausible that he'd begged to come on this trip. Had he really said, "But that's what I want, Dad. To see that kind of place. I mean, that's what the world is like, right?"

He'd only said this because he'd known his father would never refuse such a plea: he was always yakking about how screwed up everything was and how lucky they were, especially Peter, even though he was a fat, friendless high school junior who'd just bombed the SAT. Lucky, lucky, lucky. At least those kids picking around in the trash weren't aware that their lives were shit. They probably just thought that's what life was like. Meanwhile, Peter was doomed to a life that'd never be what he wanted, just like his father. Not that his father was honest enough to admit this. His father had always been delusional and just look at his friend, Alain, draping his gun, like a shiny penis, out the window. The guy was pretty obviously a gangster. But, then, thank God he was there. Imagine if his father was driving. They wouldn't have gotten past the first roadblock. Those men would've stepped into the road and hauled them out of the Range Rover, into the suffocating heat. They'd have been forced to their knees and the men would've been screaming in that awful patois, and Peter would be slapped, his pockets pulled out, the watch ripped off his wrist. Then one of those kids would've stepped up, his bare feet slapping against the scalding concrete, and, smiling, the boy would lift his gun and push its greasy muzzle against Peter's slick forehead and he wouldn't even hear the shot.

Peter's fear was too palpable to pretend it wasn't there, but he didn't want his father to know about it, so he tried to pretend he was doing fine, instead of basically shitting himself all day and night.

On his first full day in Haiti, three days ago, he'd wanted to see something of the city. Before heading off with Alain, his father had warned him not to go too far from the hotel. "Out of the good neighborhood," was how he'd put it, but it was hard to see what that meant when Peter went out through the gliding glass doors. Maybe he'd meant out of the area where there was nothing but high stone walls topped with barbed wire, or glass, which made the whole street feel like a prison. Even there, though, Peter had been afraid. There were vendors who shouted at him in the French that bore no resemblance to what he'd learned in school and men in jeeps swerving close to the curb, as if trying to run him down. Worst of all were the soldiers, many of them younger than Peter. They looked as though they were considering whether they should beat the living shit out of this fucking American kid in his jeans, his Nike tennis shoes, that ridiculous fanny pack (which he'd worn ironically, but as soon as he was out on the street it was clear this was no place for irony). Two blocks from the hotel, he'd stopped to catch his breath. A mistake. One of the soldiers across the street noticed him. The soldier was tall and thin and no older than sixteen. His blue uniform didn't fit: baggy pants were cinched up around his narrow waist and the sleeves of his shirt were rolled up several times. He smiled at Peter and waved. Peter couldn't move, couldn't even feel his legs. Smiling, the soldier thrust a finger up his nose, the smile mixing with winces as he dug around, then he slowly drew the finger out, bringing with it a sagging line of glistening mucus. He held the finger up and grinned, then, before Peter could turn away, unzipped his pants and pulled out a wrist-thick dick. After waggling it at Peter, the soldier pissed a loud, thick stream into the street. Peter finally broke his look from the soldier and ran back to the hotel.

Since then he'd spent almost all his time in his room, with occasional trips down to the lobby, where he pretended to read the newspapers. Twice he'd gone to the restaurant and ordered cocktails, charging them to the room, eavesdropping on the American businessmen who leaned close over their tables. Probably they were CIA. Or mercenaries. He tried to track the particularly nefarious faces, but they all seemed to blur together: big, square heads with military haircuts and wide shoulders, as though they were all former college football players.

The second time he'd been in the bar, sitting against the wall that smelled like cigarettes, trying to read *The Plague*, his father had come in with two men. They ordered martinis. Seen from a remove, it was clear that his father was the little man, the powerless one, short and pudgy, with a coating of office fat. A few long strands of his white hair were draped over all his shiny scalp. Tortoise-frame glasses slid down his nose and he squinted instead of pushing them up. While the men sipped their drinks, his father had talked on and on, surely one of his boring stories.

Frustrated at not being able to hear, Peter eventually got up and walked right past the table, but still his father didn't notice him. "It was at these ruins outside Damascus," his father was saying. Peter had heard this story many times: how his father had been jumped in the ruins by a couple of crooks, but he'd kicked one in the stomach, and the other had run away, terrified at the American's unexpected bravery. Each time he heard the story Peter rolled his eyes, but he always listened, hoping to catch his father in contradictions that'd prove the story was a lie. But he never found any kinks and sometimes wondered if maybe it was true. Or maybe his father was just a terribly precise liar. Or, maybe, on some level, his father believed all his bullshit was true.

Now in the car, Peter tried hard to focus on Camus's sentences and though they seemed simple enough, he had no idea what they meant. He turned the pages. He wanted to appreciate the irony, reading *The Plague* while trapped in a dying city, but any pleasure he might've felt was diluted by the fact that he wasn't anything like Camus's doctor. But that wasn't Peter's fault. What could he do? His father said, We're going up to the château, and was Peter supposed to stay in the hotel alone and write about the events and maybe meet a correspondent for *The New York Times* in the lobby and over dinner show the man some of his writing and the guy would be so impressed he'd fax it back to the office and they'd print it? Or maybe the journalist would be a woman and she'd be so impressed that she'd come up to his room to work over a few edits and they'd lean together over his pages and he'd put his hand high up on her thigh so he could feel the pulse of a deeper warmth just inches away and she'd turn to him, eyes fluttering shut, and they'd roll back onto the sheets.

He covered his erection with his book and rubbed the pages in a slow circle.

When Donald looked back again, his son seemed to be sleeping, just as they were given an open view of the city, penned in by the aircraft carrier.

"These roads," he shouted. "They're almost as bad as D.C." Peter might've cracked an eyelid, though he couldn't be sure.

"Oh, come on!" Alain shouted, speeding up. "Don't insult my country."

Donald laughed and stared at his son—the boy's eyes were clenched shut— then turned around to find that trees had swallowed the muddy, gutted road. Branches slapped against the windows like frantic, scrabbling hands.

❖　　　❖　　　❖

Disgusting, Peter thought, as the fridge exhaled cool mist into his face. The top glass shelf brimmed with cheeses and vacuum-packed meats. The next shelf was devoted to a cluster of foggy bottles of exotic beer and wine. Alain had all this, while kids had to pick through garbage until they were handed guns so they could scare all the Americans badly enough to allow them to think, *See, there's really nothing you can do to help. Better just let them rot.*

His dad was always going on about helping, but really, when the world was like this, when it was full of guys like Alain, how could you possibly help? Over the years, Peter had met many of his father's students. They were always polite, intelligent, and gentle, pulling him into elaborate dances that made him blush and trip, asking him all sorts of questions about his high school—that rich, elitist, Jesuit place full of meatheads his grandmother paid for—and somehow managing not to appear bored by his surely incoherent replies. Then they'd graduate and another crop would arrive. But what good could education do anyone in a place like this? This country was obviously totally fucked.

Alain led them out onto a slate patio that overlooked Port au Prince. Vertigo surged through Donald's gut. The city was a smear in the morning haze, as though someone had tried to erase it.

"Coffee?" Alain said, clapping his long hands. "Or, maybe you'd like to rest?"

"Coffee sounds good," Peter said. The boy was squinting, as though he'd spotted something below.

"Actually, is there a phone?" Donald said. Alain was acting like they'd skipped out on work to relax. Meanwhile, twenty-five young men and women were about to be shipped back into the hands of the Macutes. Some of them would be killed immediately. Others would disappear. But if they could just hold on for another year, Aristide would be back.

"Sure, just inside there," Alain said, as though it was a stupid question, then turned to Peter. "Milk? Sugar?"

"Just black," Peter said, grinning, as though this made him a man.

Donald watched his son and Alain sip coffees as he dialed. They should've stayed at the hotel with the other Americans and the international press. What did he really know about Alain? Only that he was from a wealthy family and, in addition to running a series of gyms, worked in "protection." The first time Donald had come to Haiti, Alain had picked him up at the airport—somehow plucking him from the crowd of dazed passengers—and asked if he could run a quick errand before going to the hotel. "It'll just take a minute. And you'll see something of the city," he'd said, already driving out into the suburbs. Eventually, they turned in through the high iron gates of a grocery store, guarded by men with machine guns. Pulling around to the loading dock, Alain left the Range Rover idling as he leapt up onto the platform and shouted at an obese man in a tent-like T-shirt. Alain cuffed the man on the side of the head, then grabbed his shirt and pulled him close. Shining lines of sweat ran over the man's cheeks and his big eyes seemed unable to blink. When the fat man waddled into the store, Alain turned to Donald with a bemused smile, as though stuck in line at the post office. The fat man returned with an envelope, which Alain glanced at before cuffing the man's head once more. As he climbed into the SUV, he held the envelope open so Donald could see the thick stack of twenties. The only explanation Alain had offered was, "In this country, if you want to get something done you always have to do it yourself."

At least Peter had no idea about the reality of the situation. The boy probably just admired Alain, thought him tall and handsome and strong, unlike his droopy, bespectacled father, worrying over the calling codes.

"I mean," Peter said, "what I really want to do is travel, you know? Through South America."

"Like Che!" Alain said, smiling over the rim of his tiny cup.

"Well," Peter said, spilling coffee down his chin. "I don't know about Che. I mean, I've read *The Motorcycle Diaries*—"

"Of course, of course," Alain interrupted, laughing.

He couldn't tell if the man was mocking him, or if that smirk was just permanently lodged on his face. At first, when Peter met Alain, he'd thought he was an idiot. But, Peter had to admit now, Alain seemed to actually know things about the world. He had an edge that wasn't immediately apparent, but which, once you spotted it, seemed very sharp and hard. Or maybe that was only in contrast with his company, these two lumpy Americans. At least Peter was young. He could change. At least he wasn't ruined and trapped like his father.

"But, yeah," he said. "I mean, I guess kind of like Che in that I want to really see the countries you know? Not just the tourist routes."

Alain was smiling at him, as though he saw through the thin fabric of Peter's idea of himself. But maybe he also saw (as his father never could) that ultimately Peter did genuinely wanted to see the world, and that this desire was something in itself. And rare. Alain might be a corrupt aristocrat, but Peter couldn't help but admire him. Compare him with Peter's father, whose starched white business shirt was sagging with sweat. His father's mouth worked noiselessly at the phone he clutched with both hands, as though it was a wriggling bird. Then look at Alain, with his shining black skin, his muscular arms, his perfectly fitted suits, the white collar of his shirt startling against his black skin, staring out at the ruined city below, completely unperturbed by anything.

Alain said he'd done something like that, though he'd gone to Africa. He said he'd accidentally crossed into Uganda and had been picked up by soldiers on the side of the road. "They drove me around a little, then dropped me off at a whorehouse. They wouldn't leave until I went inside. When I was in one of the rooms, a soldier came and watched at the window."

Peter could almost feel the legs of a whore wrapping around him—a Chilean whore, or maybe Brazilian. Of course, no matter how much he might travel, he'd never end up like Alain. First off, he'd never be able to just go around paying whores and feeling okay about it. But goddamn did he want to. He really, really wanted to.

"More coffee?" Alain said.

"Actually, I'm kind of tired." Why did he say this? Was it even true? He didn't want to go inside. He wanted to stay out here talking with Alain, having a real conversation for once. But now, as usual, he'd fucked it up.

"You remember where your room is," Alain said, flipping a hand at the glass doors. He tugged at the cuffs of his shirt beneath the sleeves of his suit coat and went inside. Peter stayed out on the patio, letting heat settle over him in layers until his arms were slicked with sweat.

Donald tried to finish up his call as Alain slid open the glass door. He hadn't wanted to call Margie. He should let her worry: wasn't it her favorite pastime, fretting, nibbling at Donald and Peter's relationship until he felt awkward around his son? *What does she say about me?* he wanted to ask. He wanted to tell his son not to listen to her, wanted to say that there was always another side to the story, if you just listened.

Alain stood just inside the door, close enough that he could surely hear everything.

"I told you, everything is fine. Don't worry."

"I just can't believe you took him down there. What do you think you're doing? You've always thought you're some kind of stupid hero, but now you're bringing Peter into it and I don't—"

"Right, right," he said. "Okay, well, he'll give you a call." Donald hung up the phone and said, "Peter's mother."

"Does she work at the office?" Alain said, glaring at the phone as though Donald had smeared shit on it.

"I just wanted to let her know where we are." As soon as he said it, the stupidity was obvious: they were on the brink of civil war and Donald was clogging up the lines, costing Alain a fortune.

"And did you talk to the office?" Alain took a step closer, closing Donald into the corner.

"Oh, yeah, nothing they can do, of course," Donald said, and then tried to laugh, though it came out as a croak.

Alain pointed at the phone. "Next time you talk to them, be sure to tell them how helpful I've been. How I've taken care of you."

"Oh, I did. And I can't tell you how much—"

"Because, I expect a little something more, for all this." Alain stepped closer, breath whistling out his nose. Beads of sweat had gathered on his upper lip.

"Right, I mean, of course. Of course they will." Through the blood rushing in Donald's ears his own voice sounded like the whine of a distant automobile.

"Good. Because I'm not some asshole who works for free, Donald. But you know that."

"Of course. Of course you're not. I mean, I know that."

Alain walked into the kitchen and jerked open the fridge. Donald's legs felt stiff and his hands were shaking. He thrust them into his pockets, but they didn't stop.

❖   ❖   ❖

Jungle might not be the right word, Peter thought, glancing back at a corner of the château, but the tangle of trees, vines, and brush certainly looked, at the very least, jungle-esque. Probably, though, it was just a forest. Ahead the path narrowed into thicker foliage (thicker jungle).

Sweat ran out of his hair and into his eyes. Probably he wouldn't feel so shitty, if he hadn't let himself get so fat. But after he'd been cut from the freshman soccer team he'd thought, *Fuck this, you ignorant assholes*, and stopped running, stopped doing much of anything except reading and writing and eating. It'd surprised him how good it'd felt to gorge until he was swollen and puffy, sprawled on his bed, filling a journal.

Out the window of his room at the château he'd seen a meadow higher up the mountain, and that's where he was trying to go, though now he wasn't sure if this was the right direction. But if he could get there, he'd walk quickly and grass would whip against his legs . . . Jessica should be with him, his best friend, the girl he wanted to marry, though often it really felt like all he wanted to do was fuck her. See, he told himself, forcing himself to start jogging, you're disgusting. This is why you're alone.

He didn't notice the man on the side of the path, half-hidden by the heavy growth, until he was right next to him and then Peter's legs twisted and he fell into sticky, clawing branches and mud. Peter rolled over, letting out a low, guttural moan. The man moved onto the trail and stood smiling down at him, only a few rotten stumps of teeth in his gums. The man's arms were bare—his shirt was chopped messily away at the shoulders—and a jagged, puffy scar ran down one forearm. The man stepped toward Peter and started speaking, gesturing wildly with his hands.

"What?" Peter shouted, scooting away through the leaves. "No, get away!" The man's voice got closer, as though he was bending over Peter, who had rolled onto his stomach and scrambled, pressing his face into the wet muck and letting out a long scream. When he looked over his shoulder the man was gone. Blobs of light blinded him for a second. "Hey!" he shouted, but there was no one. *Don't chicken out, you pussy*, he thought and wheezing, close to tears, got to his feet. He went carefully up the path, unable to catch his breath, looking to both sides and behind him, holding to the thicker trees for balance. If he hadn't been going so slowly, he probably wouldn't have noticed the hut.

The walls of roped together sticks leaned in a clear patch on the steep slope, clinging to the ravine. The metal sheets of the roof drooped like wet leaves.

A little boy, in just a frilly woman's blouse out the bottom of which poked his stick legs, came around the corner, chewing a bright green stick. The boy picked through the debris—a bashed in bucket, more metal sheets—until he cleared a bare patch of dirt on which he turned around twice before flopping down. Once seated, he began humming, a high, clear pitch.

Peter stepped off the path. Finally, the real Haiti was right in front of him. These people, this little boy, were the ones who needed the real help, not the rich kids his father brought to America. And Peter was here. He could help. The boy hadn't noticed him, was busy sketching on the dirt with a stick, chewing now and then on the other end. Peter checked his pockets and of course he'd left his wallet behind, and his fanny pack, so all he had was his little leather bound journal, which fit tight in his back pocket, and the fancy black pen his grandmother had given him for his birthday last year. It was the pen he always used when writing in his journal, he'd already replaced the cartridge twice, but he pulled it out and held it in front of him, taking a few more steps off the path.

"Hey," he said, shaking the pen. The boy didn't hear him. He was humming loudly and bobbing his head.

"Hey, you," Peter said, louder and this time the boy looked up, his humming stopped. It was as though it had been coming from a radio whose cord had been pulled.

The toes of the boy's feet were splayed, and thick yellow calluses covered his heels. His legs were lined with small scratches, red ridges rising on his black skin.

"Do you want this?" Peter said, waggling the pen between two fingers. "Don't you want it? It's nice, here, take it."

The boy leaned away, but stayed where he was, bringing the stick to his mouth and chewing with his few crooked teeth.

"It's for you," Peter said. He tried to smile and nodded. "It's a gift, for you. Here, you can have it." He stepped closer stumbling over one of the metal sheets so it clattered.

Out of the corner of his eye, in the dark of the hut, shapes moved. A voice snapped. The little boy looked at the doorway. A hand appeared on the door frame, long, brown fingers. Peter still held the pen in front of him as the hand turned into an arm and then half a face, yellowed eyes staring at him. Taking a deep breath he threw the pen at the house and turned and ran up the hill to the path, falling to his knees, clawing through the thick branches to the path. As he ran his ankles wobbled and his breath burned, but he managed not to fall until he reached the château's groomed yard.

❖   ❖   ❖

Once dark had fallen, Alain took them out on the patio for drinks. The flag-stones were bathed in floodlights around which bugs swarmed, casting wild shadows. Alain poured four fingers of whiskey into three glasses and set the bottle at his feet. The city below was lit up, vague blobs of light, a few headlights on the roads, and beyond the city, out in the bay, sat the brightly illuminated aircraft carrier, an enormous yellow 69 on its tower.

Donald watched his son choke down a mouthful, but said nothing. Since that confrontation in the living room, Alain had been acting as though he was fed up with these two Americans. He'd tossed a frozen pizza in the oven and then "went out for something," not returning for hours. Chewing the icy crust, Donald had tried to make conversation, but Peter had been his usual, petulant self.

Now the boy, who'd showered and changed into a V-neck sweater that showed off the white lump of his sternum, would get drunk and act like an asshole and chat up Alain, who—there was no point in pretending any longer—was little better than a gangster. The man had changed out of his suit into a tight-fitting, shiny black T-shirt and gray wool pants. Instead of wing-tips, he wore elaborate black leather sandals. Alain clearly saw himself as one of those who could get what they wanted by force, and of course he thought this because it was true. When Donald got back to D.C., he'd terminate the man's contract.

Now that they were all seated, Alain was staring at him from across the patio as though he knew exactly what Donald was thinking. Even when Alain lifted his drink he didn't look away. Donald smiled stiffly and blinked out at the lights, heat rising through his neck. When Alain stood he flinched, but the man just went inside without a word.

"Nice view, isn't it?" Donald said, lamely.

"What?" The boy was clutching his drink as though he was dying of thirst.

"The view, it's nice."

"Whatever you say, Dad." The boy shook his head as though this was the stupidest thing he'd ever heard.

Donald was trying to think of something to say besides, *Fuck off, Peter,* when the floodlights snapped off.

Whiskey sloshed over Peter's hand in the sudden dark and he almost called out, but, thank God, managed to squash the impulse. In the dark, the lights of the city seemed very close. He had a terrible feeling that those people he'd seen in the shack, the man with his scarred arms, the face in the doorway, were coming through the forest for them, gripping machetes, shoulders hunched as they slipped into the dark house, pointing to the shapes on the patio. Footsteps sounded behind him and a hand came down on his shoulder.

"I thought this would be better. And I have something special for you." The hand lifted from Peter's shoulder and a dark shape passed before him. The eruption of static startled him—more whiskey slopped onto his hand—and then he spotted a small, red dot and, in its glow, Alain's face. "With this, we can listen in."

"To what?" Peter said, hating the wobble of his voice.

"Your Navy," Alain said. The radio sputtered and a voice came through clear for a second, then faded. "They don't hide their signal. But why should they? There's no one here but a bunch of stupid Haitians."

Donald wasn't sure if he was supposed to laugh, but his son, apparently, thought it funny enough to giggle and this drove Alain on. "That's right, Peter. We Haitians, we're a truly, very stupid people."

The static screamed out of the radio and then an American voice with a thick Southern accent came through, reciting a series of numbers before ending with, "Over." Donald strained to make some sense of it. More numbers, a brief sentence, one of which seemed to have to do with location.

"Are they in the city?" he said. The lights below wavered and seemed to shift with the wind, as though everything had become unmoored and was mixing.

"Of course they are," Alain said. "They come and go wherever they want." Donald's eyes had adjusted somewhat to the dark and he could make out shapes: Peter's round torso, and Alain's face, lit like a mask by the radio's red light.

After a few minutes of listening, Donald thought he could make out the point of the military chatter. There were three, or maybe four, voices. One kept calling himself Eagle's Nest and another was obviously Alpha Team. After a while, Alain confirmed all this. There were recon groups in the city, checking out the situation and identifying the locations of the Macutes.

"In case they want to invade," Alain said. "But then they should just blow the whole place up. Better for everyone, am I right?"

"Well, that's what we're good at," Peter said, surprised at the volume of his voice.

"Exactly. That's why you're so rich, right? Because you blow everyone else up?"

"Anyone, everyone, bomb, bomb, bomb," Peter said. Sitting there in the dark and talking like this was thrilling. Peter was on Alain's side against America, against his father, against all the bullshit of his life. Fuck America. Fuck his school and the goddamn SAT. It was all imperial violence. He got to his feet and went to get more whiskey. As he bent to grab the bottle he sensed Alain leaning forward, perhaps with a balled fist, ready to strike. Peter's legs felt heavy and loose, as though his bones, wet sand, had fallen into his feet.

Donald watched his son return to his seat, slurping at his refilled glass. Those soldiers down there weren't much older than the boy, but were from a whole other world. They were brash and wild and capable and direct, while Peter felt entitled to complain endlessly. He knew nothing about life. Everything had been handed to him and he picked over it in search of a flaw. When he was younger than Peter was now, Donald had sold papers on the street and worked for the park service and waited tables and worked in a book store all to make enough money so he could go to college, and once there, he'd worked sixty hours a week at similar, crappy jobs. Peter's one job in sixteen years had been at the local country club. He'd lasted three weeks: according to Margie the boy had come home early one day, weeping, saying the other guys were bullies and he wasn't going back.

Donald had had such hopes for this trip. He'd connect with his son. He'd show Peter the truth of his life, his work, how vital it was, that there was a whole world out there, available with a little effort. Peter had spent most of the flight down reading, but Donald had managed to instigate a brief conversation about where Peter might go to college. The boy had said, "I'm thinking, I don't know, maybe California. You know? I want to get away from DC. To see new stuff."

At that moment, Donald felt this was a part of himself rising up in his son. Margie wanted the boy to live at home when he went to college, probably to the University of Maryland, or Catholic, or George Mason, somewhere within forty minutes, so she could keep him in her clutches. But with his father's help the boy could get away, find himself, shed this ugly moping solipsism. But, that hope had gone sour over the course of the trip. Every night after his meetings Donald had come back to the hotel room to find Peter passed out on his tangled sheets in his boxers, the air sour with alcohol, a vaguely sexy movie flickering blue light.

Now Alain was telling the boy about his time in the army, about the time he'd had to put down looters after a hurricane. "Wow, that's incredible," Peter said, his voice full of the admiration Donald longed to have directed at himself, though he knew it never would be again.

The back and forth between Alpha team and Eagle's Nest was interrupted by a series of thuds and then a new voice came on, screaming.

Voices piled atop one another. Someone said, "Fucking shithead," and then there was another round of shots.

"What is that?" Donald said.

Through a clatter, a man managed to scream out that he was pinned down. "You've got to send someone to fucking get me. You got to send somebody fucking right now."

"We hear you, Beta," Eagle said. "We are assessing your position."

Peter held his breath. Adrenaline ran up and down his arms, catching for a moment in his neck before spilling into his head. He imagined himself back in Port Au Prince, weighed down by fatigues, body-armor, a gun, moving in formation, scanning the rooflines, the alleys and then there'd be the whistling hiss of the bullets striking the wall, dust and plaster ricocheting into his mouth and eyes. He'd lift his heavy gun to his shoulder and pull the trigger and the dark shape he'd sighted atop the building would disappear into a blaze of fire.

After another series of shots, Beta started screaming. "They know where I am, you fucking pieces of shit! Get me the fuck out of here. Now, get me out of fucking here."

"Who is that?" Donald said. Still, Alain ignored him.

Eagle told Beta to stay where he was—"No shit, you asshole!"—while they tried to get a vehicle out to him. "Try harder," he screamed.

"You poor Americans," Alain said. "You are so brave behind your guns. But alone, you are like babies. Each of you, a trembling little baby."

It was terrible to hear that tone—the same tone Alain had used in the living room, the same tone he'd surely used with that man on the loading dock. Alain could step across the stones and stick a knife in Donald's neck and he'd never see it coming.

"That's exactly right," Peter said. "Bunch of stupid bullies."

"Who love to kill the Haitians. Brown people. Anyone, as long as he's brown. Am I right, Peter?"

"That's right. We're a bunch of dumbshit racist pigs. Pigs, Alain. Someone needs to come and bomb the shit out of us," said Peter, nearly shouting, his voice slurred.

Alain laughed wildly. This was why they'd sheltered Peter. This was why Donald and Margie had hidden him away in the suburbs, in private schools, in the idea that he was smart, special, lovable. Because the alternative was a world of men like Alain.

There were more gunshots and more obscenities screamed by Beta until finally Eagle said, "Beta, there is no vehicle available. You'll need to get yourself out."

"Myself! You motherfucking ass-shit-whore-fuck—" He went on that way until a new voice broke in.

"This is Sleeping Cobra, I have your position, Beta." There was an accent in the voice, a lilt, Peter thought, much like Alain's, as though he was both here with them on the patio and also down there in the city. Peter tried again to imagine what it must be like to be pressed into a doorway with gunfire coming down on you. Would he feel totally removed from himself? Or would he feel the sick uselessness of his flabby arms, his fragile jawbone, ready to shatter?

"Who the fuck is that?" Beta shouted. "Eagle, who is that?"

"We read you, Sleeping Cobra, please state your position," Eagle said.

"I see you Beta, and I see the hostiles," the Haitian said.

"Who are you, asshole? Eagle, who the fuck is this guy."

Eagle demanded verification of identification from Sleeping Cobra, but the questioning was smothered by a series of explosions. Peter leaned forward, heart pounding, sure he should be able to see what he was hearing. The lights below pulsed and wavered, betraying nothing.

Beta was screaming again, his voice trembling with tears and Eagle demanded to know what was going on, but both were drowned by another series of concussions.

"You're clear now, Beta. You can move," the Haitian voice said.

"What the hell is going on?" Beta's voice was cracked and small.

"Stay where you are," Eagle said.

"The hostiles are down." The Haitian voice was calm, as though reporting the weather. "You can move."

They listened for a moment more, but neither Sleeping Corba or Beta said anything. Alpha team began reciting coordinates again. Alain turned the volume on the radio down and laughed. "You see, Donald, what I am saying? You need us, you Americans. You need the Haitians."

"It's true," Donald said. He was shaking too much to sip the last of his whiskey.

"Who was that guy?" Peter said. "I mean, that Cobra guy, who was he?"

He felt stronger, having heard that, than he had since, well, ever. Ever in his whole stupid life. And he knew whose fault that was. The man responsible for making him afraid was sitting a few feet away. How many times had his dad done that little shake of the head: *no, son, that's wrong. You don't know anything.* But the truth was now clear—his father was the one who didn't know anything. His father was the idiot, the liar. This was the goddamn world. Men blowing each other to shit in the streets. *Finally*, he wanted to shout. *Finally the truth!* Peter could stand up and go over and punch his father in the face and the stupid ass old man would never see it coming.

"He's like me," Alain said. "A man who saves Americans who don't deserve it."

For the first time since they'd come out onto the patio Donald was glad for the darkness. Soon, the people below would come up the mountain after them—the Macutes in their pick-up trucks, the little boys with their guns, eyes bloodshot, bare feet slapping on the asphalt, as they went house to house, dragging people screaming into the streets, prodding them with the butts of their guns, then making them kneel in the shrubs. Then they'd step quickly up behind them and hack through their necks with a machete. But maybe with the lights off they'd pass right by Alain's house. The dark pressed on his chest like a stone, but it also concealed him from the world. And it concealed his son, his son who hated him, his son who would go back home and brag about this trip to his friends, distort it, bend it so that it meant almost nothing, so that it became just another trial in his endless litany of self-pity, his son who sat slumped now in his seat, panting heavily, like an old, dying dog.

Developing

Not until I received the second call from the photography shop did I remember they'd called once before, back in January, but at the time I'd been out of town, far from you, Janet, and I'd erased the voicemail with annoyance, consumed at the time with the fading hope of a new job. So, when I answered the phone between classes that first week of April, seeing a local number I didn't recognize, I assumed it was the video store where we're forever returning movies late, but the woman said she was calling from Columbia Photo about some pictures I hadn't yet picked up. I was just outside the English Department building and I stopped, students swirling around me, and said, "Excuse me, what?" A broad shouldered young man with messy blonde curls hanging beneath a low pulled baseball cap charged straight at me, as though he was going to run me down. And why not? He was young and strong and in a hurry whereas what he surely saw in me was weakness, age: a thirty-something man with glasses and thinning brown hair in a wrinkled blue oxford shirt and sagging jeans, a leather bag hanging reluctantly from my shoulder. In short, a fallen member of the herd that was surely on his way out.

The woman's voice was young and I thought she was probably a student, maybe an art major, working at a photo shop (one I'd never heard of) to make some money for beer, or drugs (or maybe, just maybe, books, or in her case I suppose, film, photo-paper, even a new camera). She said I had eight pictures to pick up.

I thanked her and snapped my phone shut and immediately wished I hadn't. Eight pictures? What was she talking about? I hadn't taken photographs of the sort one picked up in a store in years, not since I bought you that tiny digital camera. I don't even own a camera that takes real, physical film photos, haven't, I realized as the hour mark approached and the students were swallowed up into the bellies of the classrooms, since I was in college myself (eons ago, as I liked to tell my students, who liked to hear that their teacher, standing up there rattling on about Ralph Ellison, had been at one time alive and maybe even like them).

I opened my phone and checked the number, considered calling back and asking, "Are you sure they're for me?" but not only had she known my name, but she also had my number, so how could they not be? And then I remembered the first phone call back in December when I'd listened to the message in the great open hallway outside the interview pit at the MLA conference, the air vibrating with anxiety, men and women hurrying by, all about to cry it seemed to me (probably because that's what I felt like doing), all in suits you could tell they hardly ever wore and weren't comfortable in and I'd listened to a woman's voice tell me I had pictures ready for pick-up and I'd thought, *What the fuck is this?* and deleted it angrily, wishing it was a piece of paper, so I could rip it up and stuff it into a trash can because that's what I'd felt like doing with my resume, my cover letters, all the bullshit I'd brought in hopes of a real job, of getting out of this instructorship I've been stuck in for seven years, this instructorship that pays just enough to live on, so we never go hungry, are never really absolutely short on money, but which makes it impossible to do the things we really wanted from life: like travel, or have a baby.

◆   ◆   ◆

I can't say I didn't *think* about the pictures again until the next week, because who knows, maybe I did think of them during one of the long winding patterns of thought that had to do with all the things I was supposed to do, like grade my students' research papers. But it wasn't until you asked where your camera was that I remembered the pictures explicitly and for some reason, as soon as I did, I knew I wouldn't mention them.

Thinking on it now I know I was making the right choice, but then it made no clear, rational sense, was just a powerful, overwhelming feeling, *Don't tell her.* Of course it wasn't articulated in that way, in words, was simply a feeling of protectiveness for this one thing in my life I wanted to keep for myself.

You wanted the camera to take pictures of the purple crocuses blooming at the base of our rose-vine on the front porch. Remember the hopes we'd had when we bought that house years ago? Surely the neighborhood would improve and at first it'd seemed to be doing so. The crack house next door was bought, remodeled, and sold to graduate students and we were sure we'd make a killing one day selling our own place. But then the neighborhood had stalled, dipped up and down, so that for a few months things would be looking up, but then there'd be weeks full of drunken, filthy men heading shirtless up to bars on the Business Loop, throwing failed lotto tickets and beer cans into our yard so they caught amidst the flowers we planted each spring.

"Isn't it in your office?" I said, referring to the camera.

"I looked," you said, smiling at me in the way that meant, *Can't you look for me?* You were wearing your gardening outfit, old, tattered khaki shorts and a baggy black tank top, your hair pulled back under a green handkerchief you've had as long as I've known you, all this making your pale legs and arms and shoulders look even skinnier.

The coffee table in your office was covered with piles of books, all on the verge of toppling onto the heaps of clothes you'd worn once and tossed around to be refolded, only to have them migrate from the couch, or the leather chair in the corner, to the floor where they mingled with the dust and hairballs. I lifted your purse, the one you'd bought in New York four years ago, the last real trip we'd managed to take together, and as soon as I did I knew the camera was in there (you'd been using this purse the day before, I'd noticed, and so how could you not know the camera was there?) and it was then I remembered the call about the film. I looked back to tell you about the odd call and when I saw you smiling (surely you too already knew the camera was in the bag) I knew I wouldn't tell you. The words didn't exactly "catch in my throat," but they caught in my mind, in what felt at the time like my forehead.

I smiled and said, "I think I found it." You pulled the slim black leather case out and said, "How'd that get in there?" An adaptation of our oldest joke: I'd spent the night at your apartment and the next morning I said, "How'd that bed get so far from the wall?" You pointed at me and said, "I blame you." I'd felt then that surely I'd be happy for the rest of my life, knowing of course that happiness couldn't be promised forever at any single point. But I'd felt a happiness that rushed up and down my body, a new, thicker, richer, more sustaining blood.

I said I was going to run out and get a six-pack at the gas station and asked if you needed anything.

"Nope," you said, studying the image of the flowers you'd just taken.

I hurried back inside and flipped through the phone book—my hands were shaking—to Photography and found there, second from the top, Columbia Photo, with its address, which I memorized quickly, then snapped the thick floppy pages shut and hurried to the car, as though I was betraying you.

◆   ◆   ◆

I don't think I'd ever noticed the photography shop before I pulled into its cracked, weed-tufted parking lot, but then I'd rarely been to that side of town, to those neighborhoods that'd once been intended as a safe (white) retreat from downtown. But the neighborhood had been left to decay when the real expansion began in the southwest of town—enormous, quickly built mansions and restaurants, a Whole Foods, three gyms, a sushi restaurant—so all that was left in this neighborhood was a Ben Franklin, a copy-business, and the photography shop, a rusty metal camera sign above the door.

Chemical smells I remembered from high school photography class permeated the long, rectangular room: those pleasant, thickly sweet smells of the developing solution. The store was one long, mostly empty room, shelves scattered here and there holding a few frames and, on those nearest the door, a few lens filters: yellow, red, blue, white. Against the long wall were a few glass cases with cameras that looked antique and at the far end of the room was a counter, behind which I could see a few clanking white machines.

I went to the counter and looked for a bell. No bell, no buzzer, and so the only option was to call out, "Hello?" but for some reason I felt I shouldn't.

Along the wall beside the counter were a few framed photographs: one was a family portrait, father, mother, two sons, and a baby girl, all dressed in white polo shirts and white pants; another was of a mountain landscape, the peaks predictably covered with veins of snow, the lower ridges thickly forested; the third was of a sunset over calm, iridescent water, the last few boards of a pier were visible, darkened in contrast to the glow of the falling sun. They weren't very good pictures (the sunset was, I thought, in soft focus).

Eventually I had no choice but to lean against the counter and shout, "Hello?"

A young woman with thick, black hair poked her head around the corner. She was wearing a black T-shirt with a smiling yellow tiger's face on it, pulled tight by her breasts that seemed to point out to the sides. Her teeth pushed out her upper lip, as though she was forever skeptical of that last thing you'd said.

"Oh," she said, "I didn't know you were here."

"Sorry, I'm here to pick up some film."

"Sure, sure. Hold on," she said, ducking back out of sight.

I couldn't be sure if hers was the same voice I'd heard on the phone, but there was certainly something familiar about her. Maybe she'd been one of my students, or maybe I'd just seen her around over the last ten years.

This feeling of familiarity intensified when she came back into sight, wiping her hands on the hem of her black shirt. I almost asked, "Have we met," or, "Do I know you," but didn't want to sound like a letch, with just the two of us there in that big, empty store.

"What was it you needed?" she said, studying her fingernails.

I told her I was there to pick up some pictures and she asked my name and when I gave it she said, "Oh, of course. I was wondering when you were going to come. I mean, they've just been *sitting* here." Her tone was almost scolding, but just not quite, so I smiled and nodded, though she wasn't looking, was busy digging through a cardboard box half-full of photo-envelopes, all just tossed together in a random way, as though she'd meant to haul them out to the trash.

"I was out of town," I said. Why would I lie, Janet? But you've seen me do this, these meaningless lies that are no better, in the end, than the truth. I've always had the sense that lying protects me somehow, puts up a little wall between me and the world.

One hand full of photo-envelopes, the other thrust down in the box, the girl looked up and said, "Oh, yeah, where were you?" Her upper teeth were just visible beneath her pushed-out lip, and they were stained a dull yellow and slightly crooked.

My throat felt tight. My hands were clammy and I put them in my pockets where they seemed to get colder. "Oregon," I said. You, of course, will know why this was the lie I chose. You, and maybe only you, know how badly we've always wanted to move out there, Portland, with the mountains, the ocean, the liberal population, not like our own state that seemed, as we often put it, so intent on reducing women to second-class citizens.

"Really?" the girl said. "Where in Oregon?"

"Portland," I said. I looked away from her toothy smile and noticed the yellow tiger on her shirt wasn't in fact smiling, was, rather, in mid-roar.

"My parents are from Portland." When I looked up she was nodding happily, as though we were old relatives, finally meeting up after years of sporadic phone calls.

"It's a beautiful place."

"Oh," she said, nodding vigorously, then reaching into the box and grabbing the top-most envelope. "It really is." She glanced down at the envelope and said, "Let's see. That comes to eleven seventy-eight."

I handed her a twenty, (the envelope was slim in my hand and when I glanced at it I saw my name, my cell phone number written on it) and my hand was shaking, but if she noticed she didn't say anything.

"Come see us next time," she said, turning and disappearing behind the wall.

◆   ◆   ◆

I wish you could see the pictures so I wouldn't have to describe them (they're out in the glove compartment now). How can I do them justice, how can I explain the way they made me feel and I know that of all the people in the world you too would respond as I did, as I have? You alone would understand why I've had to do the things that have led me here, to this room, from which I'm writing you.

Back in the car I locked the doors and sat with the windows rolled up though it was a warm April day. The pictures were in a flimsy mini-album. The first was a double-exposure, sloppily overlapping images. The top half is of a woman sitting at a computer head turned toward the camera. Other than the glaring computer screen the only thing that really catches the light (her back blends with the chair and into the dark wall behind), is the woman's face, though it's cut off so all you can see of it is a chin, a smile, the bottom of a nose. She's wearing a sweater with the sleeves pushed up. The bottom image is all darkness for three-fourths, though on the far left there is a slice of a bright room and what looks, if you studying it hard enough, to be a food rack in a kitchen. Clearly these weren't my pictures, but for some reason I didn't go in right then and return them.

The second picture is of the front of a house. The address, 1007, is visible and you can make out the glass door, the railing on which potted plants sit, up to a little attic window that looks like it doesn't quite fit the hole made for it. And if you look close enough you can see what you first assumed was the front of the house is in fact a porch, with the second level of the roof rising up behind it.

In a way the third picture is as badly taken as the first: it's completely out of focus and too dark to make out anything other than two people (women), leaning together and it might be that one of them is pointing at the camera.

In the fourth there's a woman, the same woman, I noticed immediately, from the top-half of the first picture, standing at a counter in a kitchen, cooking, wearing that same sweater, the sleeves still pushed up, looking over her shoulder, smiling at the camera. How can I tell you how beautiful she is, Janet? Her hair is cut in a boy's style with bangs and you can tell it's blonde from the way it catches the light. She's tall (or maybe the counter is short) and her legs are thin and you can see, turned slightly toward the camera, the rounded curve of one breast. I know I shouldn't be telling you these things. Though this picture is the clearest of the first four, it is still poorly taken, for the counters above her quickly fade into darkness and the light over the sink is too bright, bringing unnatural attention to two bottles of wine on the counter, one empty, one full.

The fifth picture is of the same beautiful woman with her short blonde hair, smiling at the camera straight on this time and cupping with her slender hands the head of a beautiful, sleek, black dog with a white snout. The dog is looking skeptically at the camera with great intelligence.

Pecan pies are the subject of the sixth picture, two arranged on a counter and by this time there is no doubt that the woman with the blonde hair cooked them and then, when I turned to the seventh picture, is when I saw myself. The picture is slightly blurry so for a moment I didn't realize it was my own face, shot up close. I'm looking down and my glasses (as always) are sliding down my nose. My mouth is slightly open, as though I'm reading something, or about to look up and say something. I look heavier in the picture, I thought there in the car, but when I looked quickly in my rearview mirror I saw the picture is accurate; the mistake was inside my head.

How can I explain to you how calm I was when I saw myself there, Janet? And how does it make any sense to claim that I knew that the picture of me was taken in the same house as the pictures of the pies, of the woman with her short blonde hair, with that sleek, tall dog, in that house with 1007 as its address, with its porch, its flower pots, its glass front door? The final picture confirmed this. There I was in the center of the image, laughing (wearing the same shirt from the previous image), bringing a glass of what looks like whiskey to my mouth. Standing just beneath the overhead light I'm brightly illuminated and all the other people are shadows. Looking closer I saw my eyes are closed with drunken happiness.

I looked back through the pictures quickly. Painful as it surely is, I must for once tell the truth: each time I saw those pictures of that beautiful woman in the kitchen and at the computer, I felt I was falling deeply and idiotically in love.

Slowly, reason came over me, spreading up through my neck and covering over that little glimmer of happiness until the thought finally stated itself clearly, *What the fuck?* Who the hell was that woman? Whose house was that and what was I doing there? Who'd taken those pictures of me? I looked at the envelope, but the writing wasn't my hand, was likely that of the tiger-girl inside, bubbly, with a circle instead of a dot over the i in my name. There was no address, just my phone number.

I looked up, ready to get out of the car—the air inside had thickened and I was sweating—but when I did I saw that the *Open* sign was turned off and the bluish haze of the fluorescent lights had been extinguished. Squinting to be sure I was right I saw it was clear the place was closed. Well, I thought, I'll come back later.

◆   ◆   ◆

If I were a better person I'd have put the pictures away and not thought anymore about them. Maybe that was just some party we'd been to years ago when I was still in the Ph.D. program and went to such parties and maybe you were even the one who'd taken the pictures. Maybe the blonde woman was a friend of yours and we'd gone to a party at her house and you'd snapped a few messy shots, then found the camera and its undeveloped film years later and so dropped it off and told me to pick it up and I'd just forgotten in the rush of the semester, the crush of grading papers for five sections of composition, in the rush to try to get a job, in the blinding hope of that interview at the small school out in Oregon near Portland and all our talk about what our lives would be like if we could move out there: hiking in the mountains, liberals everywhere as bright and healthy as grass. Then the job fell through and in the inevitable, squelching return of mediocrity I'd just forgotten to pick up the pictures.

But I knew this wasn't true. So I put them in my pocket when I climbed from the car and saw you on your knees reapplying mulch around the pansies. From there I hid the envelope in a drawer in my office desk, not a locked drawer, but a place I knew you'd never look. Over the next few days, while I was in there grading, or, purportedly, doing some of my fabled and surely-never-to-be-finished research on the political implications of *jouissance* in the novels of

Nabokov, Bellow, and Ellison, I'd take the envelope out and study the pictures, looking for anything that might tip my memory and fit them into my mind's idea of my life: What about the little ball of light that is the computer mouse in the first one? Or the arrangement of books in that final, party shot? Nothing worked, though I thought the books might be arranged alphabetically.

Two weeks went by before I began looking for the house. At first, it wasn't any kind of systematic search. I was driving to the grocery store to pick up a few things for the risotto you wanted to make and I noticed that the houses I was driving past looked a lot like 1007. I slowed and turned onto a smaller street and checked the numbers. They were in the low hundreds, so I followed the street to the cul-de-sac into which it eventually spilled and the numbers only got to 814.

Over the next few weeks every time I went out in the car to run an errand I took a new route until I found houses that vaguely resembled the style in the photo and then I'd slow and look for 1007. I found three houses over the next few weeks with that number, but none had that lopsided attic window, none the white railings, the glass door. Eventually I was inventing reasons to go out and search and, as the semester drew to a close and the grading mounted, I began to neglect everything else.

How could you not have wondered what I was doing, out in the car all that time? Maybe you did. But you didn't say anything. Maybe you assumed I was doing research at the library, or conferencing with students. Maybe you were just glad to get me out of the house. Your sister had gotten pregnant during those weeks and you were always on the phone and I could feel your disappointment with our life.

But surely you remember how long ago we'd agreed, with my meager instructor pay and your hourly wage at Barnes & Noble, that we couldn't support a baby. What about health insurance? What if the English department cut loose the adjuncts? Then what would we do if I didn't have a job? And our student loans, yours from undergraduate and my enormous pile from years of grad school decadence, would bury us. But this was all just money and people with far less than us all over the world went on having children. So there had to be something else holding us back, some understanding that we weren't ready, that it wasn't right for *us* to have a child, even if so many others did.

Now, from this new vantage, I wonder if that decision was the death of our relationship and so with it the death of whom we were. For so long that's just how I felt, as though I wasn't truly alive, as though I was floating through life, insubstantial and only glimpsed now and then by others, warily, a shadow that sends a little shiver up their arms so they turn away and think, *No, I didn't see anything*. I'd become a figment, not just in the minds of others, but in my own mind and, most importantly of all, to you, Janet. It's surprising we held out as long as we did, that we managed to make a life and believe in each other for all those years when we were going nowhere but down into nothingness. Love, of course, is what held us together. And when that went, as it did somewhere along the line, so too did our sense of one another as real people, so too did my sense of myself. Until, that is, I started searching for that house, that woman. Suddenly I was a person again, with a purpose. I felt others saw it: that my students looked at me differently, glancing between the pages of their unread, battered books and me, thinking, maybe there's something here, maybe he's actually trying to tell us something. How could you not see this? Maybe if you'd seen it, if you'd acknowledged it in the slightest, I wouldn't be here. But to you I was still and would always be nothing.

At dinners during those weeks you never asked what I'd done that day, even when I'd spent four or five hours searching methodically, highlighting a map I'd bought just for this purpose, a map I often accidentally left in the car where you might see it, all my insane yellow boxes and lines and Ts. I'd ask how your day had been (How'd that staff meeting go?), but you never asked, "Where were you all day?" As though you simply didn't care. Maybe, perhaps even likely, this is just the excuse I use now to explain how I can be sitting here in front of this little white Apple computer, writing you this letter, from this room. But no, all that time I felt the distance between us widening like wet, loose earth when the wall that so long held it up is finally taken away, spilling down into the rushing river.

And there was, for once, so much to tell you, so much beyond the typical, quotidian nonsense we normally shared. How, for example, I'd been fired, or, to use the official language, they'd *decided not to renew my contract*. There were the budget cuts, the director of composition explained, and there were, to be honest, too many complaints about my classes from students.

"What kind of complaints?" I said, though of course I knew the answer.

"Mostly there's a feeling amongst many of your students that you're not grading fairly and that your classes aren't topically relevant to first year English." The director was looking down at a sizable sheaf of papers, all of which looked, from my vantage, like printed out emails.

It was true that I'd long since stopped caring if my courses adhered to the departmental guidelines, which discouraged the use of primary texts. I found this obscene and idiotic, purely and utterly antithetical to the study of language and culture, and after struggling for years to adapt, I simply gave up, assuming I would slip unnoticed beneath the demagoguery of departmental politics. As to the grading question, I knew they simply resented the fact that I held them to any kind of standard of academic competence. I was supposed to doll out As and Bs and maybe a few Cs and if there were truly illiterate students, a few who'd somehow slipped through the not-very-rigorous admissions process, then I was supposed to possibly, if there was no alternative, fail them. Instead, I'd failed half my class the previous term. But they'd all deserved it, really. But did anyone care? Did anyone, when I sent an email to the Department Listserv after my "notice" (if that's what it was, it actually felt far more casual than that, as though I was an empty envelope on the counter they'd been meaning to toss out for weeks), take my side? Maybe I'd been too harsh in the email. I did call the director of composition a condescending asshole. You know how sensitive and tender those English department folks can be about curse words. If asshole is even one. The response to my missive was silence. I was a small, dirty fish, drifting to the bottom of the deep, cold, empty sea where my meager flesh could be picked over by crabs until there was nothing left but a flimsy, pale frame.

◆　　　　◆　　　　◆

You must be wondering why I persist, page after page in this fashion, in not explaining myself. *Where are you!*

Today, as you know, is the final day of the semester and I spent a few hours at my desk, picking up portfolios from my students who stood awkwardly around my desk, nodding after they handed me their folders, as though now that that was out of the way we were friends and I was supposed to invite them out for a drink. Instead I said, "Well, have a good semester," and looked down as though about to start grading.

Three students hadn't turned in their portfolios and I was sure that afternoon I'd have a couple harried emails explaining the incredible circumstances that came between them and the deadline, but I marked them down for Fs and turned in my grades.

Instead of going straight home, I decided I'd go to the store and get a six pack, maybe even a twelve pack, or a couple of bottles of wine, to celebrate the end of the semester, the end of my half-assed tenure at this mediocre school in the middle of nowhere and over those drinks, I'd tell you what had happened, how utterly screwed we were now. I hadn't even meant to take a back road, through one of those neighborhoods down Broadway, the kind we drive past and shudder and think, *Who'd live there?* caught between the old and the new in the absolutely banal. But Broadway was closed. An accident and apparently a big one. They were diverting traffic down Stadium, so I went that way, then took the first right and wound over toward the store.

How long did I drive down that street before I noticed that the houses looked a lot like those in the picture, the same style with numbers in the low hundreds? I went a couple more blocks and there it was: the white house with flowerpots on the railing. 1007. I pulled up in front: there was the ill-fitting window in the attic, there was the porch, the glass door, the porch floor, which, I saw now in the full color of life, wasn't white, as I'd assumed, but painted a very light gray.

Even before I checked the photos, I knew this was the house. Not only did I know this with an irrational, powerful certainty, but I knew I'd been here many times. The arrangement of the colored flowerpots, purple, red, yellow, sky blue, purple again, was familiar, was the kind of thing you don't notice you know because you see it so often. You'd love those pots, Janet, the mint, flourishing in the largest, and the spindly rosemary.

There's no shame, I suppose, in telling you how frightened I was when I got out of the car. Or maybe it was excitement. At any rate I felt a dizziness, a lightness, a disorientation so powerful I don't remember the walk from the car up to the porch. I stood on the top step. No voices, no television. Pressing my face close to the glass so my breath misted I looked in through a little square window on the door. I saw a yellow wall, a stereo atop a bookcase, and beyond this first room the corner of a table in a room whose walls were painted light brown and, beyond that, a green room with red curtains.

I rang the bell and heard its mechanical buzz. There was no response. I knocked on the purple door and looked in through the window.

How can I explain what I did then, Janet? It sounds insane even to think it, much less write it here. How can I explain then that I reached into my pocket for my keys and, feeling a soothing calm, found my house-key (our house-key) and slid it into the lock? Would you believe me if I told you then that it fit perfectly, and turned with no resistance, and the lock retreated with a welcoming thud? Our second key worked the knob and I stepped inside.

On the couch was the black and white dog from the pictures and she began slapping her tail against the leather, ears back, as though she was excited to see me, a bright pink tongue flicking up over her nose in welcome.

"Hey, there, baby," I said and she jumped down and leaned against my legs. I stroked her shining fur, ran her floppy ears between my fingers like folds of satin.

I'm telling you so much about the dog because there's really no way to convey the confusion of what I saw, the abundance of detail—the little gray television in the corner, the glass table covered with plants, the soft-frosted glass orb of the lamp, the leather couch and matching chair and mismatched turquoise footrest, the full bookshelves (novels, arranged alphabetically)—was at once disorienting in its newness and also deeply familiar. It was like the feeling you have when entering again for the first time in years an elementary school (to vote, or for some community meeting) and you see those slim gray lockers, those tiny water fountains, and in the bathroom those ludicrously low urinals, the building smelling of the glue that has stuck the glitter to the pictures that droop all down the stone hallway. I had that same overwhelming sense that I'd spent time here in another life, like a childhood one can remember only in pieces, the edges of which have softened so they're limp and loose and less and less a part of who we are. The dog clicked away from me and climbed carefully back up on the couch and settled contentedly atop a red pillow.

The kitchen, like the living room and the hall through which I passed, was large and bright and clean, an island in the middle with an enormous chopping block and hanging above it was a rack of Le Creuset pots and pans, the kind you'd always wanted, the kind we talked about splurging on, before we realized how far outside our budget they lay. The floor was gray tile and the granite counters were wiped clean, the sink silver.

Most of the pictures on the fridge were of a little girl with auburn hair: sitting in a swing on the beach with her little rounded shoulders burned; in a backyard as a toddler, playing with the black dog who'd greeted me. And there were pictures of the dog as well, frisking with toys, or splayed out goofily in the grass. On the side I found what I was looking for, a picture of the blonde woman from the photographs I'd picked up at Columbia Photo, though in this picture her hair is longer, grown in a bob down to her chin and she looks even prettier. I slipped the picture out from beneath the ladybug magnet. It was in color, unlike the eight I'd picked up, and then I saw, looking again at the fridge, the picture of me. I was holding the little girl in my arms on the beach. My legs, in the picture, are tanned and my hair is dusted blonde from the sun.

I put the picture of the woman back and went through the brown dining room to the green room with red curtains. An office, with a desk and a stiff-backed wooden chair. There was a computer closed up on the desk, the same computer on which I'm typing now. But before I went to it, before I opened it and started this letter to you, Janet, I went through the room carefully, along the bookshelves and I studied the pictures on the walls. There were three framed photographs. One was of the little girl, the blonde woman and me, all wearing white T-shirts and smiling at the camera, posing, I think, on the lawn of this house, the corner of which is just visible on the far left. There are also two vacation photos: one of the mountains, the far peaks covered in snow, the trees the bright green of mid-summer; the other is of the ocean at sunset, the water a rippling orange and red, the darkened end of a pier just visible in the foreground. I lifted these two pictures off the wall and read on the back, *Oregon, 2005*. I'd been there and I know that when I'd pushed the button on the camera until it clicked and that image was captured, I'd been then happy and alive in a way I haven't been for years, since, perhaps, we first met. Can you remember it? Do you remember what it was like to be in love like that with nothing but hope in front of you, and years and years to go before disappointment slowly crept up and became your life?

✦   ✦   ✦

I'm waiting now, which accounts for the length here (it's been hours and the evening is deepening and if not for the clocks being set forward, it'd be dark already), for the woman and the girl to return. Reading this over (and editing it—you know me), I see I haven't explained things. I realize it makes no more sense that I'm at this desk than it did before I wrote these words. But I feel you deserve to know.

Please, Janet, don't look for me. What I've written here is full of little, undetectable lies. The house number, for one, isn't 1007. And the town isn't our town. Maybe I'm writing this from a hotel in Texas, on my way, as I've always joked, to Mexico (I'm not, I'm here in this room just as I've claimed, but I won't tell you where this house is). Maybe, tacked to a board above this desk is a letter, a job offer from a small liberal arts college in the Northwest.

These final words are being written after I've pasted the Word file into email and gone through and made sure all the italics are in place. I'm ready now for you to read it. But I'll wait until I hear a car crunching in the drive, a key in the door, the door opening and little feet running, and voices calling, "Daddy," or, "Honey, we're back," and then, when I hear those voices, I'll hit Send.

Hidden in the Trees

I.

At five-thirty when the alarm went off, Max was already out of bed shouting, "Get up! We'll miss the bus, let's go. Hop to it!" He was wearing jeans and his khaki shirt, as always. Jenny watched with one eye—the other seemed to be stuck shut—as he popped a rubber band around his silver ponytail.

"Hop to it?" she said, trying to blink her eye free, reaching for the jeans she'd stepped out of a few hours ago.

"That's right, sweetheart. Hop your silly ass to it." He grabbed his backpack and leaned across the bed to slap her on the hip.

In the thin morning light the streets of the town looked different, smaller, quainter, less like a tourist trap, as though this was the real city beneath the noise and sun and stupidity of the foreign crowds. Belizean women hurried by, arms heaped with baskets, long dresses swiveling around their ankles. There was a small crowd of locals in the square, gathered around a bus that was covered, wheel wells to roof, with a mural: saints, angels, and sinners gazed up at an enormous, grinning Jesus with rays of light, or power, shooting from his head.

"The town doesn't look so bad, right now," Max said as they joined the crowd. "But give it a couple of hours and this place will be full of idiots." He scratched at the gray bristles on his cheek with a frown. He was, he'd said, thinking of growing a beard.

Yesterday they'd arrived in this little beach town, which, Max had assured her, had only been built for the pleasure-seeking snorkeling hordes of idiot Americans that milled around in flip-flops. Fools who'd pay anything for a room. It wasn't until all the other tourists had been whisked away that a young man with a sloppily corrected hair lip agreed to Max's terms: ten dollars a night with their own bathroom and a fan.

As they followed the man past cafés and a crowded bar with enormous stacked speakers thumping reggae into the street, Max put an arm around Jenny and tugged her close. "Three days of this tourist bullshit, then we're out of here."

"Fine," she said. His fingers were digging under her ribs and she tried to pry herself loose. "Three days. But don't ruin those, okay?"

"What are you talking about?" he said, pulling her tighter, taking her breath away. "When do I ruin anything?"

Their room was the nicest accommodations they'd had in months: painted light blue, with a bright white ceiling from which hung a fan that spun soundlessly. Lacy curtains hung at the windows that went nearly from floor to ceiling and there was a gleaming, tiled bathroom. As soon as they were alone, Max pulled down his shorts and stood with his long penis dangling from beneath the flaps of his khaki shirt. "All right. Let's get down to the beach, slather ourselves with some chemicals, and work on that skin cancer. That's my idea of a good time. What do you say?"

"You're a real jackass, aren't you?" she said, covering herself with a towel though she was still dressed. She wanted to lock herself in the bathroom, curl up in that cool, smooth, immaculate tub.

"What are *you* talking about, Jenny? I'm here to have fun. Let's have some *fun.*" He swung his hips so his penis knocked from thigh to thigh.

"Sometimes," she said, fastening the towel around her skinny chest, "you're a real asshole, you know that?"

"That's why you love me," he said, unbuttoning his shirt, then taking a long, approving look at his body. He was forty, twelve years older than she, but just as thin, with ropey muscles from his long neck to his square, solid calves. Sharp tan lines made him look as though he'd been cobbled together carefully: dark, almost chocolate forearms turning suddenly bright white half-way up the bicep. There was a perfect curve of tanned skin around his neck, where his T-shirts ended, so it looked as though his head could be lifted cleanly off his pale shoulders with their white ridges of muscle, the hollows of the collarbone distinct. The same lines marked Jenny's arms and neck and thighs: this was the first time they'd left the mountains and come down to the coast.

"No. That's not why I love you," she said, stepping into her suit, shimmying it up over her hips.

Three months ago they'd flown from Boston down to Panama City and had started their travels north. The plan was to meander around until they reached Mexico City and from there take a bus to Houston, then catch a flight back to Boston. This was the third trip abroad they'd taken in the four years she and Max had been married: the first had been to Europe, Italy and Greece, with two nights in Turkey (to break her in for the real traveling, he'd told her), then to Southeast Asia, and now Central America. Already, as they moved farther and farther from the equator, Max was talking about Africa. One had to be careful there, but that was no reason to avoid it. Hell, it was all the more reason to go, as far as he was concerned. Which, she'd quickly learned, was all that mattered. But that's what had attracted her to him: he knew what he wanted.

She'd met him at a friend's gallery opening and had immediately wanted to be with him. She'd wanted not only Max but his elaborate bundle of plans and ideas. They'd gone out to dinner and he'd started to tutor her in disgust. He'd talked politics, pop culture, the fearfulness and anxiety of American life. Only a nation of idiots, he'd said, would elect someone like Ronald Reagan. And then reelect him, and then elect his idiot Vice President as they had just a few months before they left for Panama.

Through Panama, Nicaragua, and Honduras they'd avoided the large cities, sticking to small towns, remote, desperately poor villages where they often paid to sleep on the floor of some local's shack, huddled together under the wool blanket Max tied with string to the outside of his pack. On such nights they ate dinner with the family Max had paid, sitting on the dirt floors around a fire that clogged the hut with smoke, the children avoiding them at first, hiding in the corners, then gradually coming out, and eventually they'd be sitting in her lap, putting their filthy fingers in her mouth whenever she yawned or spoke. Then the family would bundle into the one or two beds in the hut while she and Max stretched out on the ground.

Though she never said anything, she was terrified on such nights, no matter how cute the kids had been, no matter how friendly the hosts. She and Max were always surely the only gringos for miles, for dozens, possibly a hundred miles. The people they rented floor space from, or others who'd heard about the two travelers, could kill them, take their heap of money (more than most of the people they met were likely to make in six months or a year), and dump their bodies in the impenetrable forests. No one knew who they were, or where they were. Jenny often felt in these villages as though she didn't exist and she hated this feeling, this sense of absence.

It was just the kind of thing Max would've told her, had she said any of this to him, she should be embracing. "All this American bullshit about the self. Fuck the self," he'd told her in Indonesia two years before while they were smoking hashish on the beach in front of a bungalow they were renting for twenty-five cents a night. "It's the biggest crock of shit in history. It's how they keep us afraid, worried, pliant. If you just accept the fact that there's no self, that you've got no identity," he paused to take a long drag on the joint. "Then really, you're free. Free in a way you can never be in America."

He'd handed her the joint, squinting carefully, watching her response. Probably she'd nodded too vigorously, because he'd let the smoke out with a disgusted puff and dropped the subject.

This was the state of their marriage: he pontificated, she disappointed him with her provincialism, her clutching to the emptiness of her life before they'd met. They'd married at the courthouse with the judge's secretary as witness. Her mother cried when she found out and when Jenny told Max she felt bad about not having invited her parents he said, "For what? I thought we were just doing it for the tax break." She hadn't been able to tell, from his smirk, if he was kidding.

He was wealthy: his mother had died young and rich and left it all to him, though his father had tried unsuccessfully to hone in on it. Now, Max had told her, he and his dad didn't speak. Max was able to give Jenny a security she'd never had, not even as a child, growing up in a tiny town in the far northwest corner of Vermont. But, she'd discovered once they were married, this meant leaving her past behind, starting a new life with him. It meant cutting off old friends and even her parents.

It hadn't been as hard in the end as she'd feared, but then her life before they'd met had been rapidly getting out of control. For months she'd been sleeping on friends' couches until they kicked her out, shooting heroin whenever she could get it. Jobless, on the verge, she often thought, looking back, of dying. She'd wanted to die. Then she'd met Max and he'd taken her in, made her quit heroin, helped her through rehab, gave her life meaning and direction. His love was strict and demanding and just the kind she'd needed to save her. It was easy to notice the negatives as they popped up day to day, particularly while traveling, but there was a larger goodness about Max that she'd seen early on, which fueled her sense of duty and love for him. And, she knew, he needed her. Or at least he needed someone to bounce his ideas off, someone to protect, but someone who wouldn't complain about his need to travel, his moods, someone who wouldn't make all the demands on him you might expect in life. "You'd be surprised how many women are perfectly willing to submit to cliché: give me a house, give me some babies. Everyone of those bitches I've told you about." When he'd said this he'd smiled at her and pulled her against his sweaty chest, kissing the top of her head. "But not my Jenny. You're perfect, you know that?" She'd closed her eyes, floating in a kind of bliss.

Eventually the bus driver opened the door and the locals shoved up the steps, handing over fistfuls of coins. Max had booked this ride to Tikal yesterday afternoon, while she'd gone down to the beach. When he told her at dinner, a small local fish place he'd found on his afternoon walk, she'd said, "But I told you not to fuck this up for me, Max. I just want to sit on the beach."

"Jesus, Jenny. We'll stay another day. Don't worry. You'll get plenty of time on the beach." He'd looked down at the flimsy paper tickets. "I thought you'd like to go. It's Tikal, you know. Not exactly the middle of nowhere."

There was this about Max that fed her love as well: for all his brashness, for all his shouting and swearing and anger, he loved her, sincerely, not in the easy, empty way so much of the world imagined love to be. He'd confessed as much when they'd been together three months, telling her this never happened to him, falling in love, and that he didn't really know how to feel about it.

"Feel happy," she'd said, kissing him, wrapping her legs around his in their bed.

They took seats toward the middle of the bus. Jenny pulled down the window and watched the sun rise up over the tile roofs while Max read the coverless Vonnegut novel he'd found in the hotel courtyard until, with a choke, several sputters, and a final roar, the bus came to life and pulled away, thudding over the speed bumps meant to temper the tourists on rented scooters. The buildings slumped lower and lower, roofs going from tile to wood to corrugated metal. Two white and brown dogs sniffed along the gutters and glanced up, seeming to look her in the eye as the bus passed and pulled into the dense forest, foliage thickening into patterns of shadow.

She leaned her head against the seat, letting her neck go limp so she bounced along, wondering how many days Max was likely to want to spend in Guatemala. They'd go to Lake Atitlan and he'd probably want to head farther west, to the areas hardest hit by the civil war.

She woke when the roads turned to dirt. "You've missed some good jungle," he said, pointing at the confusion of vines strangling thick trees. Dust clouded up and stung her eyes.

"I think we're in Guatemala. Or close." He seemed happy, took her hand and held it in his lap. The bus was more crowded, nearly full. All the passengers besides them were locals, some, the Guatemalans she presumed, in colorful woven clothes. Their talk was punctuated with clicks and clucks. A few men and women held crates with shuddering chickens that shed dirty little feathers and a goat on a rope leash stood in the aisle.

The road, after climbing steadily for a few miles, surged up a mountain. The bus's engine strained, whined. Jenny watched the trees, waiting to see something exotic or unexpected, something she could carry back in her memory to America, so that when everything was over she could think: on that bus I saw, hidden in the trees of a Guatemalan jungle, a leopard, a bright bird. This was, after all, what travel was for: to see that which so few others did and to carry the memory of that through life, to remember the elsewhere, the otherwise.

The ground leveled and they pulled into a clear patch of land. There was a single clapboard building on the side of a hill and a green military truck was parked beside a ditch filled with black water. A soldier stood in the road, waving them down. She felt terribly nervous. It was the men with the green uniforms and their machine guns. She'd read all about the civil war before they'd left, about the massacres in the mountains, the death squads, Reagan's support of the dictators.

"This must be the border," Max said, leaning across to look out the window. He pointed up and said, "Jesus Christ."

"What?" she said. On the hill an enormous machine gun pointed down at them. It moved, sun glinting off its long barrel, the man behind it hidden by black metal. Beside the gun a flag had been planted: a severed white hand with red drops of blood falling from its jagged stump against a black background. She tried to breathe evenly but couldn't.

"Calm down," Max said. He patted their entwined hands. "We'll be fine." He looked calm, but she wanted him to admit he was afraid. Only an idiot wouldn't be afraid. Only an idiot would be looking past her out the window as though nothing was wrong.

Dust settled on her teeth and she tried to breath through her nose. Soldiers shouted at the driver. The driver threw up his hands. Two men climbed, shouting, onto the bus, machine guns around their necks. They screamed at the first few passengers who stared straight ahead, mumbling their responses.

"What's he saying?" she whispered.

Max squeezed her hand and said, "Keep quiet."

One of the soldiers leaned out the door and shouted something to the men on the hillside who laughed and nodded. The bus was still idling and the air stank of diesel. The soldier stepped forward, grinning, and grabbed the goat's rope leash, jerking it away from an old woman, and then led the animal off the bus. The men on the hill laughed and clapped and rubbed their stomachs, pointing their guns at the goat, laughing harder.

The remaining soldier came down the aisle. Jenny looked at her legs. They were so thin, frail in the dirty jeans she'd been traveling in for months, but which now seemed to rub in a hundred places like sandpaper. Max squeezed her hand again, but said nothing. The soldier began shouting, close. She saw Max look up and couldn't stop herself from doing the same. The soldier smiled at her, his mouth missing most of its teeth. He pointed at her.

"What?" she said, softly.

The soldier pointed out the window, and then at her again. "I'm sorry," she said, shaking her head. This was the wrong thing to do, a mistake, she knew it immediately. Max let go of her hand.

The soldier shouted again and pointed his machine gun at her, the bitter smell of marijuana and alcohol falling over her with each word. She was smiling, she tried to slacken it, but her face had dried like a plaster cast. The gun was pointed at her forehead.

Why weren't the other people breathing, or even moving? Everything had been reduced to the soldier and his gun. He lowered it, as though coming to his senses, and spoke in a calmer voice, pointing at Jenny, then gesturing for her to stand and come with him. The few teeth he had looked as though they'd been smeared with dung. She shook her head. If she got off the bus she'd be left behind and the soldiers would drag her into the shack and rape her, one after the other and then again and over and over, and then they'd kill her. She'd rather die on the bus.

The soldier coughed, raised his hands, and spoke in what she imagined he thought of as a reasonable tone, pointing out the window, miming the examination of documents, then nodding and smiling and pointing at her. She gripped the seat so her fingers cramped. Sweat ran under her arms and over her stomach.

Then Max began to speak. He pointed at her and shook his head and waved his hands in front of his face, shaking his head over and over, his Spanish quick. When she looked back at the soldier he was frowning, skeptical. He pointed at her, but Max shook his finger and continued talking. He pointed at himself and nodded, then finally the soldier snorted, turned, and walked up the aisle, his gun swinging over people's heads. The bus shook as he climbed down. The engine roared and they moved down the road, past the outpost where she could see the soldier talking to the others, the goat chewing grass on the hillside behind them. A wind blew through the jungle canopy and soon the road behind them was obscured by a storm of dust.

II.

When she'd been with Max for a month she'd gone back, one night, to heroin. He was out to dinner with a friend and she grabbed her jacket, pulled on her sandals. Her feet, clammy and stiff all day, seemed to warm, to sweat, as she hurried out of the apartment. The bar in Back Bay was crowded and she went to the pool room in the back. Her old dealer was there. He hugged her and kissed her forehead and told all the men in their sleeveless shirts with tattoos that this used to be his little princess.

"Where have you been?" he said, holding her against him, rubbing her back. "Where've you been all this time? I've missed you."

"I've missed you too," she said.

He shot her up in his van, an old white thing with the windows painted black, ratty, greasy pillows heaped on the metal floor.

When she went home that night Max was watching television in a T-shirt and boxers. His feet, in the knit wool socks he wore to keep warm, were up on the coffee table and he took them down, slowly, as though he was injured. As she leaned against the door frame he patted the couch and said, "There are blankets in the closet."

She'd started crying when he left the room, curling up against the door. She'd almost left. She could sleep on her dealer's floor, maybe. But she didn't leave and the next morning Max took her out to breakfast and told her if she ever did that again she'd have to move out.

"Which would be a shame," he said. "Because I like you."

"I like you too," she said, poking at the quivering translucent skin of the bright yellow yolk. The tines broke through and the yellow ran up against her hash browns.

"So, don't fuck it up by being a coward," he said.

She hadn't. He'd driven her to NA meetings, though she wasn't sure she needed them, only felt occasional physical longings, but she did whatever he said, whatever he thought she needed, as long as he didn't leave her.

III.

Three days after Tikal they were in Guatemala, at Lake Atitlan. Max decided they should head across the lake from the city of Panajachel to one of the small towns at the foot of the volcano that hadn't yet been ruined by the tourists. There were, he said, hundreds of people who could take them across to Santiago Atitlan and, if they were patient, they'd almost get to go for free.

They went down to the stone dock early. The sun seemed to take up the whole eastern half of the white sky. Through the glare she could see the three volcanoes that ringed Lake Atitlan, towering over the other mountains. They looked, rising so steeply out of the earth, like wildly spreading tumors. While they peeled oranges for breakfast Max told her about the region's role in the country's many civil wars.

"In the early eighties the military staged some actions, or whatever you want to call them, attacks, in those mountains. Killed a lot of people, including a couple of American priests."

In a few hours these mountains and even the enormous volcano would be obscured by the thick, low clouds that had plagued them all through Central America and which seemed to be worse in Guatemala than elsewhere. She'd complained about it, two days before in Antigua, and Max had told her to stop whining like a goddamn baby for once.

He'd been angry with her since they'd been stopped on the border going to Tikal. When they'd reached the ruins she'd been unable to move, had wanted to scream, to cry and break something—the windows, maybe—to tear out the seats, but she couldn't even lift her arms. They were the last passengers and the humps of the empty seats looked to her like burial mounds, rows and rows of the dead, covered with slick new grass.

"Come on, Jenny," Max had said, "It's fine. We're here, see?" He pointed out at the parking lot full of enormous tour buses, the windows fogging up with air conditioning.

The driver shouted at them and Max said they either had to get off, or go back across the border, so they climbed down into the heat.

Tourists haggled with men hawking gaudy green statues and faux jade jewelry. Max took her to the jungle's edge so they could sit for a minute in the shade.

"What did you say," she asked. Overhead, two monkeys rattled the branches, leaping and screaming.

"What?" Max said, glaring at the parking lot. Then he nodded and said, "Oh, yeah. I lied." He took her hand and squeezed it. "I told him you were sick. I said he couldn't take you. I said you had AIDS. I think it just confused him. He was stoned, you know. So I guess that helped."

While she rested he talked about the military in Guatemala. "Sure, it's bad now, but you should've been here ten years ago before anyone had heard of the problems. I was here for maybe a week and I'll tell you what, I was scared shitless."

They walked around the ancient temples and Max said he wanted to climb one.

"I think I'll wait here," she said.

"All right. Look for me up there," he said, then turned and jogged up the stone steps through the laboring crowd.

Once he reached the top Jenny turned and hurried to the parking lot. The third bus driver she found agreed to let them ride back on the big, air-conditioned bus. Max was waiting for her at the foot of the temple. When she told him she'd booked them back on one of the tour buses he was angry.

"We have tickets, you know," he said, digging into his jeans and pulling out the flimsy strips of paper.

"Max, please," she said.

He must've been able to see how frightened she was, because he relented but didn't stop complaining. He marveled at the obese Americans and crumbly British in the plush blue seats around them. "It's like a gallery of the grotesque," he said, loud, so the old man in the next row turned around and coughed angrily.

She knew she'd disappointed him by being so upset, by overreacting, by making them ride with exactly the kind of people Max had come to Central America to avoid. Nothing had happened, he all but said. They were fine. Sure, there'd been a moment there, but Jesus Christ, this wasn't Topeka. That kind of thing was bound to happen. But look how she was acting. Back at the hotel in Belize Max had complained that the air conditioning on the bus had made him sick. "Or maybe it was all those geezers. Hot spots of disease, those tour buses. I'll take the slums any day." They'd left Belize the next morning and headed into Guatemala.

130

Eventually, Max talked one of the boat-drivers down. The fiberglass hull they climbed into was so thin she could see the water smacking and pushing beneath. Two other Americans joined them, paying twice what they had without complaint. They looked like college kids, or just out. After shooting a few hesitant smiles at Max and her they finally introduced themselves. Libby and Jim.

Libby was a tall, thin girl, extremely awkward—she nearly fell into the lake trying to climb into the boat—string hair clumping together with dirt and grease, possibly the start of some unfortunate dreds. Her face was long and too square. Her jaw looked almost masculine. The girl, with all her smiling and thoughtful looks at the landscape, put up a facade of worldliness and happiness, but just beneath the surface, Jenny was sure, lay heaps of anxiety and self-consciousness. Jim, on the other hand, looked as though there was nothing going on beneath the surface of his deeply tanned, blocky face. Growing his dark, thin goatee had probably used up every last drop of his creativity. Enormous blots of raw acne stained his cheeks, as though someone had gone at him with needles in his sleep. He probably hadn't cried about anything except sports since he was six. These kids wore almost the same outfit: baggy green pants that cut off at mid-calf and tank tops, though the girl's was black and Jim's white and filthy.

To her surprise Max talked eagerly with them, shouting over the motor and the slap of the hull on the water.

They'd both recently graduated from college and had met in Antigua and decided to travel together. From the way Libby stared at Jim, Jenny could tell the girl was in love, but the boy wasn't. He kept smiling at Jenny, as though he might seduce her right out from under Max's nose. She wanted to slap him. She watched the other boats skimming over the lake, let the wind blot out the words.

As a result, she didn't know until they reached Santiago Atitlan that Max had suggested they should all stay at the same hotel, a place he'd heard about in Panajachel. The two kids beamed as though they'd just won a prize, which was how people often felt around Max.

As they followed the switch-backing road through town little kids raced out of the stucco buildings wearing bright, identical, hand-woven shirts and puffy black pants. Each town on the lake, Max explained, had its own design, like jerseys. The kids danced and kicked a soccer ball, shouting, "*Quetzal, solo uno quetzal,*" then striking a pose, running hands through their thick black hair. Libby and Jim obliged, pulling out coins and taking photos with manual cameras. Part of Jenny wanted Max to turn and yell at the Americans, tell them this wasn't a zoo. But when he did look back, which, as far as she could tell, was only once, he was smiling as though charmed.

One would've thought that after four years together she'd know Max, but, as was made clear again as they hiked up past low houses with tin roofs, trails of gray smoke slipping out through the gaps, she knew almost nothing about him. She'd always taken his inscrutability, his seeming-inconsistency (why were these two American kids any better than any of the hundreds they'd come across and routinely scorned?), as a mark of intelligence. Surely there was a pattern, hidden, out of view to one as obtuse as herself. But maybe that wasn't true. Maybe he had no idea what he was doing, who he was, what he really wanted and maybe that was why he crashed around the world.

In the hotel courtyard Max told the American kids about the civil war. Rain poured into the garden and cats could be heard fighting for cover on the roofs.

"They'd round up all the men, from the little boys to the crippled old men, and stand them against the side of the church. Then the soldiers would take turns guarding them, making the men watch while they went through the village raping all the women, the little girls, the grandmothers, then shooting them when they'd finished. The men were herded into the church, where they'd been piling up the women's bodies, and shot. Then all of it was burned, the church, the whole town."

Libby, a hand over her mouth, looked as though she might cry.

Max took the joint from Jim, dragged on it, and stared at the pouring rain. He let the smoke out slowly, rubbed his bristly cheek and said, "I've always wondered why they did it that way. It doesn't make any sense. It wasn't a warning or anything because they ended up killing everyone. But still, they made the men watch while they raped and killed their wives and daughters and mothers. All that cruelty for no reason." Max shook his head and looked at the smoldering end of the joint, as though reading some tiny text that, in the next breath, would be gone. He sighed and passed the joint across to Jenny.

"Oh, my God," Libby said. The girl's baggy pants were pulled up past her knobby knees; there was a puss-filled scab on the arch of her right foot. It didn't look to be healing, the skin around it was puffy and red streaks of infection ran up the girl's ankle.

Jim shook his head and reached for the joint Jenny hadn't hit yet. "Yeah, man," he said. "I've heard about that shit, man. Sucks."

She wanted to slap him, drag him out of his chair and kick him. *Sucks?*

"I don't feel well," she said, standing up, not looking too long at Max's glare. "I'm going to lie down."

When she reached the stairs she ran up them and closed her door, but even then she could hear the murmur of their voices through the clattering rain. What if she left Max? Would her life inevitably spin back out of control, or would she be able to take the belligerent self-regard he'd taught her and make her way more steadily through the world? She couldn't be sure. If she knew for certain she'd survive, she'd just leave him. All the security and substance he'd seemed to embody was, it turned out, a lie. They just traveled, kept constantly on the move. No place was good enough. There was always the next thing to see. That was no way to live. It wasn't, anyway, she knew now, how she wanted to live. But a part of her felt that if she left him, if she was again on her own, she'd go right back where she'd been before they met only worse this time. And in a few months they'd find her dead somewhere, a warehouse or even someplace as clichéd as a dumpster. She wanted to be strong, as strong as Max, but the truth was she wasn't.

The rain had stopped and it was dark when Max knocked on her door and asked if she was ready. "Jim and Libby want some of those shirts," he said, pulling at the front of his own khaki one. "I told them I'd help them find a good deal."

"Maybe I'll just stay here," she said, bunching the limp pillow under her head.

"Come on, Jenny. Quit moping." He ran a hand over his chin and scratched his neck. She wished he'd shave. He looked like a monkey.

Water ran in the gutters and between the wide stones of the street, dripping heavily from the roofs, making everything shimmer.

"You don't want to buy anything down here," Max said. "Too close to the church. You're going to get ripped off. A lot of the stuff down here isn't even hand-woven, they just dye it." He pointed to the steep street that went up the volcano. "If we head this way for a while we'll find a good deal."

"Cool," Jim said, jogging every few steps to keep his stubby legs in line with Max. Jenny followed alongside Libby, who was limping.

"So," the girl said, "where are you guys from?"

"Boston," Jenny said, not returning the question.

"I'm from Houston," Libby said, smiling, as though that's where they were heading, home. The girl wanted to be friends. Don't get too attached, Jenny wanted to tell her. Max will tire of you in a few days at best.

"I mean, Jim's not from Texas. He's from California. Los Angeles. I met him in Antigua, at this great bar."

"Uh, huh." Libby's limp was making them fall farther and farther behind the men. "Max!" Jenny shouted. "Wait up."

"Just meet us up there," he shouted back, pointing into the pitch dark.

"Yeah, if you go back, you totally have to go there. It's great." Libby was smiling but must've seen Jenny's look, and stammered. "I mean, you know. It's kind of touristy."

"I'm sure it's nice."

"We're going up to Tikal, next," Libby went on. "Have you guys been there?"

"No," she said. Max and Jim had disappeared into the dark ahead, though there weren't any roads but this one, which was gradually turning from stone to thick mud. Below she could see the lights of town, and across the water the wavering blot of Panajachel. The air was thick, though a cool breeze blew steadily, making the hair on her arms rise.

Libby prattled on about how they were maybe going to go down to Honduras to do some scuba diving, because she'd heard there was this island, Roatan, that was awesome.

"My dad is really mad that I'm not coming home. He wants me to go to law school and then probably work at his firm. He's going to freak when he sees this." She pulled up her shirt to show Jenny a tattoo on her stomach, the shape of which was indiscernible in the darkness.

Jenny wondered if maybe Max was trying to teach her a lesson: if she wanted to be a coward, if she was going to make too much of what happened back at the border, then he'd show her the kind of person she was veering toward. Did she want to end up like Libby, with her infected foot, her ridiculous hair, her drooping tank top? Because that was the choice: it was either all in or all out. But maybe it didn't matter what one wanted because eventually life, or someone, was going to line you up against the wall and put a bullet through your head, be it a death squad or cancer or a speed-freak truck driver on the interstate. For so long she'd wanted to believe that Max was offering an escape, a chance to really live. Now she saw it was just another kind of death, richer in delusion and anger, but ultimately the same.

Libby grabbed her arm, stumbling on one of the large loose rocks in the road. It was almost impossible to see, and Jenny hoped they wouldn't fall into the ditch. She held the girl's arm, guided her along and, as a small bulb of panic began to rise in her throat, she finally saw a scatter of lights ahead.

"Thank God," she said and Libby laughed, a high, pinched squeal of anxiety and relief.

The houses were smaller here, leaning toward the lake, the walls clapboard and tin and strips of wood tied together with rope. Through the gaps she could see cooking fires, the shadowy faces of the family all listening to them walking past. Afraid.

The road leveled off slightly and widened and there was a small *tienda* with a faded, flaking Fanta sign hanging lopsided on one wall. Max and Jim were nowhere to be seen. They'd probably already talked with someone, headed off to a house to haggle.

"My foot is killing me," Libby said, hobbling over to sit on a stonewall.

"Nice view," Jenny said, pointing back at the lake.

Two men came out of the *tienda*, cigarettes lit, and looked at the women. Both wore big, baggy T-shirts with brown stains under the arms.

"I guess we'll wait here," Jenny said, trying to keep the nerves out of her voice. The men were smiling at her and when she caught their eye shouted something and laughed wildly.

"I wonder where they are?" Libby said, peering up the hill, as though she didn't see the two men who shouted at them again. Maybe she didn't. What was there to notice: it was just two men outside a shop shouting at a couple of gringo women. There was nothing special in it, nothing threatening, really. It happened all the time. But Jenny's hands were damp and her jaw wouldn't relax. She tried to stop her legs from shaking.

"Somewhere," was all she could say and Libby frowned, then looked back at the lake.

"So beautiful," she said, dreamily.

The men had moved to the street and Jenny saw now they were wearing camouflaged pants and black military boots, streaked with mud. They walked toward the women, whispering, then one of them flicked his cigarette so it tumbled past Libby's face, nearly catching in her clumpy hair.

Jenny looked down at her hands. The men were only a few feet away. She curled her fingers into a fist and dug the nails into her palm. When she finally looked up she saw, on the waist of one of the men, a holster with a gun inside. The man was grinning and nodding, a fresh cigarette between his lips. When the lighter spouted she could see a long scar that ran from one ear to his jaw, a fine, shining line. The men stared and smoked. Finally, the scarred man said, "You like dick?" in broken English, staring at Jenny.

"Sorry?" Libby said, shaking her head, as though the man was asking directions to a place she'd never heard of.

"You like dick?" the man said again, smiling. His teeth were so white and clean Jenny thought they must be dentures. "You like dick?"

She wondered if he knew what it meant. It was probably the only English he knew. She looked him in the eyes, and shook her head. "No," she said. "I hate dick."

"Yes!" the other man shouted, grabbing his crotch and shouting in Spanish, then laughed so hard he bent over.

"You like dick?" the scarred man said, directing it this time at Libby, who bit her lip, clutching the folds of her pants with both hands. "You like dick?" the man repeated, eyes narrowing. He blew a stream of smoke into the girl's face.

Tears fell down Libby's cheeks and she nodded, pulling her whole lip into her mouth, as though she wanted to eat it.

"You like dick, yes?" the man said, taking a drag from the cigarette, then holding it up close to Libby's face, illuminating in red the fine hairs on the girl's cheek.

"Yes," Libby said. Her bony arms were shaking.

The man nodded thoughtfully, took another drag on his cigarette, then flicked it down the hill. "You like dick," he said, matter-of-factly. He turned and walked back toward the *tienda*. The other man smacked his lips at Jenny and followed.

The women sat in silence, Libby crying, her hands still clutching her pants. Jenny watched the *tienda*, but no one came out. She felt surprisingly calm, as though nothing had happened, as though everything was fine.

"Jesus," Libby said, her sobs subsiding slightly. "What the fuck is wrong with them?" Her words released another bout of tears and sobbing.

Jenny stood up and brushed her pants, looked out at the lake, then up at the darkness of the volcano. "Come on," she said. "You're fine."

"No, no I'm not," Libby said. Snot dripped in a string down from her nose to her pants. "I'm not fine, I'm not."

"Yes, you are," Jenny said. "Stop acting like a baby, come on." She didn't want to touch the girl. She was repulsed, disgusted. Who acted like this? That was nothing, she wanted to tell Libby. Nothing. Nothing compared with what all these people on this mountain lived with. They hadn't been raped, they hadn't been shot, they hadn't been tortured and locked in a shed for weeks, gagged, knocked to the floor three times a day when men came in, sweating and angry and drunk to fuck them. They were safe. They were fine. They would go back to the hotel and sleep between clean sheets.

"Stop crying," Jenny said. "Grow up. Cut it out." She grabbed Libby's arm and shook her. "Come on, shut up."

Libby tried to choke down her sobs, but couldn't. Snot piled onto her upper lip.

"Come on, we're fine," Jenny said. "Where do you think we are, anyway? Kansas?"

"I'm sorry," Libby sobbed. "I'm sorry."

"You should be," Jenny said, then turned and started down the hill, back toward town. She didn't look back, but knew Libby was already following her down into the dark.

In the Ravine

Soon after I moved home to my parents' house it became clear my dad was obsessed with a gang of men who were growing marijuana in the State Park. That was his word, "gang." That's what he called them as he ranted on at dinner, or over morning coffee, or throughout the day as we scraped paint off the front porch. My dad had been going for hikes in the State Park since he'd taken a job as a provost at a small, private college in rural Ohio fifteen years ago. He always took his dog with him, and the newest in a long line of shepherd mutts, Chester, had been with him the day he first ran into the "gang."

When he'd arrived at the park my dad had waved to the ranger and turned down a narrow gravel side road that led to a tiny parking lot where he always left his car. Not far down he found a pick-up truck blocking the road. My dad stopped and signaled for them to make room. The men in the truck just stared back.

In his telling, my dad was always sure to emphasize that there was nothing official looking about the truck. No Park Service insignia, and the truck was electric blue and jacked up on oversized wheels with chrome hubcaps. My dad honked and waved. The passenger side door opened and a man in tight-fitting jeans, a jean-vest, and no shirt hopped onto the gravel and walked slowly up the road. The man stood a foot or two back from my dad's window and said, "Road's closed," staring at Chester who was trembling in anticipation of the walk.

"Why?" my dad asked.

"Just is," the man said, smiling. Though my dad didn't say, I imagined the man's teeth were crusted brown. Lurid tattoos covered his arms.

"Says who?" My dad gripped the steering wheel tight.

The man lifted the front of his vest to reveal a gun tucked into his pants and said, "Colt 45."

My dad stared until the man snorted. "Don't be a dumbfuck, old man," then walked back to the pick-up.

"What I should've done," my dad said over dinner the night I arrived, "is driven right over that asshole and smashed into their stupid truck." Maybe he was gripping his fork murderously as he said this. That seems right, but honestly I can't remember, remember only feeling a little embarrassed for him. Each time I saw him he looked immeasurably older. He'd had thick, curly hair most of his life that had gone silver and then thinned out so only a narrow strip remained. The surrounding expanse of his scalp was marked with age spots. And he'd gained weight. His chest was swollen up as if someone had pumped him full of air. When we'd hugged at the airport his watery breasts had pressed against me.

After he said this about smashing the drug-dealers he looked at me. I tried to smile. I'd just arrived from New York, was still dazed from numerous "farewell" parties. I hadn't slept the night before, had ended up with three people I barely knew, drinking whiskey on a bare mattress, watching cockroaches skitter out from under the fridge.

"That would've been wonderful, Fred," my mom said, spooning mashed potatoes onto my plate.

"But how do you know they're growing marijuana?" I said, doing my part.

He explained that kind of thing happened all the time in the Midwest. He said this as though I knew nothing about the Midwest, which I guess was true. I'd grown up outside Washington D.C. and had been away at college when they moved to Ohio, so I'd only ever visited over holidays, not having the time to take off from my various, low-paying jobs in D.C., then New York, then Boston for six months, then D.C. again, before the final stint in New York where I'd spent two years in a tiny studio in Brooklyn. That's where I'd been when my mom called and said my dad was having heart trouble. He was on some new medication and was under strict orders to get lots of exercise. She wanted to know if I'd come visit. He was feeling depressed and I'd always perked him up.

This was true, but that perkiness had often come with an edge, including the time we'd nearly come to blows in the basement, facing each other down about who knows what, and I remember saying, "Hit me, you old fucker," and then my mom was pushing us apart and telling us to cut it out. She turned to my dad and said, "If you touch him, I'm leaving you." But it was true we'd been getting along better recently. We'd taken a camping trip up in Vermont three summers earlier and hadn't bickered at all. On that trip I'd noticed my dad lagging behind on the trail. I hadn't really minded, as that'd given me the chance to smoke a joint every few hours, something I'd felt I needed to do to keep from falling all the way apart.

In Ohio, my dad seemed anything but depressed. In fact, he seemed frantic, as if he had too much energy and nowhere to put it, which I guess could be a symptom of depression. The day I arrived he said I'd come just in time. For what, I asked. To work, he said. Together, we were going to fix up the house. We'd start with the porch, and everyday after that's what we did. We woke late, had a few cups of coffee, then worked through the mid-morning into the heat of the afternoon, at which point we stripped off our soaked shirts and worked bare-chested, my father's swollen gut thick with gray fur, while my own was slim and pale, only a slight sagging at the hips giving away my age. We talked about all sorts of stuff, but the drug dealers were a frequent topic.

"You know what someone should do?" he said. "Someone should get a shotgun and drive those assholes out of there."

"I doubt Mom could get behind that idea," I said, shaking my hands to get the blood flowing.

"Well, she wouldn't have to know, would she?"

"So, you're thinking we'll go down to the gun-shop, then go wage war on these guys?"

My dad stopped scraping and looked over his shoulder at me. "Yes, Donny. That's exactly right. That's exactly what I'm suggesting."

"Well, at least you have a plan," I said, grinning maniacally until he turned back to his own patch.

At that moment, and at many other such moments, I tried to see some evidence of his ailing heart, but I never really found any. He wasn't out of breath any more than most people his age, didn't have the shakes, or any obvious unsteadiness that I associated with illness, all of which I probably got from TV and movies. The only evidence I'd seen in my four days there was that in the evenings when he sat down to watch the news—first the local news, then the evening news on CBS, then the PBS Newshour—he fell asleep a few minutes into this last one, the recliner pushed back, his socked feet in the air, his pant leg pulled up, revealing a shiny, hairless calf. But even if I couldn't see it, he was dying, and I wanted to be there to help.

Beyond our time working on the porch, I tried to keep busy when my dad drove to campus for meetings. I spent a few afternoons decluttering the shed, where I found three lawn mowers, two of which worked, the other so rusted I could barely wheel it to the street as my mother suggested, where it was immediately snatched up. I hadn't done physical labor in a long time, having lived for so many years in studios, except the time I'd lived in a one-bedroom with an aspiring actress who ended up moving out while I was at work. She left one afternoon and I never heard from her again. Her disappearance seemed to confirm an unsettling truth: my life amounted to nothing. Like her, I could vanish without a trace. All that kept this from being true was my relationship with my parents. They'd notice, and they might even come looking for me, and this attention made me real.

Over the years I'd considered moving back in with them many times, but had avoided it like a final surrender. As I struggled to pay rent, bills, credit cards, as I got rid of my television, couch, books, and eventually even most of my clothes, which I sold on the stoop of my building in Bushwick, I told myself at least I was still making it on my own, though it was pretty depressing that by "making it" I apparently meant I wasn't homeless, though as I winnowed down my life, that didn't seem an altogether impossible future.

What had I meant my life to be? I'd wanted to be a writer, I guess. Then, when I saw *The Wire* I thought, *Oh, fuck, that's exactly what I want to do.* How did I go about pursuing this? I wrote some awful screenplays and bought some books about how to sell them. I met some people in television and they curled away from me like hairs from a flame. Now I know the very insubstantiality of my ideas about what my life should be like was the reason it turned out so, well, insubstantial. I wrote movie reviews for a short-lived weekly that was given out free at subway stops, but mostly I drank and smoked pot and tried not to notice how many of my friends drifted away and became lawyers, editors, teachers, while I stayed where I was, which, I began to understand too late, was what people meant by wallowing.

I'd hoped that at my parents' house there'd be no time for wallowing, but apparently, you can only do chores for so long before you're left to wander from room to room, picking up books, like the first edition of Wallace Stevens's *The*

Man With the Blue Guitar that your father bought after his dissertation was approved. You flip through a few poems, set the book down again, turn on the TV, pat Chester on the head as he pants near your arm, and when you fail to find something even remotely interesting to watch, you turn off the TV and settle down on the guest bed with John McPhee's *Coming Into the Country*, a book your dad has been trying to get you to read for fifteen years and which now that he might be dying you start to read only to drift off after a few pages into a fitful sleep full of dreams in which you're unable to sleep and when you wake up the only way to not be up all night is to smoke some of the pot you carried in your crotch onto the plane despite the police dogs swarming all over JFK. This was not how I'd hoped the summer would go.

By the third week I started to see my presence was more of a burden than a comfort for my parents, breaking up as it did their habits. I had nowhere to go and nothing to do outside the house, so I kept coming into the kitchen for coffee in just my boxers while my mom was cooking, or I was hogging the TV, which my parents pretended they didn't want to watch. Dinner conversations were strained and my parents occasionally spoke in low voices while I stared off at the bookcases, as if we were strangers in a cramped New York restaurant. So, when my dad asked if I wanted to go into town to pick up a sander, I said sure, great, hold on, let me get my shoes.

Chester darted around our feet in the driveway, spinning in circles before hurling himself into the car and clambering into the back. We went past the neighbor's farm with its peeling white silo and stumpy cows, and I said, "So, what is there like a Lowe's out here or something?"

"We're not getting a sander, Donny," he said, as if I was being intentionally obtuse.

"No sander? We really could use a sander," I said, feeling a little flutter of excitement rising through me. *Yes*, I thought. *Let's do it.*

"We're going to the park."

"Okay," I said. I was ready for anything. Anything, frankly, was better than nothing and nothing was where I'd been for ten years. Like my mom, I'd been worried by my dad's obsession with the drug dealers. I'd met a few drug dealers and knew you didn't fuck with them, not for a second, not for half a second. I knew men like that were willing, were often eager, to beat the living shit out of some measly toad like me. I'd only just avoided that on one occasion, which I don't like to think about, but which had me hiding behind a burned-out shell of a car in an empty lot in Bed-Stuy while two men hunted me, calling out,

"Hey, fucking little white bitch, get your pussy ass out here." But now, in the car with my dad, seeing his courage—what he was doing was stupid, but it was also courageous—filled me with what I can only think of as hope. He was resolved. I could be resolved too.

We drove a few miles, then my dad said, "Open the glove-box." That was an antiquated word he used that I'd always found endearing, along with "ice-box." He'd been raised by Irish immigrants in Saint Louis, and hadn't altogether let go of that world.

Beneath a clutter of maps and dusty pens was a small back gun. I touched the handle, then snapped the glove-box back up.

"I'm not going to use that," he said. "Not unless I have to."

What was there to say? Maybe I should've tried to talk him out of it. Instead I just stared out the window at all that land rolling past.

By the time we reached the park dark clouds bulged overhead and a few drops flicked against the windshield. My dad waved to the man in the brown booth and we drove down the asphalt until it turned to gravel and the road split. Stopping, my dad pointed to the right.

"They're down there. I haven't seen it, but I'm sure it's there. Look behind you."

On the floor in the back were a hoe and a shovel.

"We're going to dig it up. We'll park down there and walk in."

"How are we going to find it?"

"We'll find it," he said. "It needs sun, so there aren't that many places to hide it."

The road narrowed. Trees pressed their branches together and blocked out the sky so it seemed we'd plunged from mid-day to late evening. My dad drove faster than he probably should've, so fast that it was hard to see the road with all the bouncing over the deep ruts, and when we came around a turn and saw the tree across the road we both shouted and lurched against the dashboard.

Chester thudded against my seat and let out a whimper, and my dad whooped, slapped me on the shoulder, and said, "That's them. Has to be them." He whistled. "What a bunch of motherfuckers."

He spat the words, thrilled by the sound of them. He'd never been able to swear in a natural way, something I'd always found funny, but there in the car, his cursing seemed a sign of how stupid we were, of how much trouble we'd likely get ourselves into and how clearly we needed to get the hell out of there.

"Well, here we go then," he said, opening his door.

"What are you talking about?"

"We're walking." His voice had assumed a clipped, military formality, something he'd done when he lost patience with me as a kid.

"Walking where?"

"We can't drive, as you might've noticed." He leaned across and opened the glove-box and the gun fell between my feet. I considered chucking it into the tangle of bushes, but he said, "Hand me that," so I did.

He stuffed the gun into his belt, then doused himself with bug spray. By the time I was out of the car Chester was bounding around and burrowing into the bushes. My dad told me to bring the tools. We climbed over the tree in the spot least bunched with broken branches and started down the road. He kept fiddling with the gun he'd tucked into his pants and I was afraid he'd shoot himself in the leg.

Mosquitoes drifted around our heads and buzzed into my ears, the only spot I hadn't sprayed, and overhead the sky continued to thicken with clouds.

After twenty minutes or so, my dad stopped beside a barely broken trail. "Down there."

Each moment presented itself to me like a little offering: *Now you can stop him. Now. Now.* But I just went along, an accomplice. This was always my role. I was the affable drunk, the one who always had connections to get pot, the one who might even, for a Thanksgiving get-together, bring along mushrooms. I was the one on the edge of the group, the one who'd taken to wearing a bright red headband for an entire year, as if I was afraid otherwise my friends (none of whom were still my friends) would lose track of me. That had in fact happened a few times. I'd gotten too drunk and the people I was with had left while I was in the bathroom, or while I was talking with a stranger and I'd realize I knew no one in the place. A few years later I might see one of those old friends at a coffee shop with his wife and fat little baby and I'd say, "Hey, Pablo," though that wasn't his name, had been his nickname, and he'd look up with annoyance and a bit of fear, as if I was there to get something from him, as if he owed me something, which, with a dismissive frown, he let me know was not the case. He didn't owe me shit. I was nothing to him. His wife would look up, her blonde hair bunching on the collar of what was surely a thousand dollar coat, and eventually Pablo would say, "Oh, man, hi, I didn't know you were still in the city." And I'd laugh and say, actually, I wasn't, I was out in Brooklyn, and this former friend turned lawyer/banker/rich asshole would nod with such excruciating boredom and confusion—*Why in the world should I care about you who means nothing to me?*—that I'd begin to stammer, and then leave. Outside, my hands shaking, trying to get my cigarette lit, I'd see him talking with his wife, and though I couldn't hear anything he was saying, I knew exactly what it was: *I really have no idea who that guy was. Isn't that weird?* His wife would glance through the glass wall of the coffee shop and see me standing there, a cigarette between my teeth, a little spout of flame not quite touching the tip, and I'd see not just revulsion in her look, but hate.

The bugs were even thicker on the narrow trail, which I assumed was because we were moving toward the water. Chester kept running ahead, then back up to check on me.

"Dad, how much farther?"

"Buck up. And keep your voice down."

On a steep slope I slipped and the shovel banged against the side of my head. The trail got steeper, and I kept losing my grip on the tools. Finally the ground leveled, the trees thinned, and we entered a field.

My dad started looking more carefully, parting the sheaves of grass gently, as if they were Chester's fur and he was combing through for ticks. Which were probably everywhere in that grass.

I was the one who found them. I pushed aside a clump of grass and there in front of me were twelve marijuana plants, sagging with sticky buds. They smelled tangy with a bit of strawberry underneath. I reached out and touched one and was about to pluck it when my dad said, "You find something?"

He came to where I was standing and looked with gratified disgust.

"Told you," he said, then grabbed the handle of the shovel.

No, I thought, *you can't*, and I didn't let go of the shovel. I had another thought at the same moment: I could harvest these plants. They were ready and I wasn't even sure why they hadn't been picked. I could take the buds to New York and sell them and the money I'd get from that, which would be thousands of dollars if I played it right, with that money I'd have enough to live on for a while, time in which I could figure out what I wanted to do with myself, time in which I could really settle down, find a job, make some connections, stop living as if I was going to die in a few weeks.

"Let go," my dad said. When I looked at him I could see he knew what I was thinking, and in that instant I realized that my dad, and so my mom, knew who I really was. They weren't fooled. They didn't think I was bumbling, as many of my generation did. They knew the truth: I was a degenerate, an outcast. I lived on the cusp of a criminal life. I could end up dead and they'd only find out months later when my body was dredged from a poisoned canal.

I let him take the shovel and I hoisted the hoe. Did I consider, as I seem to remember, bringing it down on his head, on his thin silver hair, on his age-spots, crushing his skull, leaving him there in the field, or maybe burying him quickly, taking the buds and getting out of there, dumping his car in Pennsylvania, catching a bus to the city before making the sale and leaving the country for Tangier, or Mexico, or Kenya, anywhere I could disappear? I could see myself sitting on the veranda of some crumbling colonial mansion with a man I'd met at a local bar who'd laughed at my jokes and invited me to see his property. While we sat there, looking out at the orange and yellow landscape, his servant would bring drinks brimming with opaque ice and we'd sip them and I'd listen to his stories about lions, about the locals, about the giant they said lived in the caves we could just make out until the shadows of evening swallowed them.

My dad told me to loosen the soil at the base of a plant, then he crammed the shovel down in a widening circle and, groaning, sweat all over his red face, he broke the roots. The plant sagged and fell. After the third plant we traded jobs. We didn't speak, except for the occasional command, "Right here, the root's here," or, "No, tilt it this way." When we got to the sixth plant it started to rain, a sudden downpour that soaked us through, but we kept working until our arms were heavy, our shoulders hunched, and all the plants had been pulled from the earth. The rain was already filling the holes we'd made.

"What," I said, panting for air, "do we do now?"

"What?" my dad shouted. It was hard to hear with the rain.

"What do we do with them? The plants?"

He studied the carnage, his thin hair plastered to his head, his blue shirt clinging to his body, and then he said, "The river." We dropped the tools and loaded the plants into our arms. Even with the rain I could smell the buds and I had the urge, as we stumbled through wet grass, to eat the one nearest my face, to just wrap my lips around that bright green lump and swallow.

My dad stumbled into the river, almost falling on the wet stones, then heaved his plants out. They fell at his feet and waved their leaves in the shallow water. Chester splashed around and bit one of the stalks. I dropped my load and one by one we threw them out into the current where they spun lazily and moved off toward the waterfall. Before I lifted the last plant, as my dad was resting with his hands on his knees, I plucked off two of the larger buds and jammed them in my pocket.

After tossing the last plant out into the river I sat down on a stone and hung my head and wasn't sure I could get up, much less walk back through that field and all the way up that slope which with the rain was surely now pure mud.

"Good job, Donny," my dad shouted over the rain, putting his hand on my shoulder.

"Tired."

"But that was good." He squeezed my shoulder. "That was good."

"Think we'll get paid?" I glanced up, but when I did rain fell into my eyes and I blinked it furiously away.

He kept his hand on my shoulder and I wanted to fall back into his arms. I wanted to cry, to fall to pieces with him there to hold me.

The walk out was as bad as I'd feared and I cut my knees and then my hand on the sharp shale rocks. The car was where we'd left it, the gravel road ribbed by thick gray streams of water, so that when we tried to pull out the wheels spun before catching.

My mom asked where we'd been, what had we been doing hiking in the rain? Look at poor Chester. What were we, idiots? She made us coffee and brought us towels and told us to take warm showers. By the time I came downstairs my dad was already reclining in front of the television. From the kitchen I could hear my mom making dinner.

"Think she needs help?" I said.

"Hey, you've worked enough, take a break. Take a seat."

I sat on the couch, making sure not to crush the buds I'd transferred to the pocket of my dry pants. After my parents went to sleep I thought I'd bake them a few minutes to dry them out, then smoke a little. I felt I'd earned it, and my dad seemed to feel the same way, smiling over at me instead of at the TV.

"Why don't you get us some beers?" he said.

My mom rolled her eyes at me when I went to the fridge. I told her it smelled great and she just hummed. By the time I got back to the living room, my dad was asleep. I watched the irregular bobbing of his Adam's apple, the way the flesh bunched beneath his chin, the faint flutter of his jugular. His mouth was open just a crack, and in a lull between commercials I heard a raspy breath as he twitched in a dream. I set a beer on the floor beside his chair, then put my hand just above his throat. When I closed my eyes I could almost feel the heat from his skin, the bristle of his evening shadow, the soft lace of wrinkles. I could almost feel the movement of the life inside of him, his blood, the blood being pumped by his damaged heart, blood that ran in me as well. But my mom clattered a pot in the kitchen and I hurried back to the couch and watched the news in silence.

Famous for Crabs

The longer Henry taught, the clearer it became that his was the last generation that would remember a world before technology had thoroughly consumed everyone's life. This fact made him feel pleasantly anachronistic, as did the wool tweed coats he'd started wearing during his first year as an assistant professor. He imagined he now looked something like the white haired professors he'd studied with in college: they'd lectured enthusiastically and earnestly about biological theory, pausing now and then to bemoan the disaster science writing had become since the ubiquity of the personal computer. He couldn't pretend to that charming a level of technophobia, but he still felt, bubbling up in his throat like a not-quite swallowed mouthful of beer, that all the dozen, or perhaps two dozen, times he checked his email every day were a complete and total waste of time. Weren't there better things he could (and should) be doing with his day? Like reading the journals he insisted the department subscribe to, or writing that now long overdue article, or taking a look at those peer review essays?

Despite all these responsibilities, he apparently had plenty of time for Facebook, that moronic website everyone he knew had recently become enamored with, primarily, it seemed, so they could spy on friends from the past they hadn't bothered to keep in touch with, which was exactly what he used it for. Since joining the website he'd reconnected with dozens of old college and high school friends. Well, not *friends*, but former friends. He tailored his information so they could all easily see that he was now a professor of biology at a liberal arts college in Maryland. They'd see he was married, would see his little girl was five years old, and that his wife was still beautiful. And no one would know they'd grown so distant from one another that he took every excuse—a cold, his wife's cold, insomnia, real or faked—to sleep on the living room couch with the dog curled at his feet, cramping his back.

It was through Facebook that he'd ended up getting back in touch with Brian, whom, in college, they'd all called Tower. Though Henry and Tower had lived together for three years, they'd fallen out of contact as soon as college had ended. Over the past seventeen years, Henry had only heard about Tower through common friends: apparently, he'd moved back to Richmond and bought an enormous house in the suburbs where he lived, alone. Henry had laughed when he heard this: it was so exactly Tower, so within the lines of convention and yet so distinctly outside them. He'd often imagined his old friend in his big white house, every window dark but the one that flickered with a sickly blue light as he hunkered over a video game controller.

The vividness of this image was perhaps what had propelled him to look Tower up on Facebook and then, when he had a paper accepted at a conference at MCV, he'd sent an email and suggested they meet up. Tower wrote back and said that'd be great and to call any time, or just show up and why not just stay out at his house? There'd been no chance Henry would do that—his hotel was paid for by a research travel grant—and, anyway, the main reason he went to conferences was to have a few days alone, a few dozen hours of quiet where he could remember what it was like to be able to think. Whenever he first entered those anonymous conference hotel rooms he felt light and ageless and could pretend that maybe he in fact was the person he'd always imagined he'd become—a well respected and even admired academic—and not the person he seemed to be, a tired, grumpy, thirty-eight year old man caught in an unhappy marriage that was held together by a shy daughter who often seemed almost afraid of him.

At one conference a woman had said, "Oh, I love your work. You're famous for crabs, you know."

"Well," he'd said, "that was my childhood dream." Though he'd smiled to show he was joking, her face had lapsed into a confused frown.

"I'll bet. I wish I was famous for crabs." She'd been drunk and not very attractive and yet, for a few minutes, he'd considered sleeping with her. Ultimately, he'd resisted the urge and went back to his hotel room where he'd almost ordered porn, remembering just in time that he'd be turning in receipts for reimbursement.

He knew this visit with Tower was a childish grasping after his old self, not to mention a rather bald-faced opportunity to show a faded friend that he, Henry, was successful. He was a professor. He wasn't just another idiot like the people who owned the enormous houses in the planned communities that scrolled past, one indistinguishable from the next, as he followed the directions issuing from the rental car's GPS. The melodic voice told him to turn left at the next light onto Charing Road. This took him past a red brick arch that declared, *Charing Estates*. After two blocks—well, they weren't properly blocks, as the development appeared to be aiming for a pastoral feel, with winding roads that came to two way stops—he could see there were three, or maybe four, different styles of brick and wooden houses, all enormous, almost all with electric Christmas candles in their windows. On the red door of a green wooden house hung a negligent wreath: *Happy Thanksgiving*. They'd probably already received a chastising letter from the community watch.

He slowed to pass two old women with enormous butts shaking in tracksuits on which they'd taped yellow reflective strips that sparkled in the headlights. Tower had always been strange, but this was almost too much, living out here, surrounded by fat, old Republicans. Though, Henry supposed, slowing for a stop sign and leaning up to look more carefully at the street signs, Tower had always seemed both feebly old and, at the same time, terribly young. He used to slip away from parties and they'd find him up in his room in the dark, sometimes playing a video game, or sometimes just sitting at the window in his hideous green armchair, staring out the window at the people in the yard below. The way he'd turn his head at such moments—from the TV, from the window—seemed to suggest he was lost. This was part of what they'd all liked about him, his vulnerability and lack of irony. Tower had simply been himself, strange and inscrutable and lovable.

The house was red brick, with four large windows and a bright green front door. The front yard was immaculately tended, the trees kept appropriately far from the house, and the stone path was free of weeds. The black driveway whispered under the tires.

As he pulled around back, the garage door slid up and yellow light spilled over the asphalt. Tower emerged, waving. Despite the cold, he wore only a white

T-shirt and khaki pants that rode up around his bare ankles and feet. He looked heavier, but other than that he was exactly the same as he'd been all this time in Henry's mind: he still wore those round wire frame glasses, and his floppy brown hair was still parted down the middle. And, of course, he was still enormously tall, at least six-four or five. Beside him, in the garage, was a gleaming silver Lexus.

"Welcome, welcome," Tower said, stooping his shoulders to shake hands, as though greeting a toddler. "Found it okay, huh?" His voice was the same, soft and barely audible.

"GPS," Henry explained. Tower nodded and, still holding Henry's hand, peered into one of the rental car's windows. This was another thing he remembered about Tower: his comfort in silence. He seemed to feel no urge to fill the empty spaces of conversation with chitchat or bullshit. This took some getting used to, but once you'd adapted, the silence became strangely soothing. As the rental car's engine clicked, they turned and looked at the house. The backyard was surrounded by a wooden privacy fence, but Henry caught a glimpse of something blue through the slats.

"Jesus Christ, is that a pool?" He wanted to punch his friend in the arm, or hug him.

Tower smiled and stuffed his hands into his pockets. "Indeed it is."

"You've done it, Tower, I'll give you that."

"Done what?" Tower frowned. Up close, Henry could see the wrinkles and age in his friend's face.

"All this," Henry said. "I mean, look at your fucking house."

"I'm not sure what you mean." Tower crossed his arms over his chest. His look wasn't the pleasant befuddled frown Henry remembered, but something thicker, almost angry.

"I mean, this is great, Tower. This is a beautiful house." He was disappointed in the stumbling, placating tone he'd adopted. He hadn't come here for awkwardness.

"Tower? Nobody calls me that." Could Tower really be as angry as he seemed? A deep crease between his eyes suggested this was true.

Henry stepped back toward his car. "So, what do they call you?"

"Guess." That odd, familiar grin spread across Tower's face, as though he was hearing a joke no one else could.

"I have no idea."

"Brian. They call me Brian." The smile was so big now it seemed almost unintentional, like an expression you see on homeless men hunkering in the warmth of subway stations.

"Well, I guess that makes sense."

"Come on, it's cold. Let's go inside."

The house was almost exactly as Henry had imagined: other than a black leather couch and an enormous flat screen TV there was no furniture in the living room. Video game controllers tangled their wires on the bare wood floor.

"So, this is my house." Tower gestured at the TV, as though that was the real point of pride. His front teeth seemed to protrude more than Henry remembered. The ceilings were barely a foot above Tower's floppy hair, which was shiny with grease.

"This is something," Henry said. "This place is huge."

Tower sighed, as though he'd expected more, and then took Henry on a quick tour. In each darkened room Tower waved his hand and pronounced its function: "Dining Room," "And this is the office," "Florida room." Each room contained a few odd pieces of furniture. In the dining room was a gleaming, dark wood cabinet, the glass shelves empty but for a single green plastic soldier hurling a grenade. In the office there was nothing but a rolling chair and a sagging poster from the movie, *Trainspotting*. In the Florida room a king sized mattress slouched where it'd been propped against a wall.

"And there's the upstairs," Tower said, gesturing at the stairs as though only an idiot would bother with that, then he led Henry into the kitchen. "Hey, you hungry?"

"Sure. Should we go out?" Henry wanted to get out of there, to go to some bad, overpriced place in a strip mall and talk for an hour, then drive back to the hotel and sit up late watching movies.

Without answering, Tower led him into the kitchen. "I guess we could go out," he said, leaning against the island, rubbing his hands. "Or, we can drink some beers,"—he jerked open the fridge to reveal shelves loaded with several cases of Budweiser—"and order pizza."

Before Henry could say anything Tower grabbed two beers and tossed one across the room. Henry bobbled the can, but didn't drop it. Tower chugged and gasped for breath. "Too bad we don't have three more people. We could play some asshole."

"Jesus, I haven't played asshole in, what, I guess ten years." Henry cracked his can. Foam spouted wildly and he took a bitter sip.

"Are you kidding?" Tower chugged again and banged the empty can down on the counter. "What, you some kind of pantywaste?"

"That's right, Tower. A big fucking pussy."

"I knew it. You always were a pussy," Tower said, pulling out two more beers.

Laughing, Henry drank, choking on the foam and dribbling down the front of his sweater.

"See," Tower said, bouncing a can in each hand. "A little domesticated pussy-man."

"Let me try that again," Henry said, then threw back his head and chugged until the beer was gone. He crumpled the can in his fist and let out a whoop.

With another round of beers, Tower led the way outside. "My land actually goes way back there," he said, gesturing beyond the pool to the trees, "but it was way too expensive to put up that much fence."

"Well, this is what, like half an acre? I think you're probably fine." Nail heads crept up from the warped deck boards. Henry stomped on one, as though he could drive it back down.

"Come on," Tower said, heading down the steps and across the yard. The ground was slick with fallen leaves and pine needles.

"Aren't you supposed to close that up?" Henry said as they skirted the pool's edge.

"You know, I kind of like swimming in the cold. I mean, isn't that supposed to be good for you?" Tower said, skimming his foot along the water.

"Is it? What like the polar bear club or something?"

"Right, right," Tower said, nodding happily, as though they agreed and Henry wasn't sure they didn't. "I guess I'm like one of those polar bear guys."

Squeezing between two overgrown bushes, Tower pressed his face to a gap in the fence. "Back there," he said, pointing, "there's this woman, she's always taking off her clothes and standing in front of the window."

Several hundred feet away stood a house exactly like Tower's. "All that land is yours?" Henry said.

"Half of it. But I never go out there. Bunch of deer run through it sometimes." He kept his face pressed to the slats.

He probably came out here every night, hoping to glimpse a middle aged woman's breasts, deer hooves clattering on the fallen trees of his neglected land. Instead of pity or disgust, Henry felt a swell of affection bordering on jealousy, as though this was what he wished he could do instead of all the things that were, somehow, what made up his life. There was a kind of freedom in this life.

"Come on, come on, come on," Tower whispered into the fence. "Where are you?"

◆   ◆   ◆

While they waited for the pizza, they played video games and soon Henry became so entranced he lost track of how many beers and slices he'd had.

They talked about old friends. Tower had kept in touch with everyone: James was a lawyer, Marcelo was a lawyer, and Nick worked for the government. Tower was working for an internet company, developing websites for local businesses.

"Mostly code writing, you know?"

"Actually, you know what? I have no fucking idea what that means."

Tower nodded and picked a lump of cheese off his slice, dangling it so a ball of orange grease trembled then dripped down into the box. *I'm kidding,* Henry wanted to say. *It's a joke.*

"So, when did you buy this place?"

"A couple years ago." Tower squinted at the television, his fingers darting over the controls. "I guess it was three years ago. I just got sick of living in some stupid little apartment like I was still in college."

"Well, this is a little nicer than that dump on 14th Street," Henry said, remembering what it had been like to sit in that filthy living room. The wall above the fireplace had been blackened by a fire they'd made one night of the previous tenant's accumulated mail. Tower had always woken up last, coming down some time after noon in a white T-shirt and boxers, scratching his ass and blinking through a hangover. He always went straight to the kitchen where he'd slurp four cups of black coffee.

"My parents died," Tower said, "and I inherited some money."

"Oh, I'm sorry," Henry said, a little surprised that this was true. Beyond even appearances, Tower was alone, and yet he was making the best of it, was making a life.

"They lived not too far away. I grew up like a mile from here."

Were those tears in Tower's eyes? Henry felt he should scoot across the couch and hug him. When was the last time he'd felt so strong an urge to comfort anyone other than his daughter?

"And you're still chasing crabs, right?" Tower said, leaning over his controller.

"That's right," Henry said, flopping back into the couch cushions. He was getting demolished in every game. Stretching his cramped hand he said, "Actually, I'm famous for crabs."

"I'll bet you are," Tower said, scratching furiously at his crotch.

"No, seriously," Henry said as his avatar was shot in the head again. "I mean, I actually am kind of famous for crabs. I mean, in the stupid little world of people who care about migratory salt water crabs in the coastal regions of Costa Rica. With those people, I'm like a superstar."

He reached for one of the three beers at his feet and opened it. "I suck at these games. Was this always true?"

"Wait, don't change the subject" Tower said, clicking through options on the screen. "You were telling me about crabs. I can't tell you how totally fascinating that is."

"Yes, it's true, crabs *are* utterly riveting." Henry laughed uncomfortably, pushing down a little swell of anger at being required to mock himself.

"Didn't you live in Costa Rica for awhile?"

A memory seized Henry: one night, when he'd been living in the jungle so as to track the movements of the crabs, he'd needed to get up to town for kerosene. The road had been too muddy to drive, so he'd ridden the plodding donkey. The mud had been so deep the donkey had sunk to its knees. Atop the hill, he'd looked back through the forest to his cottage, the single lamp just visible through the shaking trees, and he'd felt a surge of disbelief: *This is my life.* He was living in a rain forest, deep into a study that was intensely his own. There he was on the knobby, bouncing back of a donkey climbing through a mud-slide, rain crashing through the leaves overhead, and he was more alive at that moment than ever before or after.

"For a year, yeah, I did. That was pretty amazing. Maybe the best thing I've ever done."

Tower slumped on the couch, mouth ajar so his big teeth were visible, and he nodded, as though he understood completely. Henry had assumed that, like everyone else, Tower would've changed since college, that he'd have become more static and predictable. But it wasn't true. Here he was, living incongruous-ly in these empty rooms and, on the surface, his life was pathetic, but dig an inch and it turned out Tower had a real self, a self capable of sustaining itself through time, whereas the rest of them, including, unfortunately, Henry, were no more than mutable shadows, shifting along as the sun passed overhead, grasping at whatever they were supposed to want next: a job, furniture, a wife, a child. Tower proved what everyone suspected: there wasn't any single, clear way to live. Fear, conformity, and laziness structured most lives.

"Costa Rica. That's awesome," Tower said. "I was thinking of going there for vacation."

"You should," Henry said, catching himself before he accidentally said *we* should.

For the first time in months, maybe years, he felt alive. Blood seemed to course more eagerly through his head and his eyesight seemed sharper, like the time his daughter had scratched his cornea and the following day his sight had been startlingly crisp in the wounded eye. Then the eye had healed and he'd needed his glasses again. But this time, he told himself, he'd hold onto this feeling. He wouldn't allow himself to forget that life could be this, this—he could think of no other word—real.

He looked up and noticed that the window was drifting with white. "Oh, shit," he said, pointing.

"I know. They're saying like four inches." Tower drank deeply from his beer and belched.

"Wonderful," Henry said. He should leave. But he was having fun. And he was already too drunk to drive. Not that that ever used to stop him. Once, he and Tower, drunk and stoned and at 6:00 a.m., had driven out into the country, the grass blue with frost, the sun breaking pale over the horizon as they sang along to Cat Stevens, windows down to keep them awake.

"Need a beer?" Tower said, grunting up from his slouch.

Henry shook his head and closed his eyes, letting his mind whirl.

"See," Tower said. "Total pussy, like I said."

Henry giggled and found, as Tower left the room, that he couldn't stop.

❖　　　❖　　　❖

By the time they went out front to smoke, snow had coated the yard and the cul-de-sac. The cold air singed Henry's arms and neck, but in a pleasant way, as though the beer had stoked a stove in his pot belly. He'd been happy to hear Tower hadn't given up his pack-a-day habit, and now that they were out in the cold, Henry wanted to know more about his friend, to have all the emptiness of the past fifteen years filled in, as though, if he could just understand Tower, the unhappiness of his own life might vanish.

"So, have you heard anything from Sara?" The cigarette tasted awful, but he didn't let himself stub it out.

"Jesus," Tower said, staring blankly out at the snow. "Sara." He stepped off the stoop and stood on the path. Snow accumulated atop his head. "Sara. Sara."

Ducking his head and pumping his arms, he ran up the path in his bare feet, then spun, nearly falling, and ran back to the stoop. "Sara," he said, shaking his head. "That's really weird, to hear you say her name, you know?" He grinned and then stuck his cigarette between his teeth. "Man, Sara."

Henry should've known better. Sara was also the only girl they could even pretend Tower had dated, though they'd never, so far as he knew, been on anything like a date. Sara was from Russia and she'd spoken English with a thick accent, smoked her cigarettes in an elegant European manner, and had a perpetually greasy forehead. One night, while Tower wasn't around, she'd started flirting with Henry. He'd turned her down, but after that night she'd stopped coming around. Tower had been heart-broken, spent almost a week in his room, listening to the Smiths and the Cure. Henry had never been sure if his friend knew the real reason for Sara's sudden disappearance.

Rubbing a hand over his head, Tower said, "Look at all this stupid fucking snow. Let's go."

In the living room, Tower went back to the video game, but Henry was no longer in the mood. He did his best to drink another beer, but his eyes kept drifting closed.

"You're not going to drive in that shit, are you?" Tower was hunched forward, pounding at his controller.

Unable to open his eyes, Henry said, "Well, I've got a panel at nine."

"Why don't you stay here tonight? You can drive back in the morning."

"Where would I sleep?" This was the last thing Henry wanted to do, but what were his options?

"In my bed. It's a king, you know" Tower said.

"Well, I—" Henry started before he was cut off.

"What, you think I was serious? Jesus, you idiot, I have a guest room."

"Maybe I will," Henry said. "But I better call my wife."

"Yeah, right. Don't want the old lady to worry." There was an edge in Tower's tone that made Henry pause. Tower was glaring at the television. Sweat, or maybe it was melting snow, ran down his forehead and along his fat jaw. The muscles of his arms and shoulders bulged beneath the thin white T-shirt that had, Henry saw now, a hole at the neck and yellow stains at the arm pits.

"No sir," Tower shouted. "No need to go worrying the crazy old wife. Wouldn't want to worry the old bitch."

Swallowing a surge of anger, Henry went into the dark kitchen, holding up his phone to get a single, wavering bar of service.

◆ ◆ ◆

Though it was almost eleven and his wife was surely sitting up, watching TV, she didn't answer. He left a message, telling her to call and let him know that they were all right. Why did he feel panic rising in his throat? Why did he so vividly see their front door pried open, splintered wood scattering the foyer and beyond that, an empty house, the only sign of struggle a fallen lamp whose loose bulb flickered? She'd probably just seen his number and hadn't felt like talking. Everything was probably fine. He called a second time. When it went into voicemail he hung up.

To put off facing Tower, he went to the cramped, mildewed bathroom in the hallway. Atop the toilet was a Victoria's Secret catalog, warped and yellowed. The hand towel was stained with rusty blots of blood, from shaving, surely, though when he opened the mirror, there was nothing on the narrow glass shelves except a loose, crumpled string of floss.

Back in the living room, Tower was lying on the couch and the television was off. Without the lights and noise, the room's emptiness took on a different tone. The absence of drapes was obscene. The legs of the couch had dug furrows into the wood floor. Grit gathered along the seams of the walls. A vacuum cleaner stood near the back of the room, its yellow hull darkened with a layer of grime. Henry considered saying goodbye. If he kept the windows down he could probably manage. Anyway, it'd be better than staying here.

"You know," Tower shouted, as though they were in a crowded bar. "I never understood that fucking Sara girl."

Here came the predictable descent into drunken self-pity. He closed his eyes and rested his head against the wall.

"I mean, she wasn't very nice, was she?"

"Actually, you know what? I always thought she was kind of a bitch," Henry said. He opened his eyes to find Tower sitting up and staring at him.

With one hand Tower rubbed his clenched jaw, then pushed himself up and walked toward Henry. "You thought she was a bitch? You really did?"

Henry could see now why most of the girls they'd known in college had always felt uncomfortable around Tower. He'd often seemed to be leering at you as he was now, and he always got too close, as he did now, as though they were waiting for a train together on a crowded platform. His long arms and his big chest suggested an absence of control, as though he might accidentally swing out an arm and catch you across the face.

"She treated you like shit," Henry said, a hitch in his voice.

With a loud sigh Tower shook his head and said, "Oh, fuck it. You need a beer?"

"I think I'm okay."

"What, you're not done drinking, are you? Come on." He slapped Henry's shoulder. Then did it again, harder. "It's good to see you, you know?"

"It's good to see you, too."

"Wow," Tower shouted, and though Henry had braced himself, he flinched. "What sincerity, Henry. You always were a goddamn fountain of human feeling. Now come on, you need a beer." Tower put his arm around his shoulders and steered them into the dark kitchen.

Handing Henry a beer, Tower leaned against the open fridge, propping the door open with his toes. Mist and yellow light drifted out. Otherwise the room was dark.

"Did I tell you that I saw her recently? Sara, I mean. I saw her," Tower said, squinting at his can.

"No. You didn't tell me that."

"Yeah. Here, actually. I mean, in Richmond. Here too, I guess, because she came back here to see my place."

Henry nodded and shifted his weight. The digital clock beside the sink read, *1:45.*

"You tired?"

"No, I'm fine. Go on. Sara came to your house?"

"Why the hell do you give a shit?" Tower said, stepping away from the fridge so the door swung shut. Tower moved, a loose silhouette, to the window where he was framed by the pool's blue glow.

"That stupid fucking pool," he said, shaking his head. "Look at that. I forgot to close it up again."

Though he hated being there in the dark, Henry went to join his friend. The skin of the water quivered under the falling snow. There were only two lights on under the surface, one in the dark blue of the deep end, the other in the white of the shallow end.

"We went swimming." Tower shook his head and looked at Henry, his face half-lit in the glow. "It was her idea. The idiot. And, she didn't have a suit, so she went naked."

Tower chugged from his beer and crushed the can in his fist. "It was her idea. She wanted to do it." He opened the door and stepped out onto the dark wooden deck, shifting his bare feet around in the mounds of white. "She could hardly swim. I mean, she was flopping around like a spaz. I had to jump in when she started thrashing around in the deep end." He lifted one foot and rubbed it. "And, you know what, you're right. She *was* a fucking bitch. I always hated her." Tower crammed his hands in his pockets and hunched his shoulders. "Well, I mean, maybe not at first. But eventually, I really hated her."

"I don't blame you," Henry said. He'd left his shoes by the garage door and his toes were starting to ache.

Tower let out a bark of a laugh. "Do you remember that time she gave you her phone number?" What looked like tears ran down his cheeks.

"Yes, I do." When they'd first met her, Sara had slipped Henry her number when leaving one night, written in tiny print, the scrap of paper folded so many times it almost looked like a spitball. Henry had shown it to everyone and Tower had joked along with everyone else.

"What an idiot, right? I mean, she was still an idiot when she came over here. She asked about you." He turned to point at Henry with a shaking hand. "So I asked her what her obsession with you was, you know. I mean, I told her I had no idea what you were doing, that we aren't friends, but still, she wouldn't shut the hell up. She was, blahbitty fucking blah Henry, Henry, Henry. It's too bad you didn't get in touch earlier. I could've told her how you're famous for crabs."

Tower finally dropped his finger and took a long, deep breath, puffing up his chest. "You wouldn't believe how hard it was to get her to shut up. But I did." He rubbed his hands together and blew on them. "I finally got her to shut her big mouth." He coughed and rubbed his hands quickly together beneath his chin. "I told her not to go in the pool. But she insisted. So, you know, I think it was her fault, really. But I'm not going to kid you, Henry. I did my part."

Melting snow had plastered Tower's hair to his head in stringy clumps and the way he smiled made his teeth protrude. He turned and looked at Henry again and said, his voice low, but loud, "Did you hear me, Henry?"

"I heard you."

"Did you hear what I said? Because I want you to understand. I don't want you to not understand what I'm trying to tell you, Henry." Tower took a step toward the kitchen, big hands dangling at his sides.

"I understand you, perfectly."

"Do you? Because it's pretty simple, really. I hope you understand. I really do." Tower took another step toward the open door.

Henry turned and almost ran into the living room. Where the hell was his coat? Where were his keys, his wallet? Hadn't he handed those to Tower as well at some point, so they didn't fall out of his pants on the couch?

"What are you doing?" Tower was standing in the doorway to the kitchen, a puddle spreading around his feet. He dragged on a cigarette and blew a blue stream at the ceiling.

"Where's my coat?" Henry's voice was shaking and his hands were weak and loose, as though they'd turned into the softest plastic.

"In the closet." Tower blew another stream of smoke at the ceiling and rolled his eyes and giggled.

Holding his breath Henry squeezed past, nearly slipping in the puddle, and fumbled in the hall closet, found his coat and, in the pocket, his wallet and keys. Near the door, he found his shoes and forced his feet into them, crushing the heels.

"I think I'm going to go," Henry said, cramming his arms into the sleeves. "I have to be up early."

"But the snow." Tower was smiling, and he was blocking the doorway again. Henry knew that if he tried to push past, Tower's cold hands would close around him.

"I'm fine. It was good to see you, you know? It was good to see you, Tower."

"Jesus!" Tower shouted. "I told you nobody calls me that."

"Okay," Henry whispered.

Tower stepped out of the doorway. Turning his back on the man scared the hell out of Henry, but it was the fastest way out of there. He slapped at the button and the garage door slid up.

"Thanks for the beer," he said, unable to keep from glancing back. Tower was standing in the doorway, fiddling with the hem of his T-shirt.

"Whatever, man. Drive safe."

"Right, I'll be fine."

The car's wheels spun in the snow and he muttered, "No, fucking go, just go," and eventually they found traction. He backed toward the garage. Tower was standing beside his silver Lexus. He lifted a hand to wave, the same hand he'd used just months ago to hold Sara's head beneath the water while her body twitched, while her dark, silent mouth worked frantically, the pathetic pink slip of her tongue flopping out until she was still, and even then he held her under, to be sure. With that same hand he'd dug the hole in the land beyond his fence, pushing aside fallen trees and clearing away leaves. He'd have dug deep down to be sure a frost wouldn't push up a hand, a foot, and then he'd have piled the earth back in and replaced the fallen trees and spread out the leaves, so no one would possibly notice, especially not come fall when the leaves fell and the ground hardened.

The headlights barely pierced the blowing snow and Henry leaned against the steering wheel, blinking hard to see, but everything beyond a few feet was a blur.

THE EMPTY HOUSE

AFTER THE PLATE OF UNDERCOOKED BEANS and crumbly tortillas, Ryan had half an hour before his bus for Huehuetenango, so he ordered coffee. The waiter, an old man with gray hairs hanging from his nose said he had something special and hurried into the back. By that evening Ryan would see his old friend, Jim. It'd been eight years since they had spoken and in that time Jim had become a Maryknoll priest, a missionary, posted here in Guatemala—there really was no accounting for life, Ryan thought. The old man came out of the back with a cup, taking small steps.

"Nescafé," he said, setting the cup down and putting his hand on Ryan's shoulder. "*Bueno. Muy bueno.*"

"*Gracias*," Ryan said, touching the handle of the cup, but the old man stood squeezing his shoulder until he lifted the cup, sloshing a bit over the rim, and took a sip. It was bitter and grainy. He smiled up into the tangle of nose hairs and said, "*Deliciosa.*"

"Nescafé," the man said, delighted. As he went back to the kitchen he glanced over his shoulder, miming sips.

Here Ryan was in a country covered with coffee plantations and he was served instant coffee, which probably cost twice as much as local grounds. And this wasn't a Western tourist hotel where the need to impress Americans might drive the owners to such stupidity; he was in a shitty little café near the Guatemala City bus station. There were only two other patrons, both young, scraggly looking men, both of whom looked asleep over their yellow plastic tables. But this was one of the pleasures of traveling: you were always allowed to marvel at the incongruities that, when they faced you in your everyday life, say, in the suburbs, you simply rolled right past, thinking, big deal, let's get moving. That would be him in a few weeks, back in America, at his sister's house in Florida. Florida! As though they were all retired and worn down and exhausted by life, which, he felt sure, his sister, younger than him by two years, would be soon enough, since she was getting married in a week and would probably have a kid, buy a Volvo, start saving for college and then if she were in a coffee shop and they served her Nescafé, well, she'd probably just be annoyed. What is this shit, she'd think.

Nescafé, he thought again, sloshing the last bit of coffee around in the slick of grounds, with a sinking feeling that he'd overplayed the moment. The irony wasn't as dense as he'd hoped. Anyway, what good was irony, without anyone to share it?

Hooking his blue duffle bag over his shoulder—though travelers were now all using new, internal-frame backpacks, he stuck with his old Diadora bag with a sense of Luddite pride—he went up to the bead curtain that hung between the dining room and the kitchen and called for the check.

In the blue haze of the station men clambered atop buses, shouting at the crowd that tossed up luggage. The drivers, some in gray uniforms, others in white shirts and jeans, chatted together off to the side, smoking, together summoning the strength to plunge these buses out onto the crumbling roads that clung to and wound around the sides of mountains through remote areas purportedly— though who could know how much of the "official news" to believe—full of revolutionaries and bandits.

The highways all over the country, Ryan knew, though he'd not actually traveled much in Guatemala, were spotted, particularly at the sharper turns in the passes, with clusters of white crosses where whole buses had overshot the road, breaking a window through the jungle canopy, crumpling on the mountainside. He'd seen many such crosses in Chile and Peru, up in the Andes, on buses just like these. He wasn't about to be fazed, or worried. Or maybe he was a little bit worried, a tiny, niggling fear that crept through his stomach. But he was used to this fear, and in a way, he thought, it was a comfort: proof, amidst the chaos and violence, of his individual, coherent self. The fear was the same each time he boarded a bus or was stopped by the police, and so it was a reminder that, despite all he'd seen and all he'd learned about the terror of the world, at the core he was still Ryan. Himself.

Stuffing his duffle beneath the seat, he flipped through the *Time* he'd bought in Antigua. He scanned the table of contents for familiar names, but didn't recognize any. Most of his friends had gone into television, thinking, rightly, that's where the money was. He was one of the few to stick with newspaper work, and one of the very few to have left the country. For six years now he'd been covering the political troubles in Chile and Argentina. The culture of fear. Though, looking through *Time*, you wouldn't have any idea this was happening. He'd always half-expected his work to make him famous, to win him Pulitzer Prizes, get him on staff at *The New York Times*. This hadn't happened. Four of his articles had been picked up for the *Herald Tribune*, over six years. This wasn't bad. Better than most. But it was never enough. The world just didn't care.

The bus left the middle-class neighborhood around the station, rattled past two large shopping centers, then turned onto a narrow side street. They went through what seemed to be a shipping district: streets were full of trucks, idling up on the curbs, or pulled halfway into warehouses. Men with machine guns herded a crowd of peasants onto the backs of cargo trucks while a fat man in a tight suit brandished a clipboard. After the warehouses the bus passed along the edge of a market where people were screaming at one another across tables loaded with fruit and flies. From there the neighborhoods deteriorated until they were passing the slums along the mountain, shacks with plastic walls, heaps of trash sending up translucent waves in the sun. Then the bus was free of the city.

Earlier that morning he'd taken a different bus over the mountains from Antigua, where he'd been "on vacation" for a week after a long flight from Santiago. He'd managed to make himself into a real tourist, he'd thought: taking a tour of the heavily guarded jade factory, visiting the crumbling cathedral, and breakfasting each morning in the flower flooded patio of his pension, listening to the elderly British couple at the next table whisper over cups of tea about whose fault it was that they'd missed their charter flight to Tikal or some other failure in their trip. Nights he'd gone to bars, surprised at first by the hordes of gringos there to study Spanish at the language institutes despite the civil war. But then the gringos had their own take on reality. A few had told him earnestly that the civil war was overrated. It wasn't really a *war*, you know. He'd been disgusted by their obliviousness. He was glad to be back on the trail of a news story, a potentially radical and important one.

Jim was a Maryknoll, which meant he was teaching literacy skills to the poor and instructing them in the proper way of Catholic worship, ordaining local priests and, although of course he'd never admit this, encouraging dangerously leftist ideas. The political naiveté of the Catholic project in Guatemala was the seed of Ryan's projected article. Though he sympathized with the ideals, it was suicidal. There were rumors of recent massacres in the mountains just outside Huehuetenango. Whole villages dumped in the woods. The military blamed the EGP; the Catholic clergy blamed the military. The military blamed the clergy for supporting the EGP. The clergy said they were doing humanitarian work. According to a reporter Ryan had spoken with in Guatemala City there was a rumor a young woman had escaped, taken for dead amidst the pile of bodies by drunk, blood-lusting soldiers. Eyewitnesses were rare. If Jim could hook him up with this woman not even American newspapers would be able to ignore the article. Ryan could, with some luck, make the world care. At least for a moment.

Along the highway, the jungle was flattened back a hundred feet. There were gleaming puddles of water in the deep tracks of heavy equipment. Yellow backhoes leaned on piles of earth. Men squatted in the shadows of the wheels, smoking. He knew the trees had been pushed back to reduce the risk of guerrilla ambushes, and that the forests were also ravaged by a beetle that burrowed into pines and cut off the sap flow. The remaining trees were whittled at in the night by local farmers for fuel. He thought this would be a good way to open an article on Guatemala: a new, unused highway and a disappearing forest.

◆   ◆   ◆

It's possible that not all the buses are quite so broken down as the one I rode to Huehuetenango when tracing the path Ryan, my older brother, must have taken back in 1982. For one thing, it was years later, 1997. The civil war had ended the year before.

I got on the bus early and had a seat, but soon people filled the aisle, bumping each other with bags of vegetables and fabrics. The driver climbed along the side, thrusting his hand in the windows, demanding fares. I gave my seat to an old woman with a chicken in a wooden box. Not far out of Antigua the young woman beside me in the aisle threw up, splattering my shoes, strings of saliva hanging from her lips, her face pale. She grabbed my shirtsleeve for balance. She dry heaved a few more times, then straightened up, wiping her mouth. She was younger than I'd first thought, maybe around my age, mid-twenties, wearing a loose T-shirt that said Nike in flaking black script. Her long black hair was pulled into a thick braid that went all the way down her back.

"*Gracias*," she said. I kept my hand on her arm. She smiled weakly and tucked her head down, shoulders shaking before she got sick again. For an hour we went on like that, me holding her up, she throwing up and dry heaving. It was the closest I'd felt to any Guatemalan while I was down there. When we reached her stop, a small town whose name I didn't know and couldn't find on any maps later, she said something to me, more than just thanks, and I nodded, though I hadn't understood. I wanted to hug her. I didn't want her to go. Maybe, I thought, I should get off the bus, talk with her, make sure she got home all right. But this was just an excuse, I knew, to avoid going to Huehuetenango.

I'd put off going there until the very end of my trip to Guatemala. I don't want to give the impression that I had any real, tangible hopes of finding my brother still alive in Guatemala. He'd appeared on a list from the State Department, marking him as missing. Disappeared. They'd called my parents two months after the wedding to tell them Ryan had been in the country, but had not been heard from since the day his plane had landed. They knew he'd gone to Huehuetenango, apparently to visit an old friend working as a priest there. That was the last they'd heard.

I went down to Guatemala to see the place where, in some ways, my family had broken apart. But traveling alone down there was harder than I'd anticipated. The country was rough, my Spanish was bad, and after getting violently ill for a week in Panajachel I spent most of my time in Antigua which was crowded with tourists: Swedes and Americans and Danes shopping in the boutiques, drinking all night in the gringo bars and clubs, admiring the city's beauty, the pastel painted walls of the Spanish colonial mansions, the ornate lampposts over cobblestone streets. Antigua felt, beyond the architecture, European and safe.

This is not to say that one doesn't still encounter fear, even there. Once, walking with my camera, taking pictures of flower-dressed ruins destroyed in an eighteenth century earthquake, I strayed too far down through the city. I lowered the camera and noticed an old man, face down in the street, as though he'd stopped for a sip of sewer water and died. His hands, flopped out above his head, were cracked and looked as though they were made of chalk. I turned to find my way back uptown when a group of young men spotted me and began following, shouting faggot, pussy: *pinche huecho, concha.* Each time I glanced back the four flung out their arms, like birds defending a nest.

Thinking back I'm not sure how afraid I should have been. Maybe the boys just wanted to scare me a little, or maybe they wanted to take my wallet, stuffed with Quetzals, my watch, my camera. I hurried past gringo bars and the central park with the ornate fountain, three angels, heads thrown back, hurling white arcs of water. It was near the fountain that the boys fell off my trail. That should have been the end of my fear, but, a moment later, on the far side of the park I passed the police station—two cops were outside smoking cigarettes—and then the fear only got worse, became terror. The boys might have mugged me, at worst kicked me a few times, but these men, with their big stomachs and machine guns, could arrest me on a pretense, murder me, and no one would stop them.

Even in my short time down there I knew this sort of thing happened. I'd met a young Danish man in a bar who'd been thrown in prison for insulting a drunken policeman. In his cell the guards had kicked him until his liver ruptured. His skin had tainted yellow. Patches of green flesh sagged beneath his eyes. He flew back to Denmark for surgery the next day, or that's what everyone at the bar said.

I left all this out of the emails and postcards I sent home. I mentioned the flowers; the way people from each of the five towns in the mountains around Lake Atitlan wore different brightly colored woven shirts, like jerseys. I wanted my parents to know I was all right. I was a gringo, and so I could be scared and worried about myself but I'd always be safer than most. But how could I say this to my parents, my mother in particular?

There was, throughout my childhood, a shrine to Ryan in his old bedroom. The room hadn't been left untouched—he hadn't really lived there since he left for college—but on one dresser were several photographs of him: his graduation from college, a picture of him in New York before he went to South America, then one he'd sent from Santiago of him on at a rooftop restaurant in the early morning, the sheer, snow capped tops of the mountains not yet cloaked in smog. There were the postcards he'd sent along with his news articles in a binder, arranged relatively chronologically. This little shrine wasn't hidden away, or something to be ashamed of. Nor was it something every guest was shown. It was just there.

Ryan went to college when I was five and I only remember glimpses of him: a bag of candy corn he gave me as a present one Thanksgiving—probably just left over from Halloween—while he was in college. I left the candies in their bag on the windowsill, liking the way the streetlight glinted silver off the plastic, until the following spring when they melted in the sun and my mother threw them out; his long hair toward the end of college that our mom hated. "Where are my scissors," she kept saying at his graduation, lifting up long frizzy locks and snipping them with her fingers. Then he moved to New York and was busy with reporting, then he was off to South America and didn't return home for years.

Though Ryan wasn't physically present, he permeated my life. My mother cried often when I was young, and though I can't be sure it started with Ryan's disappearance, I assumed they were related. I remember once going upstairs to tell her I was going to play soccer and finding her sitting on the edge of the bed, sobbing. Her whole body was involved, shoulder shaking, head bobbing up and down, hands clutching at her pants, then coming to her face, then grabbing her hair.

"Mom?" I said, and she looked up, still sobbing.

"Honey, yes, what is it?" she said. It was terrifying to hear her voice, trying to be so normal in the midst of all that awful shaking grief. I couldn't remember why I'd come up there. She came across the room, wiping her tears. She put her hand on my head and asked again what I wanted. I hated Ryan then.

One of his articles, a short thing published in the *Herald Tribune* about the American expatriate community in Santiago says it's tempting to imagine ourselves the victims, to imagine the violence is because of us, about us, but it isn't and one needs to always remember the thousands in the mountains, in the cities, who have no voice, whose fear will never be recorded. But what good was this to my mother?

Ultimately, I went to Guatemala with two hopes: perhaps I could find out who *I* was—I'd always felt my self was in some ways missing and was connected to the mystery of what had happened to Ryan—and maybe my trip could bring a kind of solace to my mother. Perhaps, through action, through really engaging the world I could forge clarity out of the mess of life.

❖   ❖   ❖

Ryan's bus slowed as it reached the small town of Chimaltenango. An old man climbed aboard; his gums were stained black, as though a bottle of ink had spilled in his mouth. He held a sack of avocados on his lap like a favorite grandchild.

As the bus pulled clear of the town a clutch of children gave chase, dragging strings tied to plastic bags, trying to fly them. Ryan waved to the kids and one let out a triumphant shout, leaping in the air, his bag jerking along the ground.

He hadn't seen Jim for eight years and wondered if he'd recognize him. But of course they'd be the two gringos at the bus stop. He imagined Jim with the long hair he'd had in college, curling into a loose cloud, though this was hard to match with a pinching white priest collar and those sticky black polyester pants and shirt.

It was difficult to connect Jim, who he'd always thought of as the smartest of his college friends, with the fact that he was now a Maryknoll. Ryan had a rich, full contempt for religion. One just had to consider the situation here in Guatemala, with General Rios Montt who believed he was some kind of prophet and the massacres were the will of Jesus. But if Jim hadn't turned to religion they might never have connected again. His sister had forwarded along Jim's letter. The letter had jokingly said it was Ryan's adventurousness that had helped him decide to leave the States and work in Latin America.

Ryan had written back, saying perhaps he'd come for a visit. Jim had written an encouraging letter: maybe Ryan could even write an article about the work they were doing there in Guatemala? Sure, Ryan wrote back. Maybe.

Jim's letter had felt like a cord, trailing back into his past he'd thought long severed, suddenly pulling on him. And, over the past five years in Chile, he'd met many expatriates, had so much work, felt caught in something so important, that it was easy to lose track of those back in America living the life you'd not been able to stand the thought of; but here was another friend, someone he'd lost track of, who'd chosen a similar path. They were different from most Americans.

When he called from his pension in Antigua he'd been full of nervous energy. The letter with Jim's number was tattered from a week in Ryan's wallet and from his having read it so many times. A woman who answered, perhaps a nun, said yes, Padre was in.

"*Diga?*" Jim's voice shouted, so familiar, so wonderful to hear.

"Is this the infamous Father Jim?" Ryan said, feeling his old self, his self from college—naive, ironic, ridiculous—rising up in a rush.

"It just might be," Jim said, with a laugh. "Ryan. I'm surprised you called."

"Of course I called. I was so moved by your letter, I just had to."

"Right," Jim said, then cleared his throat, sounding suddenly older. "So, you're in Guatemala? You said in your letter you might be stopping through."

Ryan said he'd been trying hard to be a tourist for week and Jim responded politely, but there was a distance in the conversation. When Ryan asked if he should come visit, as Jim suggested the man said, "Of course. Did I say that in my letter? Of course you should."

"Jim, if this isn't a good time, that's fine. I haven't even been to Tikal yet."

"No, everything is fine. It's fine. You should come." Jim then tried to steer the conversation onto more even ground, asking about old friends, but after a few minutes of this Ryan asked if Jim was frightened.

"Who isn't?" The line was staticky. Maybe they were being taped, Ryan thought.

"Well, me," he said. Was this a lie? He wasn't sure.

"You've always been the brave one."

"That's very true," Ryan said, smiling ironically at his reflection in his room's mirror. "I am incredibly brave."

"Maybe you can inspire me, when you visit." There it was again: the old Jim.

"You haven't given up drinking, have you? Because I'm not sure I can look at you in a priest get-up without at least a few drinks."

"Ryan, I'm a priest. All we do is drink. And love Jesus. And mankind and so on." He would meet Ryan at the station, but right then he really needed to go.

* * *

The weekend before my own bus ride to Huehuetenango, I went to the Embassy in Guatemala City. They had no information, not even the records of Ryan's disappearance. Or at least they didn't show them to me. They showed me nothing, though they were polite. They asked how my hotel was. They gave me their business cards. They told me to travel safe. Back in Antigua that night, I met a guy from Chicago who here I'll call Chris. We watched the Red Sox game—this was the only bar in all of Guatemala with satellite TV—and talked about places we'd been, places we thought we were going. He asked if I'd been to Tikal. I said I'd missed it, too hard to get to. We discussed the new highway that was scheduled to open soon from Guatemala City to the ruins, cutting the trip from sixteen hours to four.

The next night, when Chris didn't show up, the bartender from Virginia told me Chris's story. He was traveling with his fiancée. They'd been up in the Tikal region a few months before and had gone camping in the mountains. A group of men had found their campsite and had tied him to a tree and forced him to watch while they raped and beat his fiancée. She was in Antigua, but never left her hotel.

Why would they stay in Guatemala? I asked. The bartender said he didn't know. "But that's crazy," I said. "Why don't they just get out of here?"

"What? Dude, how should I know?" He turned away to watch the Red Sox.

I didn't tell my parents I was going until after I'd bought my plane ticket. My father listened, didn't say anything, and handed the phone to my mother who said, "What? What's this?" I tried to explain. I told her the countries weren't nearly so dangerous anymore. "Being on an Interstate is more dangerous," I told her. I wasn't sure if this was true, but it sounded right. "You are not going, do you hear me?" my mother said. But what could they do? They couldn't stop me. I needed to get out into the world.

My mother had always encouraged me to live through the imagination, particularly after Ryan disappeared. She made me take typing instead of shop and was always happy when I went upstairs to work on one of my fantasy novels instead of going out to play. I remember once my father came upstairs, home from teaching at the university, and sat me down and said it just wasn't healthy for a kid to spend so much time alone. Out my bedroom window I could see two of my neighborhood friends chasing a couple of girls, shouting and jumping. My mother came up during this talk and told my father to leave me alone. "What's the problem?" she said. "He has an imagination. There's nothing wrong with that. I'm proud of him."

She did this to keep me safe. She'd already lost one son to the world.

But, after graduating college and working for three years in customer service jobs, I decided I needed to go to Guatemala. I'd been thinking of doing it for years, but had put it off because of my mother, and I'd hoped how I should live my life and who I was would be clearer in the working world. They weren't and eventually going to Central America was all I thought about, all I wanted.

What I found during those six weeks in Central America wasn't what I'd been looking for. Nothing had been resolved. I still had no better sense of who I was, or who Ryan had been. After the trip I stayed with my parents for a couple of months, figuring out what to do next. During those months with my parents—they didn't look at my pictures, didn't want to hear anecdotes—I wondered if I'd only gone down there for myself? Is that what all this was? Was it all just for me?

◆   ◆   ◆

With the wedding as an excuse, Ryan felt like less of a coward for leaving Chile. He'd spent too many years there, had angered enough people that if he was murdered the Embassy wouldn't be able to guess who'd done it. It was the article he'd written about a rumor of children stolen from their dissident mothers and given to military families that had caused the biggest stir. Death threats had come in, both on the phone and in the mail. He'd come home late from dinner downtown one night to find his front door open. His first impulse was to turn, run. But he pushed the door open, flicked on the light. Nothing, as far as he could tell, had been stolen, but everything was ruined: curtains torn from the walls, the pillows and mattress gutted, books pulled from the shelves, ripped up. There was a pile of pages in the middle of the room someone had pissed on. The next day Jim's letter arrived and since he hadn't bought a ticket home yet, Ryan planned his trip through Guatemala.

He leaned his head against the bus window. Dirt blew into his eyes as the stubby landscape scrolled past, dark silhouettes of mountains in the distance, streaked with webs of rain, strands cut, hanging loose.

When he woke, his neck stiff, the old man with his sack of avocados had moved a row closer. "*Buenos tardes,*" the man said, his Spanish clipped with an Indian accent.

Avoiding the old man's stares, he tried to read the few reports about the Civil War he'd gotten after two days of asking—the Embassy had given him almost no information, and what he did have was mostly blacked out. The heat bore down and he gave in to it, sitting stunned for the next several hours as they pulled in and out of ruined towns.

His flight was in three days. He'd land in Miami. His sister worked in the administration of a small private university along the western coast. Her husband-to-be worked in a Chemistry lab.

He'd only seen his family twice in the past six years. And now his sister's world was filling out with the things one's life was supposed to be filled with, while he had only his career: but it was a better career by far than if he'd stayed in America and become a lawyer, a banker, a teacher. It wasn't wrong, he thought, to take a kind of pride in his life.

In Huehuetenango the bus stopped in the street, the station no more than an office with glass doors. Jim wasn't there. Ryan waited on a bench, watching the driver toss cargo from the bus's roof. Maybe Jim had forgotten. Or was just busy.

After an hour it was clear Jim wasn't coming. According to the map the church where Jim worked was just a few blocks away. The sun lit up the tops of the buildings, reflecting off high windows. Though it was still early evening the streets were nearly empty.

The yellow and white church was at the far end of the square, bell towers visible above tall thick green trees. Flagstone paths wound between the trees and flower beds, past iron benches, all empty. Birds lined the buildings and chased each other off unlit lampposts, disappearing into the dark trees.

Ryan saw the body as the path opened up before the church. At first he thought it was a drunk. He'd seen that before, men passed out in the gutters, along the sidewalks. You just stepped over them and kept going. But as he got closer, he knew this wasn't the case. The black clothes were tattered, one pant leg pushed up over a white sock, the dark hairs flattened against the pale skin. The kneecaps had been shot out, jagged crusted wounds with bright, hard slices of bone. The face was turned to one side, but Ryan knew it was Jim. Pieces of flesh had been torn from his face. Crusted holes where the eyes should have been.

Behind him a car rattled past, small and brown, the windows clouded with dirt. He stepped around the body and went toward the church. The sun had fallen farther and light struck only the point of the steeple. The strap of his duffle cut into his shoulder. He drew close to the end of the square and then he thought, *Not the church*, and turned quickly down a side street. He stopped against the wall. The square was still empty, save the birds and the body he could no longer see. Ryan pulled the map out of his pocket. Four hotels were noted. One a few blocks off, near the local market. He patted his wallet, buttoned the front of his coat, and then unbuttoned it. Through the closed windows overhead he could hear the low murmur of voices.

The concierge was chatting and smoking with the bag boys in the lobby when he pushed through the glass doors. They all followed him to the check-in desk, as though they were all old friends, finally together. He ground his teeth until they squeaked in order to control the shakes as he signed in. One of the boys went with him up to his room, though Ryan had no bags other than the duffel, which he carried. The boy leaned against the doorway and nodded, smiling, as though he were waiting for a punch line. Ryan closed the door in his face.

He turned the lock and took off his coat and sat on the bed. His face felt filthy and looked, in the mirror across the room, as though he'd been beaten. He went to the bathroom, splashed water on his eyes, and wiped them with a thin, stiff towel.

❖ ❖ ❖

Had I found the same hotel? I found the one closest to the church, but it was fifteen years later. A lot changes in that much time. Though the war had been over for two years threat leaked from the city's run down buildings. I spent one night in the town then took the bus back to Antigua. I hated myself. Was I trying to pretend it was the same now for me as it'd been for Ryan? Did I want to *be* Ryan? Of course I did, to some degree, and this meant I wanted to face violence. But also to live. To be always on the edge, the way Ryan had put himself. Glance right and see death, spreading like a stain over life. But then why wasn't I in Haiti? I was a coward. That's why I took notes, always scribbling throughout my time in Guatemala in my small notebook, little fragments of phrasing and descriptions I've put together into this story.

❖ ❖ ❖

There was a phone on the nightstand beside the bed. He picked it up. The dial tone sounded like a horn intended to drown out screaming. He put the receiver down. There were no buses until morning. He had the numbers for the Embassy. They'd tell him to just take the next bus. The phones were probably monitored. He thought of calling his sister. No one knew where he was.

For an hour he watched television and then called for room service. The concierge told him there was no service. Where could Ryan eat? There was, the concierge said, a *restaurante, cerca, comida fresca.*

Behind the swollen blue lips of Jim's corpse Ryan had seen a line of jagged broken teeth.

The bedspread was a bright paisley pattern and Ryan sat on it with his eyes closed, running his hands back and forth, as though his fingers were inches deep in crumbling petals that loosed up a bright smell into his nose.

The last time he'd visited his sister she was living in Wisconsin, working at a small two-year junior college. She'd driven him around the depressing town, pointing out the new McDonald's, the small hotel whose restaurant had been the first to obtain a liquor license, and then she'd taken him to her small brick house on the outskirts. Beside the fold out couch she'd set out a pile of new, green towels. Maybe, he thought, smacking the hotel sheet cover, she'd bought those towels just for him.

After a few minutes he put on his jacket. He'd eat, come back, watch television, sleep, wake up, and get on the bus to Guatemala City. In two days he'd be in Florida. He'd sit with his sister and drink a beer. He'd be able to hear the water, pulling at the pilings of her dock. They could walk down, after the sun had set, having put on warmer clothes against the cool night air, and watch ghost crabs scuttle up the sand.

The bag boys were outside smoking. Their whispering seemed to chase him down the street. Curtains were drawn over all the windows, so only slices of yellow light fell onto the dark paving stones. A car rolled past and Ryan felt his legs tighten. He wasn't hungry. Had he ever felt hungry? How was that possible? What the hell was he doing out here? He should've just stayed in his room till morning. But then the restaurant was there, spilling yellow light over the cracked street. Behind him in the square church bells tolled nine times.

The restaurant had three round tables, a pair of metal folding chairs at each. On the wall was a dirty soccer pennant. At one of the tables an old man scooped watery beans into his mouth. Ryan sat down as a short overweight woman brought him a pitcher of water and a plastic plate with four thick tortillas on it. He asked for a beer. She nodded and smiled. Her two front teeth were missing. A television crackled—hysterical laughter—out of the back room into which the woman disappeared, the thick rug falling back in place. Flies drifted up off the empty tables and a large beetle hummed furiously about the light.

The old woman delivered his beer. It was warm and bitter, but he finished it before she left the room and asked for another.

It was awful to leave Jim's body in the square. But what could he do? Drag the body out of town? Bury it? Put it in his duffel and take it back to the Embassy? The military wouldn't stand for that. But then, maybe the men who'd done this had moved on, had frightened themselves with killing a gringo, a priest no less. Maybe they'd already been reprimanded by their superior or executed.

With his second beer the woman brought his beans and chicken. The chicken was covered with wilted, almost-brown tomatoes. The beans were warm and crisp on top and he ate them, sipping his beer.

❖   ❖   ❖

When I went out for dinner in Huehuetenango the food was almost inedible, pocked with puddles of water, trembling with parasites. The chicken was sticky and pink. There is no way of knowing if it was the same restaurant, if he'd even gone out to eat at all. Perhaps he'd been too afraid. Perhaps the men came to his hotel.

◆   ◆   ◆

Beetles hummed in to the light when the men opened the door. They were all young, sixteen to eighteen. The bulges of guns could be seen on the hips of two, while the third, who remained out in the street, carried a machine gun. They wore cobbled together suits. The one who stood in front, a short kid, maybe eighteen, wore a baggy pinstripe jacket and tight tuxedo pants that rode up above his military boots.

"*Señor*," he said and smiled. Dark metal braces pushed out his lips.

Ryan could barely get his beer back to the table.

"*Pardoname, señor,*" the boy said, stepping forward, his hands out. The old man at the next table stared at his plate. The kid in front of Ryan had terrible acne, clusters swollen red. He asked Ryan to please come with them.

"Where?"

"Please, sir," the kid said, smiling. He reached out and put a hand on Ryan's arm and squeezed gently. Ryan stood up and the kid nodded and said, "*Sí, señor*. Questions, yes?"

Two of the boys walked alongside him while the third, cradling the machine gun, followed. The windows along the street were silent. He could hear the crunch of his shoes on the loose stones. Ryan asked where they were going.

The kid with the acne looked up at Ryan and smiled and nodded and squeezed his arm again. They walked through town to a poorer section. The shacks became conglomerations of tin scraps. Fires could be seen through gaps in the walls, but there were no voices. "Questions," the kid said, massaging Ryan's arm, the fingers pressing down, then loosening, pressing.

The boys stopped Ryan beside a brown car with dirty windows. The doors slammed and the engine clattered and they bounced over the pitted road. The boy with the scarred face sat in the back with Ryan, smiling at him, the dark braces, slick with saliva, catching bits of light. The two up front talked about something Ryan couldn't make out. They drove out of town.

The conversation up front escalated. The boy in back got involved, leaning forward and shouting curse words at the other men. They were talking about soccer teams.

The boy turned to Ryan, grinning and shaking his head. He pointed at the driver and said, "This *pendejo* says Guate isn't the best team. Can you believe that? What's wrong with him?"

Ryan shook his head and tried to smile.

"Do you love Guate? Are you a fan?" the boy asked, his smile fading. Before Ryan could answer he said, "Because I hope I'm not riding here with two idiots."

"You dumb fucker!" the driver shouted.

The boy leaned forward and slapped the back of the driver's head lightly. "Just drive, you Guate-hating *pinche huecho*." The boy smiled at Ryan, shaking his head, as though this wasn't to be believed.

Out of town the car stopped. Sounds of the jungle, birds and howling insects, became louder as the men opened their doors. Ryan stayed in the car.

"Please come out. Questions only," the acned kid say, smiling.

Ryan considered letting them shoot him in the car. But then a last hope filled him. It was possible, after all, that they *did* just want to talk. Why would they kill another American? They could just be taking him to talk with someone who would explain that the priest had been the work of the rebels. They'd assure him they were doing all they could to find the communist murderers.

A hand pulled him out of the car and pushed him toward the jungle. He stepped into high grass. The forest was a black wall.

He stumbled and the boy behind caught his shoulder, held him steady. "*Cuidado.*"

Ryan looked at the kid. He thought of his sister in Florida, his family gathering for the wedding, all those aunts and uncles he never thought of, and his younger brother. What was his brother doing now? For a moment Ryan couldn't remember how old he was. Then it came, a sudden rush or memory: ten! When he thought of his brother, he thought of the little kid riding a bike, wobbling and happy.

The boy with the braces and acne told him to keep down the path. Ryan didn't see anything that looked like a path. Down there he'd find a man who wanted to talk. Just to ask some questions. Nothing else. It wasn't a big deal. Then he could go. "*Nueva York*," the boy said, and laughed.

"*Bueno*," Ryan said. Maybe, he thought, feeling this didn't make any sense, but feeling it deeply nevertheless, rising up, as though from somewhere behind his stomach, like a truth, that if he explained to these men about his brother things would be different. *I hardly know my brother,* he'd say. *He's going to be in Florida. Florida?* the men would ask, glance at one another. *Cuantos años?* Ten, Ryan would say and smile, because ten, they could all understand this. They knew what it meant to be ten and to have a brother and to not know this brother, because who, the men would all be saying together through their looks, knows a brother? They're like strangers, Ryan would say. Very much like strangers you encounter in a crowded city, or perhaps on a trail, out in the woods, walking past, and you both nod hello because you happen to be there, on the same trail in the middle of the forest; how unlikely to encounter another person! What are the two of us doing here on this trail, passing? And so you nod and say hello.

Ryan walked ahead of the boys who'd all stopped. There was nothing but the dark forest. Somewhere in there was a house. Thickening grass pulled at his legs. He just needed to get to the house and for a moment he thought he could make out, between two trees, a path. Already he could imagine what the house would be like; perhaps it even stood, now, at that moment, empty and dark. They'd light some candles, or switch on the generator, and wait in the empty house for the colonel to show up. It was a mistake. It was the communists. And then he would be on the plane, back to Florida, where his sister was waiting for him, where he would see his parents and his brother and he'd tell them all this story, of his run in with the military in Guatemala, of Jim's death, of the horror that was life down there and everyone, happy from the wedding, dazed with wine and cake, would lean forward and shake their heads for wasn't it unbelievable, how terrible those countries could be?

To MY PARENTS, for their stories and their endless encouragement, and to my brothers, Tom, John, and Brendan, for their friendship. To Thomas and Mary Wilkinson, for all their support over the years. To Billy Burns, for his generosity on my trips to Guatemala, and to my cousins in Ireland, the Scanlons in Galway and the Fahertys on Inishmor, for their hospitality. To my peers at the Center for Writers at the University of Southern Mississippi, the Writing Seminars at Johns Hopkins University, and the University of Missouri, and to all my teachers, especially Frederick Barthelme, Steven Barthelme, Mary Robison, Stephen Dixon, Alice McDermott, Trudy Lewis, Marly Swick, and Naeem Murr. Special thanks to Sherod Santos and Lynne McMahon, for their friendship and guidance. To my colleagues at Seton Hall University, especially Jeffrey Gray and Mary Balkun. To the Elizabeth George Foundation, for the grant that supported the finishing of this book. To all the editors who have published my work, with special thanks to Robert Fogarty at *The Antioch Review*, where seven of these stories were first published. To my children, Sylvie and Baxter, who teach me something new about love everyday. Thanks, Sylvie, for picking the title. Finally, and really first, and certainly most of all, to Amy Wilkinson, without whom this book could never have been.

Willow Springs Editions is a small literary press housed in Eastern Washington University's Inland Northwest Center for Writers, in Spokane. The staff of Willow Springs Editions is comprised mostly of creative writing MFA students under the direction of poet Christopher Howell. As part of an internship for which they receive graduate credit, students gets hands-on experience in every phase of the publishing process, from acquisitions to editing, design, promotions and marketing. Willow Springs Editions staff administers the annual Spokane Prize for Fiction competition. It also publishes each year one chapbook of poetry written in the surrealist manner.